# THE AFFAIR

ROWEN CHAMBERS

The Affair

By Rowen Chambers



Published by Waltham Publishing, LLC

Book Cover Designed by 100 Covers

# CHAPTER ONE

"I'm not sure I can do this," I say, my heart pounding, my stomach in knots.

"Of course you can." Dave sits in the chair beside me as I finish doing my makeup. "It's no different than the podcast, only instead of being in our studio, we'll be on stage."

"That's why I'm nervous," I say, glancing at Dave in the mirror. "I'm fine when it's just you and me and a microphone. But speaking in front of a crowd? Knowing people paid to be here? It's too much pressure."

Dave reaches over and takes my hand. "You're going to do great. There's no need to be nervous. These are our fans. Most of them have been listening to our podcast since the very first episode. Nothing you could do or say would upset them."

"I'm not worried about upsetting them. I'm worried about disappointing them."

"You couldn't possibly disappoint them," Dave says, and when our eyes meet in the mirror, he smiles, which relaxes me a little. "You know how much they love you. They've been leaving comments online for weeks, telling you how excited they are to meet you."

"And you," I remind him.

He laughs a little. "I think if they had to choose, you would definitely win out. I'm telling you, Iris, no matter what happens on that stage tonight, people will leave here loving you even more."

"That's kind of you to say, but I'm still nervous." I turn to Dave. "I think I'm done. Do I look okay?"

"You look absolutely gorgeous." Dave leans over and kisses me. "How did a guy like me end up with such a beautiful wife?"

I smile at him, noticing how good he looks in his gray tailored suit. "You're not so bad yourself."

"You ready?" Dave takes my hand and pulls me up from the chair.

"No, I'm still nervous. Do we really need to do this? Isn't the podcast enough?"

"Honey, we're doing this to help people. To save marriages. Keep families together." His arms go around my waist. "Remember why we started this. We used to be the couple who was struggling to stay together. We didn't know how to communicate. How to be there for each other. But we figured it out, and now look at us. We couldn't be happier." He brings me in for a hug. "That's why we're doing this. To help other couples get out of the dark place we used to be in."

Feeling his arms around me, my heart rate returns to normal and those knots in my stomach unravel.

"You're right," I say, pulling away. "Thank you. I needed to hear that. I was making tonight about me when I should be focusing on the people that came to see us."

There's a knock on the door. "It's Allen. Can I come in?"

Allen is our manager. Dave hired him when our podcast took off and we started attracting advertisers. It was Allen's idea to do these live events to expand our brand beyond the podcast.

Dave opens the door. "How's it going out there?"

"Great!" Allen comes into the room, a big grin on his face. He's one of those high-strung people that walks fast, talks fast, and is always fidgeting. "We've got a full house. Not a single ticket left."

"Now I'm getting nervous again," I mutter.

"Honey, relax," Dave says. "Just remember why we're doing this."

"You guys ready?" Allen asks. "We start in five minutes. They need you behind the curtain."

Dave comes over to me and takes my hand. "Let's do this."

I take a deep breath and let it out. "Okay, I'm ready."

As we approach the stage, I hear the roar of the crowd, the music pumping through the speakers. It's the song we use for our podcast. It's energizing and upbeat, the type of song that gets stuck in your head.

The volume lowers and I hear Allen's voice through the speakers, welcoming everyone and then giving a brief bio of Dave and me.

As I listen to him, I feel like he's talking about someone else. How did we get here? How did we go from struggling to pay the mortgage, days away from filing for divorce, to where we are now? Happily married, financially well-off, and hosting a very successful podcast about love and relationships. A few years ago, I would've said you were crazy if you told me I'd be speaking to an auditorium full of people about how to save their marriage. Yet, here we are, walking across the stage, looking out at hundreds of people anxious to hear what we have to say.

"Thank you," Dave says to the crowd, taking the microphone from Allen, a big smile on his handsome face. "We're thrilled to see so many people here tonight." He puts his arm around me. "Iris and I truly hope this night is a benefit to you and the person you're here with." He looks at me. "As many of you know, there was a time Iris and I thought our marriage was over, but we got through it and now our marriage is stronger than ever." He turns back to the crowd. "We're here tonight to help you do the same. Is everyone ready to get started?"

People rise from their seats, cheering and clapping. The energy in the room is electric. I felt it the moment I walked on stage. I'm still a bit nervous, but in a good way. My nerves are no longer from fear, but from excitement. I'm excited to help all these struggling couples find love again.

I was worried about doing this. I wasn't sure I wanted to put myself out there this way. I was perfectly happy hidden away in our podcast studio. But now? Seeing the crowd? Feeling the energy in the room? I'm realizing the benefit of these live events. People need to see us in person to feel the love Dave and I have for each other. We try to convey that on the podcast, but it's much more real when people see us in person. We're proof that a bad marriage can be saved.

"And now," Dave says to the crowd, "it is my pleasure to introduce you to the beautiful woman beside me. The love of my life. Iris."

Here it is, the moment I've been dreading. It's time for me to speak. I take a breath. I can do this. I just need to start and then I'll be fine.

I look out at the crowd, my heart pounding. I'm about to speak when I spot someone in the back of the room.

No. No, no, no, no! It can't be him.

Why would he be here? Why now?

Dave nudges me. "Iris," he says under his breath. "Go ahead."

Turning to him, I shake my head. He looks confused, but I can't explain. I can't tell him about the man in the back of the room. Not ever, and certainly not now.

He turns to the audience. "Iris has a bit of stage fright. While she takes a moment, let me begin by going over tonight's agenda."

As Dave talks, my gaze returns to the back of the room. I don't see him. Where did he go? My eyes dart left and right, frantically searching the crowd for him, but he's not there.

# CHAPTER TWO

## THREE MONTHS LATER

"AND NOW," the announcer says as we wait backstage, "I'm pleased to bring you the couple responsible for saving thousands of marriages. The husband and wife team who have transformed relationship counseling and taken it to a whole new level. Dave and Iris Larson!"

The crowd erupts in applause as the music plays. Dave grips my hand as we walk on stage at the arena. Looking out at the crowd, I see thousands of people, some clapping, some holding up cameras. A few months ago, I would've been terrified to speak in front of this many people, but I overcame my fears when I realized these events were making a difference in people's lives. Dave and I were truly saving marriages. Keeping families together. Bringing love back to relationships.

"Thank you!" Dave says, waving to the crowd, his other hand locked around mine. The crowd continues to clap and cheer, and I smile as I look out at all the faces.

Dave walks us over to the red velvet loveseat set up on the stage and keeps hold of my hand as we sit down. There's a plush white rug in front of us and red rose petals scattered around it, setting the mood for love and romance. We arrange the stage this way for every event to make the audience feel as if this is our home and Dave and I have invited them in to join us. When Dave proposed the idea to me, I thought it was a little cheesy, but our fans love it. Some have even recreated the set in their own homes and sent us photos of it.

"Thank you all for coming tonight," Dave says as the crowd quiets down. "Iris and I are thrilled so many of you have joined us for what we hope will be a life-changing experience." He looks over at me. "Our goal is for all of you to be as happy and in love as we are."

He kisses me, making the crowd go wild, cheering and clapping for us.

Dave looks me in the eye and whispers, "You okay?"

"Yes." I force out a smile, annoyed that he still feels the need to ask me this. I froze on stage *one* time, at our very first event, and he's never forgotten it. He's asked me countless times what happened that night, why I couldn't speak and had to leave the stage. I assured him it was just my nerves, but Dave wasn't convinced. He was sure something had happened. But I couldn't tell him the truth. I couldn't tell him what I saw. My husband doesn't know about Nick, and never will.

Thinking back on it now, I'm sure what I saw that night was my mind playing tricks on me. Nick wasn't there. The man I saw was just someone who looked like him. But because I can't tell Dave any of that, he keeps thinking it'll happen again.

Dave explained my behavior that night by telling everyone I had stage fright, but now, after being on stage countless times, that excuse wouldn't make sense. If people saw me leave during an event, they might think Dave and I were having problems. Our critics and the press would run with that, making up stories that aren't true. They're already making things up about us, with some even claiming my marriage to Dave is a sham. That we're just putting on an act, pretending to be a loving couple in order to prove that our marriage-saving program works.

Allen warned us that success comes with scrutiny, and that even the slightest hint there might be trouble in our marriage could lead to the downfall of our business. So I understand why Dave checks in with me at the start of each event, but I still find it annoying. If I were having problems, I'd tell him. I wouldn't hide something like that, although I might hide the reason for it.

"It's so nice to see all of you tonight," I say, smiling out at the crowd. "As always, we'd like to begin by having everyone face their partner and say our signature phrase. I'll start." I turn to Dave, grasping his hand. "Love you always."

He repeats it back to me, then says to the crowd, "Now it's your turn."

I watch as people turn to their spouse and say the phrase. It's meant to create a safe space before a couple tackles the difficult issues in their relationship. The idea is that if you know your partner will "love you always", no matter what, then you're free to share your feelings without having to worry they'll leave you. It's such a simple concept, but we've had phenomenal success with it.

As we wait for everyone to say the phrase to their partner, I find myself scanning the crowd again, searching for him. I'm sure he's not here. It's my fear making me think that. I'm terrified something will happen to take all this away. My marriage. The business. The huge success we've had in just a matter of months. It seems too good to be true, and I worry something—or someone—will take it from us.

"Now that we're all in a place of love," Dave says, "we're ready to begin the difficult work of repairing what's been broken. It won't be easy, but it will definitely be worth it in the end." He looks over at me. "Iris and I are proof of that. I know many of you know our story, but I think it's worth hearing again."

"I love you, Iris!" a man yells.

My eyes dart to the audience, frantically searching for the man, my heart pounding, fearing it might be him.

"Iris!" the man yells. "I love you! Marry me!"

The man is on the left side of the arena, near the back. He's standing up, holding a sign, but he's so far away I can't read it.

"Stay down," Dave says as I was about to get up. He steps in front of me. "I'm sorry, but Iris is taken." His tone is light, but I can tell he's concerned. He wouldn't be standing in front of me if he wasn't.

Where is this man's wife? This is a couples' event. Single people aren't allowed.

"I love you, Iris!" the man yells as the security team drags him away. "You're everything I want! Marry me!"

There's a low rumble in the crowd as people watch the man being taken out the exit door. I try to inhale a breath and notice my chest is tight and my heart's beating extremely fast. I look down at my hands and notice they're shaking.

"We're going to take a short break," Dave calmly says to the crowd. "We'll return in a moment. I'm very sorry for the interruption."

Dave takes my hand and we walk off the stage.

"He's gone," Allen says, meeting up with us in our dressing room. "Security took him outside and the police are on their way."

"How did this happen?" Dave says, going over to Allen. "Why was a guy like that allowed in?"

He shrugs. "Apparently, he works here. That's what one of the security guys said. He works at the ticket counter. That's how he was able to buy just one ticket instead of a pair."

"Do you think he's dangerous?" I ask Allen.

"I'm sure he's not. He's just some lonely guy who probably has a little crush on you."

"It didn't sound like that to me," Dave says. "He sounded like a man who has an obsession with my wife. He said he loved her. Wanted to marry her. That's more than a little crush."

"This happens all the time," Allen says. "You're just not used to it yet, but you will be as you do more of these events."

"You're saying we should just expect to have people like him interrupting our shows?"

"It's unlikely to happen at an event, but when you're out in public, you have to realize it's normal to encounter an overzealous fan."

"That man was not some overzealous fan," Dave says. "He was unhinged, and obsessed with my wife."

"Dave, relax," Allen says. "Iris wasn't in any kind of danger."

"Give us a minute," Dave says. "I need to talk to my wife."

Allen gets up and leaves the room, shutting the door behind him.

Dave grips my shoulders and looks into my eyes. "Are you okay?"

"I'm fine," I say, forcing out a smile.

"Iris, be honest with me. I saw you out there. You were white as a ghost and you were shaking."

It's because I thought the man shouting at me was Nick. I fear he's going to show up at one of our events and tell everyone I'm a fraud. That a woman like me shouldn't be giving out marriage advice and definitely shouldn't be profiting from it.

"If you don't want to do this, you need to tell me," Dave says. "We could go back to just doing the podcast."

I take a moment to think about that. Life was a lot simpler when we only had the podcast. At first, it didn't feel like a job. It felt like Dave and I were just having a conversation. I never in a million years thought it would become successful. But now that it has, we can't go back. Even if we quit the events and only did the podcast, we'd still have attention on us. I'd still worry about Nick showing up.

Quitting isn't the solution. Doing that would mean letting my fear win out. The past is the past. Nick's moved on with his life and so have I. He's not coming back.

As for overzealous fans? I think Allen is right. It's normal to have a few that take things too far. I was rattled by that man in the audience saying he loves me, but I'm not letting that end what we're doing. Dave and I are helping people and saving marriages.

"I don't want to stop doing the events," I say. "How could we, when we're making such a difference in people's lives?"

"I knew that would be your answer." Dave pulls me into his arms. "You're such a good person. Always putting others first. I shouldn't be surprised you have fans obsessing over you."

"Only one," I say. "And they caught him. He's gone."

"I hope you know I never would've let him get near you," Dave says. "I'd do anything to protect you."

That might be true, but he can't protect me from the one person I need protection from the most. The one who could do the most damage. The one who could ruin our lives.

# CHAPTER THREE

"What are you getting?" Jane asks, looking at the menu. "My friend Barb says the kale salad is to die for, but I just can't get into kale. Every time I eat it, I feel like I'm eating weeds."

As she continues to talk, I notice a man passing by the restaurant who looks just like Nick. He's tall with dark hair, wearing a gray sweater and jeans. He went by so fast I didn't get a look at his face, but just at a glance, I thought for sure it was him.

"Iris, did you hear me?" Jane says.

Tearing my gaze from the window, I shake my head. "No. Sorry. I got distracted."

"What were you looking at?" She glances out the window.

What do I say? I need to make something up, and fast.

"That man. The one from the event last weekend. I thought I saw him walk by."

"I thought you said he was in jail."

"They let him go. And now I feel like he could be anywhere. Following me. Keeping track of where I go."

Jane reaches over and puts her hand on mine. "Iris, are you feeling okay?"

"What do you mean?"

"You seem to be very distracted. Or maybe a better word for it is... paranoid."

"You think I'm being paranoid?" I say, pulling my hand from hers. "I had a strange man telling me he loved me and wanted to marry me. Are you saying that wouldn't concern you?"

She shrugs. "I'd assume it comes with the territory. The more famous you become, the more you attract nut jobs."

"I'm not famous. I'm known in the world of self-improvement. Outside of that, nobody knows who I am."

"Plenty of people know you. You have all those events. A successful podcast. You're always doing interviews on TV."

"Local TV, not national. I'm somewhat known by people here in Chicago, but only if they watch local programming."

"Those interviews are posted online, and according to your husband, a lot of people watch them.

"Dave told you that?" I ask, finding it odd he was talking to Jane about our business.

"Last week, we ran into each other at the mailbox and I asked him how things were going. He assumed I was asking about your business and that's when he mentioned an interview you'd done and how many hits it had, whatever that means. I don't understand all that tech speak." She picks up her glass of wine and takes a sip. It's not even noon, but Jane believes wine shouldn't be limited to only certain parts of the day.

Jane is my neighbor. She's in her fifties, married, with no kids. We met a few years ago, when Dave and I moved into the house next door. We could barely afford the payments back then, but Dave insisted we move out of our tiny apartment in downtown Chicago and buy a house in the suburbs.

The waiter stops by our table. "Have we decided what we'd like?"

"I'm going to have the salmon," I tell him.

"Really, Iris?" Jane says, sounding disappointed with my selection. "There are all these wonderful items on the menu and you choose plain, ordinary salmon?"

"It sounds good," I tell her. "And it's not something I make at home. Dave can't stand the smell of fish so I never cook it."

"Dave?" The waiter stares at me. "Hey, are you that lady that does the couples' events? You and your husband?"

"Yes," I say. "I'm Iris."

He smiles. "I thought you looked familiar. I saw you on TV last week."

"What do you recommend?" Jane asks the waiter, still looking over the menu.

"The steak salad. Or the blue cheese burger is good."

"I'll have the salad," Jane says, handing him the menu.

He points to me. "Love you always. That's your saying, right?"

"Yes. I'm surprised you know that."

"I listen to your podcast."

"Could you put our order in?" Jane says, giving him an annoyed look. "We're on a schedule here."

"Yeah, sorry." He takes off.

"We're on a schedule?" I ask Jane. "Do you need to be somewhere?"

"No, I was just saving you from another one of your annoying fans." She swirls the wine in her glass, then takes a sip.

"I didn't find him annoying. He was just saying he recognized me. You didn't have to be rude to him."

She sighs and sets down her glass. "Honestly, Iris, all you do is complain about these people bothering you and the one time I try to help you, I get yelled at for it."

"I'm not yelling at you. I just don't think you need to be rude to him."

"Fine," she huffs. "I'll never try to protect you again." She waves her hand around. "Next time some crazy fan bothers you, you're on your own."

She's so dramatic. It's one of the things I don't like about her. But I like her in other ways, and she's really my only friend in the neighborhood. All the other women are young mothers who are busy with their children. They don't have time to socialize the way Jane does.

"So how's Richard?" I ask, deciding we need a change of topic.

"I wouldn't know," she says, picking up her wine again. "He's never home."

Jane's husband is an orthopedic surgeon. He has his own practice and makes enough money that Jane doesn't have to work. But being home alone all day, she gets bored. I've suggested she volunteer somewhere, but she doesn't seem interested in that.

"Have you talked to him?" I say. "Maybe you could ask him to cut back on his hours."

"You don't know Richard. The man's a workaholic. I have to plan dinner parties or buy tickets to an event just to get him to spend time with me."

"You could still talk to him. Tell him you'd like him to be home more."

She shakes her head. “He’d tell me I’m being needy and that his job isn’t to entertain me.” She holds up her empty wine glass as the waiter goes by. He gives her a nod, letting her know he’ll get her another.

“You shouldn’t assume he’ll respond a certain way. Assumptions are a form of miscommunication that leads to misunderstandings and hurt feelings.”

She looks at me across the table. “Isn’t that one of your quotes? A direct quote from your little program?”

It is, but how did she know that? She’s told me more than once that she’s never listened to the podcast or read any of our materials online. And why did she call the program “little” like it’s insignificant or ridiculous?

“Yes, and it’s very important,” I say. “Relationships don’t survive without good communication.”

“And yet I’ve been married for thirty years,” she says in a sarcastic tone. “Perhaps your theories are just that. Ideas you made up based on your own experience. I’m not saying that’s bad. I’m just saying it doesn’t work for all relationships.”

She’s being rather hostile today. Maybe she’s in a bad mood.

“I understand the program’s not for everyone,” I say. “But it does work. We have thousands of happy marriages that are proof of that.”

“Including your own?” she asks with a smug grin.

“Yes. Dave and I are an example of what the program can do. We were at a really bad place years ago, and now, we couldn’t be more in love.”

She cocks her head to the side. “You and Dave never have problems? I find that hard to believe.”

“We disagree now and then, but we talk through it and move on.”

"And you tell each other everything?"

"Yes. Why wouldn't we?"

"Come on, Iris. All couples have secrets. I don't believe for one second that Dave knows all of yours."

He doesn't. But those secrets are in the past, and since then, I've been nothing but honest with Dave. And he's honest with me.

"Believe what you'd like, but I'm telling you, I don't keep secrets from Dave. I don't need to. I have nothing to hide, and I believe in being honest with my husband. It's why our marriage is so strong."

"And Dave feels the same way? You think he tells you everything?"

"Absolutely. Dave's always been honest with me. It's one of the things I love about him."

The waiter stops by with Jane's wine. "Your food will be out shortly."

"Thank you," I tell him.

When he's gone, Jane leans back in her chair and takes a sip of her wine. "Last June, when you went away for the weekend to see your mother, why was it that Dave didn't go with you?"

"He wasn't feeling well. He didn't want my mother getting sick. Why are you bringing this up?"

"Richard saw him at the club that weekend. Playing a round of golf." She sets her glass down. "He was obviously feeling better. I assume he told you he golfed that weekend?"

No. He didn't. He said he was in bed all weekend, trying to sleep off whatever illness he had. Why would he lie to me? I wouldn't care if he golfed.

"Yes, he mentioned going to the club that weekend," I say.

"But now that I'm thinking about it, he didn't say who he was golfing with. Did Richard tell you?"

"He didn't need to. I was there. I saw him having dinner at the club. Richard and I were leaving when they were being seated. I believe it was your manager. Tall man. Very thin. He was at your house last weekend."

"Allen. Yes, he's our manager. That makes sense. Dave was probably discussing business with him."

Although if he did, he should've told me. We agreed to always involve each other in any business decisions. I guess it's possible they were just playing golf, but still, he should've told me.

Jane knows he didn't. That's why she brought it up, and why she's giving me that smug grin. Is this her attempt to prove my marriage isn't as perfect as I say it is? But why would she do that? We're supposed to be friends.

The waiter returns with our food. "Lunch is served, ladies." He smiles at us. "Is there anything else I can get you?"

"That'll be it," Jane says, answering for both of us. "Oh, and I'm terribly sorry if I was rude to you earlier. I certainly didn't mean to be."

He leans down to her. "Leave a good tip and I'll forgive you." He laughs as he rises back to standing. "Enjoy, ladies!" He hurries back to the kitchen.

"It looks wonderful," I say, referring to my salmon.

"You really can't make salmon at home?" Jane asks, pouring dressing on her salad. "Dave won't allow it?"

"He doesn't care if I make it. I just choose not to since he can't tolerate the smell." I pause, feeling like I need to address this because it's really bothering me. "Jane, is there a reason you keep bringing up my marriage?"

"I just don't want you being fooled into thinking it's perfect."

"I know it's not perfect. I don't expect it to be. But I'm not going to go looking for problems where there aren't any."

"All I'm saying is that your marriage may not—"

"Jane, I've heard enough. I don't mean to sound harsh, but I need you to stop talking about this."

She clears her throat and forces out a smile. "Fine. Let's talk about something else. Where'd you get that dress? It looks fabulous on you."

We spend the rest of lunch talking about superficial things, staying away from anything personal. I'd like to be closer friends with Jane, but it's difficult to open up to her when I fear she might take what I say and use it against me. She's not a happy person and tends to want others to share in her misery. But I'm not taking part in that.

I have a very happy life and want to keep it that way. Although I'm not too happy finding out Dave lied to me about being sick when he was really out golfing. Maybe he wasn't in the mood to visit my mother. She's always asking him to do things around the house and I could see how that could be annoying. He probably just wanted some time to himself that weekend. I just wish he'd told me that.

# CHAPTER FOUR

"WHAT'S a guy to do when it seems like nothing he does for his wife is right?" a man in the audience asks. He looks to be in his forties, with dark hair, a thick beard, and a wide, muscular frame. He's dressed in faded jeans and a plaid flannel shirt while his wife is wearing a navy suit, looking like she just left the boardroom of a large corporation.

I'm always surprised by the couples I see at our events. Some look very similar to each other, while others look like complete opposites.

Dave laughs a little. "I know exactly what you mean. I think all husbands have felt this way at one point or another. Am I right?"

He waits as the men in the audience applaud, raising the volume level in the massive auditorium. Tonight is another sold-out event, our tenth one this month. Word continues to spread about our marriage coaching events and tickets are selling out within hours of going on sale. Luckily, we haven't had any more incidents with disruptive fans like the one we had a few weeks ago. The man involved was released from jail with a fine and an order to stay away from me.

"Actually," the man in the audience says, "I was hoping to get Iris' opinion on this. If you don't mind."

"Of course not," Dave says. He usually answers the questions from men, but at the past few events, men have been directing more of their questions to me than to Dave. "Iris, sweetheart, go ahead."

I smile at him, then at the man who asked the question. "The first thing to consider is if your assessment of the situation is correct. You said it seems as though nothing you do is right, but is that just your perception, or is that really how your wife feels?"

He glances at her. "I guess I don't know. I just assumed."

"Assumptions are a form of miscommunication that leads to misunderstandings and hurt feelings. It's always best to ask rather than assume."

I give an example from my own marriage, calling on Dave to recount his memory of it so he isn't left sitting there with nothing to say. He'd be perfectly fine letting me answer, but it doesn't feel right not to include him.

At the end of the event, we're heading back to the dressing room when I notice a woman coming toward us. She's young, mid-twenties, and very beautiful, with long blond hair and wearing a black suit.

"David," she says, smiling at him.

How does this woman know my husband? And why is she calling him David? He always goes by Dave.

"Heather," he says, smiling back at her. "I'm sorry I didn't get back to you."

"Don't worry about it," she says, waving her manicured

hand in the air. "It's no problem. I ended up staying late at the office."

I wrap my arm around Dave's and smile at the woman. "I'm sorry, who are you?"

"Heather works for the company that makes products for couples," Dave says. "The one that's helping us develop our own branded items."

"We haven't met," Heather says, extending her hand toward me. "Heather Scott. I work in client relations. I've been working with your husband to develop some ideas we can take to our product development team."

"Nice to meet you." I shake her hand. "I didn't realize we already had a deal." I look at Dave. "Why didn't you tell me?"

"We don't have a deal. We're still working on the contract." He smiles at Heather. "But it sounds like we're getting close to finalizing it."

"What product ideas are we considering?" I ask.

Dave laughs, but it's an uncomfortable laugh. "Honey, we talked about this. The relationship game. The couple's journal. The massage oils. We had a whole list. We just need to narrow down what we want."

"So this is actually happening? We're developing products?"

"It'll happen if the deal goes through," Dave says.

"I'm sure it will," Heather says. "We just need to work through the details."

Why didn't Dave tell me we were this far along in the process? The last I remember Dave was still in discussions with the company and hadn't decided if we were really going to do this. I didn't know he was already working on the contract.

"Heather really liked your idea for the relationship game," Dave says. "In fact, that's the product they'd like to start with."

"I think it'll be really popular," Heather says. "And the questions will make a great hook for promotion. I love that one where you have to guess what historic figure your partner would want to marry if he went back in time. Or the one where you have to list three events from your partner's childhood that influenced him as an adult."

"You like the more serious ones," Dave says, smiling at Heather.

She shrugs. "I prefer the ones that are more thought-provoking, but I also like the ones that are just for fun. So do you have time to talk? Or would you like to try to meet another time?"

Dave looks at me. "What do you think?"

"Now isn't a good time. I'm tired from the event."

"I totally understand," Heather says. "But we'll need to finalize the terms of the contract fairly soon or my boss is going to offer the deal to someone else."

It sounds like a scare tactic. I bet there isn't someone else and Heather's just saying that to hurry us into making a deal.

"Then perhaps we should meet now," Dave says. "Just for a few minutes. Iris, would you like to join us?"

I feel like I should be involved in this, but the event took a lot out of me and I'd really like to lie down for a few minutes. Discussing the details of a contract is the last thing I want to do.

"You go ahead. Just don't sign anything yet." I smile at him, as if I'm kidding, but he knows I'm not. We agreed that all deals have to be discussed and approved as a couple, which means I must've known about this, so why can't I remember?

"Nothing will be signed. We're not even close to that point yet." He kisses my cheek. "Go rest. I'll be there shortly."

As I continue to the dressing room, I hear Heather laughing

at something Dave said. It sounds like she has a crush on him, but that isn't surprising. Many women do. My husband is a very handsome man and looks much younger than his forty-four years. People often assume we're the same age even though I'm five years younger.

Going into the dressing room, I smile when I see the large bouquet of roses sitting on the table. Dave must've had them delivered. He's always surprising me like this. It's one of the many reasons I love him. It's odd he chose yellow roses instead of red, but perhaps he just wanted to mix it up. There's a note attached, and when I open it, I see our signature phrase, *Love You Always*.

The phrase came out of an argument we had years ago. Our marriage was on the verge of ending and Dave and I got into a huge fight because I'd just quit my job. We were in a lot of debt and desperately needed money so Dave was furious when he found out I'd quit that day.

I hadn't planned to quit. I did it on impulse, after my boss burst into my office and demanded I stop letting clients get better. I was working as a life coach and having great success. After a few visits, my clients felt like they didn't need me anymore. I saw that as a win, but my boss saw it as a failure. All he cared about was making money. He wanted clients for a lifetime, not a few weeks, and when I told him it was unethical to make people pay for services they didn't need, he said it was part of the job. So I quit.

Once I explained that to Dave, he understood, but it took until the next morning for us to get to that point. We fought all night, trading sleep for arguing, and around four in the morning, I brought up the dreaded D word. I told Dave we should get divorced. I was sure that's what he wanted. He never seemed happy with me. All we did was fight. So I gave him an out. But instead of taking it, he looked at me like he couldn't believe I'd even suggested it. That's when he said those words, the ones we now use in our event. We shortened them to 'love you always' but what Dave really said that night was this. "I'm not giving up on us. You're mine forever, and I will love you always."

Soon after that night, we committed to not only saving our marriage, but having the best marriage possible. We read books, saw counselors, went to marriage retreats. Then we took the best parts of what we learned and developed a podcast for other couples who were struggling. The podcast turned into our signature program, which we take people through at our live events. I never would've imagined that terrible night of fighting would've led to this, but it did, and I couldn't be happier.

"Heather and I decided to meet next week," Dave says, coming into the room. "I didn't feel right leaving you here alone when you're ill."

"I'm not ill," I tell him. "I'm just tired. This was our third event this week and I seem to be doing most of the talking."

"And you've done a wonderful job," Dave says, coming up to me. "I'm so proud of you, Iris. You've conquered your stage fright and become the star of the show."

"I'm not the star," I say, smiling at him. "We're a team. Oh, thank you for the roses. They're beautiful."

"What roses?"

"The ones on the table." I point to them.

"Those aren't from me. Allen must've sent them to congratulate us on selling out the next ten events."

"Allen never sends flowers. And the note says love you always. He wouldn't write that."

"Sure, he would. It's our signature phrase." Dave gets out his phone. "I'll call and thank him." He calls Allen's number and puts his phone on speaker.

"How'd it go tonight?" Allen answers.

"Wonderful," Dave says, smiling at me. "Iris had people hooked on her every word."

"He's exaggerating," I say. "But it really was one of our best events."

"That's great," Allen says. "Sorry I couldn't make it."

"Hey, thanks for the roses," Dave says.

"I didn't send roses," Allen replies.

"Then who did?" I ask.

"Maybe they're from Cara. She's always sending flowers."

Cara is our finance manager. She's currently in Paris on her honeymoon.

"She wouldn't send us flowers when she's on her honeymoon," I say. "And if she did, she'd sign the note with her name."

"Then they must be from someone else," Allen says. "I need to get going. You two have a good night."

"Yeah, you too," Dave says, ending the call.

I walk over to the roses. "Who would've sent these?"

"There's nothing on the note?" Dave asks. "No name?"

"No, and the card doesn't have the name of the florist."

"Maybe it was from one of our friends," Dave says. "Aren't yellow roses a sign of friendship?"

They are, but our friends would've signed their name on the card.

"Isn't there a song about that?" Dave says. "About yellow roses? And something about Texas?"

My breath catches in my throat and my heart races as I

realize what he's saying. He's right about the song, but he doesn't know why that's significant.

Yellow roses. Texas. It's a sign. A message. From him.

Nick grew up in Texas. He used to tell me about his childhood there and how he wanted to move back there someday. He purposely gave me yellow roses so I'd know they're from him.

The roses aren't a gift. They're a message. Nick's telling me he's back.

Was he the man I saw at our first event? The man at the back of the room? I told myself I'd imagined it, but maybe I didn't. Maybe it was Nick there that night. But that was months ago. Why haven't I seen him since? Or maybe I have. Maybe that was him I saw on the street when Jane and I were having lunch.

Why is he back? What does he want from me? And how do I find out without Dave learning the truth?

# CHAPTER FIVE

"I'd like to go home," I say, gathering up my things from the dressing room. I need to get away from those flowers. How did they get here? Did Nick drop them off? If so, it means he was here, in this room.

That's not possible. We hire security for every event and give them a list of who's allowed backstage and in our dressing room. Nick isn't one of them, so who put the roses in here?

"You want to stop and get something to eat?" Dave asks.

"I'm not hungry," I say, tossing my hair products in a bag. "I just want to go home."

Dave comes over to me. "Honey, what's wrong?"

"Nothing." I force a smile on my face. "I'm just tired. I'd like to get to bed." I take my things and head to the door.

"Iris, wait." Dave comes up behind me and grabs my arm. "What's going on? Why are you acting this way?"

I turn to face him. "What way?"

"Racing around. Tossing things in bags. You didn't even change clothes. Why are you in such a hurry to leave? Did something happen?"

What do I tell him? I can't tell him the truth. I decide to distract him so he'll stop asking questions.

"I want to be with you," I say in a seductive tone as I run my hand down his chest. "In our bed."

He smiles. "I thought you were tired."

"I was..." I glance down at his body. "But seeing how hot you look in that suit, I can't stop thinking about—"

"Let's go." He races around the room to get his things. I laugh to myself, seeing how eager he is to get home now that he knows what we'll be doing when we get there. We haven't been intimate in weeks. Our busy schedule has us so exhausted that we fall asleep the minute we get into bed.

Dave meets me at the door. "What about the roses? Don't you want to take them?"

"No. Someone else can have them. I don't like yellow roses. There's something not right about a rose in that color."

He looks back at them. "What if whoever sent them finds out we left them here?"

"They'll get over it." I pull on his hand. "Forget the flowers. Let's go."

The drive back to our house takes over an hour. As our audience grows, our events are taking place farther away from where we live. Soon we'll have to fly to events, which is not what I want. I've suggested we do events online, but Dave thinks they wouldn't be as effective as in person.

When we're pulling into our driveway, I see Jane walking to her mailbox. She waves at us, a big smile on her face. I wave back, but I'm still bothered by our conversation at lunch yesterday. The more I thought about it, the more I was convinced she said those things because she's jealous that I have a loving husband who enjoys spending time with me.

"It sounds like Jane's marriage is struggling," I say as we go into the house. "She seemed very frustrated with Richard when we went to lunch yesterday."

"Why? What did she say?"

"That all he does is work. It sounds like he'd rather work than spend time with her."

"Maybe he's having an affair," Dave casually says as we go into the bedroom.

"Richard wouldn't do that." I stop and look at Dave. "Would he? You don't know something, do you? About Richard?"

"No, I'm just saying it's possible." Dave takes off his tie. "Guys his age can get restless and think they need a change. Sometimes it's a new car. Sometimes it's a new lover."

"I hope that's not the case. Jane would be devastated if he left her for someone else. And what would she do if they got divorced? She's never had a job."

"She wouldn't need one," Dave says, taking off his suit jacket. "She'd get plenty of money in the divorce to support herself."

"I'm sure it won't come to that. Whenever we're with them, they seem happy."

"And yet she was complaining about him at lunch."

"Yes, but you know Jane. She tends to exaggerate things to make them sound more dramatic."

"I wouldn't worry about it. I'm sure the two of them are fine."

"She said something else." I follow Dave into the walk-in closet. "Something about you."

Dave turns to look at me. "What did she say?"

I wasn't going to tell him this. I'd decided I didn't need to.

Why bring up something that happened months ago? But I can't stop thinking about it. Maybe if I just say it, I can forget about it and move on.

"She said she saw you at the club last summer having dinner with Allen. And that you'd golfed with him earlier that day."

Dave's brows rise. "And? What about it?"

"I found it odd because you..." I pause, wishing I hadn't said anything. I don't want this turning into an argument. I should've just let it go.

"I what?" Dave asks, walking over to me.

"You didn't tell me."

He cocks his head. "I don't understand. I golf with Allen all the time. You know that."

"Yes, but I didn't know about it that weekend. It was last June. When I went to see my mother."

He slowly nods. "Yes. I remember. I did go golfing that weekend."

"You told me you were sick."

"And I was. The morning you left, I wasn't feeling well. But after breakfast, I started feeling better. Then Allen called and asked if I wanted to play a round of golf."

"Why didn't you tell me? When I talked to you Saturday night, you said you'd spent all day in bed."

He sighs and rubs his hand over his face. "Honey, I'm sorry."

"For what?" I ask, my heart beating faster.

"For not being honest with you." He lowers his hand from his face and looks at me. "The truth is, I didn't want to spend all weekend at your mother's house. She always gives me a list of chores to do, and although I don't mind helping her, I wasn't feeling up to it that weekend. We'd had a very busy week and I just wanted to unwind with a game a golf and some time at home."

"Why didn't you just tell me that?"

"Because I felt bad that I didn't go with you. And I knew you'd be disappointed that I chose golf over helping your mother."

"I would've understood." I turn and walk away from him. "We always said we'd be truthful with each other."

"Iris, I'm sorry. I should've told you."

I turn back. "What else haven't you told me?"

"That was it. I swear."

"How do I know you're not just saying that?"

He steps up to me. "Because I love you. And because our relationship is more important to me than anything else."

"Then why risk harming it with a lie? Why not just be honest?"

He rubs my arm. "I made a mistake. People are allowed to make mistakes now and then. Including you. If there were times when you weren't completely honest with me, I'd understand."

That's true for some things, but not all. If he knew about Nick, Dave would never forgive me.

His hand goes under my chin and he lifts my face to his. "Is there anything you haven't told me? Anything you've kept from me? Even something small?"

"No. Nothing."

"Honey, you know you can tell me. I'll love you no matter what."

He wouldn't if he knew the truth. He'd forgive me for a lot of things, but not that.

"Okay." I smile a little. "I wasn't completely honest about that shirt you used to wear."

"What shirt?"

"Your rugby shirt. The one with the green and purple stripes."

"You didn't like it?"

I shake my head. "It looked terrible on you. The colors were bad. It didn't fit right. And the collar wouldn't stay down. It kept curling up."

"Because it was old. I'd had it since college."

"Yes, well, I think it should've stayed at college."

He smiles. "You could've told me you didn't like it. I'm not saying I would've thrown it out, but I would've stopped wearing it around you. What else don't you like? Are there other things in my closet that repulse you?"

"No, that was it."

"Then let's move on to the reason we rushed home." He pulls me into his arms and kisses the side of my neck.

I'm not in the mood for this. I'm still on edge from seeing those roses, wondering if they really were from Nick. But I have to play along and make Dave think I want this. So I let him undress me, take me to the bed, and make love to me. But the whole time, my mind is on Nick, worried what his next move will be.

Is he trying to end my marriage? Is that why Nick's doing this? Or is he angry about my success? Angry that I'm making money telling people how to have a great marriage, knowing I was unfaithful to my husband?

"I needed that," Dave says, collapsing back on the bed, still catching his breath. "It'd been too long."

"It had," I say, snuggling up to him.

"I'm starving. Are you sure you don't want to eat? We could have something delivered."

"I'm not hungry, but you could order something. Or there's leftover pizza in the fridge."

"That sounds good. I'll have that." He gets out of bed and puts on his pajama pants.

"Hey, about this deal you're working on with Heather," I say.

"What about it?"

"Why don't I remember discussing it? I know we talked about developing products, but I didn't know we were this close to making a deal."

"I've mentioned it several times, but there's been so much going on with the other parts of our business I can understand how it might've slipped your mind."

"How long have you been working with Heather?"

"Since our first meeting. It was the morning after that man was arrested at our event. You were very upset and hadn't slept well. I told you we could postpone the meeting, but you insisted I go without you."

"I guess I remember that, but I don't remember you telling me you'd decided to work with them."

"I told you as soon as I got back from the meeting, but I'm not sure you were listening. Like I said, you were tired and your mind was on what had happened at the event."

"Why haven't I heard anything since then? Why haven't you been giving me updates?"

"Because you always tell me to handle these types of things without you. I thought I'd wait until we were closer to finalizing a deal before I got you involved."

"Well, I'd like to be involved now. Maybe you could fill me in tomorrow about the products we're proposing and the details of the contract."

"Yes, of course. We can do it first thing tomorrow." He leans over and gives me a kiss. "Get some rest. I think I'll stay up and watch TV."

When he's gone, I try to sleep, but my mind's too awake. If Nick is back in town, if he's the one who sent the flowers, then it means it won't be long before he shows up at my door. Or maybe he'll wait outside one of my events.

He's here to expose my secret. That has to be it. That's the only reason he'd show up here. He doesn't want me having success, not when it's built on a lie.

But he doesn't have proof. There's no evidence to show that anything happened between us. If he tells people we had an affair, I'll just deny it. I'll say he's some crazy person, trying to get attention.

Unfortunately, once this gets out, there will be some people who will believe it, like the ones who say our marriage-saving program doesn't work or are jealous of our success. They'll spread the story online as if it were true, which it is, but without evidence, it's simply Nick's word against mine.

What if he *does* have evidence? But what would it be? We never took any photos together. It's possible Nick took one when I wasn't looking, but a photo doesn't prove anything, unless it shows us being affectionate. Or intimate. Did he set up a camera in our room? Nick wouldn't do that, would he?

He might have saved the texts between us. I made sure to keep mine innocent, like I was texting a friend. But some of Nick's texts were explicit, making it obvious we were having an affair. Did he do that on purpose? In case he ever wanted to use it against me?

Maybe I should contact him. Convince him to let this go. I could at least find out why he's doing this and what he wants.

# CHAPTER SIX

"THAT'S BASICALLY IT," Dave says, sliding his laptop aside. "Do you have any questions?"

It's morning, and we're sitting at the dining room table where Dave just went over the contract he's working on with Heather. I tried to pay attention, but my mind kept going to Nick and what I'm going to say to him.

I've decided I need to call him. It's risky, and not what I want to do, but it's the only way to end this ridiculous game he's playing. He's obviously trying to get my attention, and he has, but for what purpose? That's what I need to find out.

"Iris," Dave says. "Did you hear me?"

"Yes, sorry," I say with a laugh. "My mind wandered. All that legal jargon nearly put me to sleep."

"It doesn't interest me either, but it's important we look it over. Our lawyer will review it, of course, but we should still know the basics of what we're signing."

"Did you see anything in it that concerned you?"

"I think we should ask for a better split of the profits, but other than that, it looks good."

"Then I trust your judgment," I say, getting up. "I need to get going. I have some errands to get done."

"Now? I haven't gone over the products we're proposing."

"Oh." I sit down again. "Go ahead."

I really wanted to leave so I could call Nick. I need this to be over. It's consuming my thoughts, and if I don't deal with it, I won't be able to focus on anything else.

"This is what they're imagining for the relationship game," Dave says, showing me a mocked-up illustration on his laptop. "I think it needs more color, which I already mentioned to Heather. She agreed, but I'd like to get your thoughts as well."

"I think you're right. More color would be good."

"Honey, you didn't even look at it. This is only the first page." He clicks through the different pages and I find my mind wandering again.

Dave closes the laptop.

"What are you doing?" I ask. "Are we done?"

He turns to me, looking concerned. "Are you feeling okay?"

"Yes. Why do you ask?"

"You're really struggling to pay attention. Did you not sleep well last night?"

"Not really. I kept waking up, thinking of all the things I need to get done." I put my hand on his arm. "I'm sorry, but can we do this later? I really need to get some errands done. Then I'll be better able to focus."

"Sure." He smiles. "Would you like me to go with you?"

"No," I blurt out. "You stay here and relax. Or catch up on work." I get up. "I should be back by this afternoon."

"You need that long to run errands?" Dave asks, following me to the kitchen.

"Maybe. I'm not sure. It depends on traffic and if I decide

to stop for lunch." I sling my purse over my shoulder and head to the door.

"I don't get a kiss goodbye?" Dave asks, coming up behind me.

I turn and give him a kiss. "Bye! I'll see you later."

Ten minutes later, I pull into the parking lot of a strip mall. I shut the car off and get out my phone. Scrolling through my contacts, I find Nick's number. I blocked him from calling me, but never deleted his number. I'm not sure why. Maybe part of me knew this would happen, that he'd try to come back into my life and I'd have to deal with him.

Staring at his initials on the screen, I almost decide not to do it. But I have to. This can't continue.

I press call, my heart pounding. It rings several times before someone picks up.

"Hello?" a woman answers. Is she Nick's girlfriend? His wife?

"Yes, I was hoping to speak to Nick. Is he around?"

"You have the wrong number." She ends the call.

*Wrong number?* It can't be. I call it again.

"Hello?" the woman answers.

"Yes, I just called, looking for Nick. I'm certain this is the right number. I just need to speak to him for—"

"There's no Nick here," she says, getting angry. "This isn't his number. It's mine. And if you call me again, I'm going to block you." She ends the call.

This doesn't make sense. Nick wouldn't have changed his number. Maybe that woman was lying. Maybe she's his girlfriend and doesn't want other women calling him. But I got the feeling she was telling the truth and really didn't know him.

What does this mean? Did Nick purposely change his number so I couldn't contact him? But why would he do that?

My phone rings. I grab it, thinking it's Nick calling me back, but it's Dave.

"Hi, honey," I answer. "Did you need something?"

"Yeah, Allen called and wants us to meet him at the studio. We need to record some clips he can use for promotion."

"Can't he use the ones we already have?"

"He needs new ones for an ad we're running online. The current ad isn't performing the way it should. I know you're running errands, but I really think this is more important."

"Yes, of course. I'm on my way home."

When I arrive back at the house, Dave is waiting to leave. We take his car and head to the studio. We used to do all our recordings in our house, but when we started making money, we rented office space in a building and turned it into a recording studio.

"This shouldn't take long," Allen says as we join him in the studio. He hands us the script. "It's similar to the current ad, but with a few adjustments."

"Where's Jeremy?" I ask, referring to our ads manager. "Shouldn't he be here?"

"He just stepped out to make a call," Allen says.

"Why are we still using him?" Dave asks. "He's always changing the ads and it never seems to do anything. We could probably stop the ads altogether and see no difference in ticket sales."

"That's not true," Allen says. "Even your fans don't always know when an event's coming up. That's why we need the ads."

"Let's not get worked up about it," I tell Dave. "It won't take long to record a few ads."

Jeremy returns, grinning at us. "You guys ready to record?"

"They're ready," Allen says, giving Dave a look to be nice to Jeremy. Dave's never liked him. Allen hired him because he's supposed to be an expert in online advertising.

The recording takes less than an hour, but Dave isn't pleased with the new script. Either that, or he's in a bad mood. He's had a scowl on his face the entire time, which is very unlike him. He rarely gets upset.

"Honey, what's wrong?" I ask as he takes his headphones off.

"Jeremy. He makes us race over here in the middle of the day to record *this*?" Dave picks up the script, then slams it down on the table.

"It wasn't that bad."

"It was ridiculous! Nobody talks like this. We sound like fools! This is why I didn't want to hire someone fresh out of college."

"Then we'll write something else. We don't have to use what Jeremy wrote."

The door swings open and Allen walks in. "Great job! I think we got everything we need."

Dave shoots up from the table and storms over to Allen. "You actually liked that? We sound like idiots!"

"You sound like people who know how to speak to a younger audience. You can't only appeal to people your age. You want to expand your reach? Grow your brand? Then you need to go after a younger crowd."

"Our brand is about marriage. Younger people aren't married."

"Some are, and some are in relationships. Your advice works for couples whether they're married or not."

"Yes, but that's not what we're known for. We're marriage coaches, not dating experts."

"Why don't we just try the ads and see how it goes?" I say to Dave, trying to calm him down.

"That's a wrap!" Jeremy says, walking into the room, a big grin on his face. "Thanks for coming in, guys. I think these new ads will perform a lot better."

"Based on what?" Dave asks, going over to Jeremy. "Do you have research to back this up? Or are you just guessing?"

"Whoa, what's going on?" Jeremy asks, seeing the anger on Dave's face and noticing his hostile tone. "Did I miss something?"

"He's just having a bad day," Allen says.

"Actually, I was having a great day until I got here," Dave says, glaring at Jeremy. "That script you wrote is ridiculous. You really think people talk that way?"

He shrugs. "My friends do."

"Yeah, well, your friends are idiots!"

"Dave!" I say, racing up beside him. "That was uncalled for." I look at Jeremy. "I'm sorry. He didn't mean it. He's just—"

"I *did* mean it!" Dave shouts. "I'm not lowering our standards to appeal to people like him!" He points at Jeremy.

"Hey, I know what I'm talking about," Jeremy says. "I've been doing this for two years."

"Two years?" Dave says in a sarcastic tone. "And that makes you an expert?"

"Dave, let's talk about this later," Allen says.

"No. He's done. I don't want him working for us anymore."

"You're firing me?" Jeremy says.

"Yes." Dave points to the door. "Get out."

Jeremy glances at Allen. "Can he do that? You're the one who hired me."

Allen shrugs. "He's the boss. He gets the final say."

Jeremy shoots an angry look at Dave. "You're an ass! And your advice is stupid." He walks out of the room and stomps down the hall.

"Did you really need to do that?" Allen says to Dave.

He sighs. "Sorry, but I've never liked that guy. He's never once asked Iris or me for input. He just assumes he knows what's best. And his personality. There's something off about him. I don't trust him."

"So now we're without an ad person," Allen says.

"I'll run the ads myself until we find someone."

Allen walks over to us. "I'm going to head out. Why don't you go home and rest, Dave? Have a drink. Try to relax." He winks at me. "You need to get this guy to not be so stressed. I'll see you two later."

When he's gone, Dave says to me, "I'm sorry I got so upset. I didn't react well. I just really don't like that guy."

"Then we'll find someone else."

"Thank you for being so understanding. I was worried you might scold me and tell me I was being a jerk."

"Well, you were a little harsh, but if you had a bad feeling about him, then it's good he's gone." I pause. "So was it just a feeling, or did something happen between you two?"

He rubs his jaw, looking like he wants to say something.

"Dave, what is it? What happened?"

"It doesn't matter. He's gone now." Dave goes around me to the recording area and gathers up our things. "Did you already have lunch? If not, we could stop somewhere."

I walk over to him. "Tell me what happened. I want to know."

He hesitates, then says, "Jeremy said things that were very inappropriate."

"About what?"

"You." His jaw tightens and I notice the creases in his forehead deepening. "I overheard him saying things about you to whoever he was talking to on the phone."

"What did he say?"

"He was making comments about your body. Crude, inappropriate things, like he was some high school kid talking to his friends in the locker room. He said if you weren't married he'd—I'm not even going to repeat it. The point is, I don't want one of our employees talking about you that way."

"I can't believe Jeremy would do that," I say, completely shocked. "I had no idea he saw me that way. I'm not even close to his age."

"Yes, well, you look much younger than you are, and you're very beautiful, so I'm not surprised he's attracted to you, but it's completely inappropriate."

"When did this happen? When did you overhear him saying these things?"

"Last Friday. He was in the editing room, working on some ads. I was going to go say hi to him, but stopped when I heard him on the phone. I almost went in there and confronted him, but decided not to. I wanted a day or two to cool off and figure out what to do. I suppose I could've let it go, but the idea of him being around you, thinking of you that way, made me furious. I couldn't allow it. He had to go."

"You did the right thing. I would've fired him too if I'd known. Why didn't you tell me?"

"Because I knew it would make you uncomfortable being around him. You didn't sleep for days after that man at the event told you he loved you. I thought it was best to keep quiet about this and just fire the guy."

"I'm glad you did. I still can't believe Jeremy would talk about me that way."

"I can." Dave brings me into his arms. "You're a very beautiful woman. You're always getting attention from men. But you're mine." He smiles at me. "And anyone who tries to take you from me is going to regret it."

Nick tried to take me from him, but Dave will never find that out. I'll make sure of it. If Nick changed his number, I'll find some other way to reach him. I'm not letting him do this. He's not going to destroy my marriage.

# CHAPTER SEVEN

"DID YOU CHECK THE MAIL?" Dave asks as we're leaving the recording studio.

"No, but I can. I'll go grab it."

"I'll meet you out back."

He heads to the parking lot while I go out the front office door to the common area shared by all the tenants in the building. There's a wall of mailboxes there and Dave and I always forget to check ours. I get out my key, unlock the box, and find that it's overflowing with envelopes of all sizes and colors.

People are always sending us cards and letters, letting us know how much their marriage has improved since attending one of our events or listening to our podcast. I love reading them. It reminds me why we're doing this, which is helpful on days when I want to give it all up. Life was so much simpler when we were first starting out and only had the podcast. The in-person events have added a lot of stress to our lives and little time for relaxation.

"Need some help?" Dave asks, getting out of the car when he sees my arms are overflowing with mail.

"If you could open the trunk, that would help."

He hits the button that pops open the trunk and I put the cards and letters in it. One falls to the ground and I pick it up. It's a red envelope with heart stickers all over it.

"Dave, look," I say, holding it up. "Heart stickers. Isn't that sweet?"

"Open it. You can read it on the way home."

We get in the car, and as Dave pulls out of the parking lot, I take the card from the envelope. It's red with a white heart on the front and no words. I open the card and a piece of paper falls out.

"What's the card say?" Dave asks, turning onto the street.

"Nothing, but they enclosed a note," I say, holding up the piece of paper.

"Go ahead and read it."

"Dear Iris. I really enjoy your podcast. You have such a beautiful voice. I could listen to it for hours. If only your husband would stop talking so it could just be you, speaking in that melodic voice."

"Wait," Dave says. "It really says that?"

"Yes." I show it to him.

"I can't read it while I'm driving. What else does it say?"

I look back at the note. "Your advice on love has helped me so much. I never knew what love was until you explained it. That's when I realized I was in love." I smile at Dave. "Isn't that nice? We helped him realize he was in love."

"*You* did. Apparently, I talk too much."

"Oh, honey, don't be that way," I say with a laugh. "Maybe he just prefers the sound of a woman's voice."

"What else did he write?"

I continue reading where I left off. "It isn't just your voice I fell in love with, but you."

"Not this guy again," Dave says with a sigh. "The police made it clear he's to have no contact with you."

"We don't know that it's him."

"Where's it from?" Dave asks.

"I don't know," I say, looking at the envelope. "There's no return address."

"That's odd." Dave takes the envelope from me. "The postmark is smudged. I can't tell where it was sent from. What else did the note say?"

I look back at it. "We'll be together soon. Until then, I wish you the very best. And then it's signed your forever love."

"It's either from that guy who was at our event or some random guy who listens to our podcast."

*Or it's Nick. The man I had an affair with. The one you don't know about. The one who's determined to destroy my life.* That's what's running through my mind, but I'm trying to remain calm so Dave doesn't suspect anything.

"I guess Allen was right," Dave says.

"About what?"

"About us getting unwanted attention the more well-known we become."

"Yeah, I guess so." I toss the note on the floor and stare out the front window.

"Honey, are you okay?" Dave asks.

I nod, but don't say anything.

"Iris, your hands are shaking. You're clearly upset about that note."

"I'm not upset." I look at Dave. "I'm just surprised. I wasn't expecting it to say that."

"I wouldn't worry about it. The man's nowhere near here. It's not like he's going to show up at our door."

He might. I'm sure Nick looked up where I live, which means it's possible he'll show up there.

"If you're really worried," Dave says, "we could call the officer we spoke to before and ask him if we have any reason to be concerned."

"We don't need to do that. I'm sure you're right and whoever wrote it is harmless. He's probably some lonely man who listens to our podcast and made up a story in his head that he and I are in love."

"That part makes me angry. I don't like other men telling you they love you." He reaches over and grips my hand, smiling at me. "I'm the only one who gets to tell you that." He puts his hand back on the steering wheel. "Do you still have the officer's number? The one we worked with before?"

"Yes. It's in my phone."

"Call him up. Read him the letter and ask him what he thinks."

"It's not necessary. He has more important things to deal with. I don't want to bother him with this."

"Maybe you're right. He'd probably say we're making too big a deal out of this. If Allen's correct and this type of thing is common with people in the public eye, maybe we should just let it go and not worry about it."

"I agree."

But I can't let it go. I need to deal with Nick, but how do I do that when I don't know where he is and I'm unable to call him?

We're home now and Dave pulls into the garage. "I can't believe I have to deal with this."

"Deal with what?" I ask as we go into the house.

"Finding someone to replace Jeremy."

I follow Dave as he goes to the kitchen. "Can't Allen do it?"

"He's the one who hired Jeremy. I don't trust his judgment." Dave takes a glass from the cupboard. "He went on and on about Jeremy being a perfect fit for us. He said he was smart, ambitious, an expert in his field. And look what happened."

"I think Jeremy was smart. And it seemed like he knew a lot about online marketing."

"How much could he possibly know when he's only been out of school a few years?" Dave fills his glass with water. "And none of his ideas seemed original. I think he was just copying what other marketers did."

"At least he was affordable. Someone with more experience is going to be a lot more expensive."

"I've thought about that." He takes a drink of his water. "It's one of the reasons we can't cut back on our live events. We need the money if we want to hire someone who actually knows what they're doing." Dave finishes his water, then sets the glass down. "I'll be in the office if you need me."

"You're working? I thought we were having lunch."

"I lost my appetite after dealing with Jeremy."

The doorbell rings. "I'll get it."

"Let me answer it." He heads to the door. "Just in case it's one of your overzealous fans."

"Honey, wait!" I race in front of him, fearing it might be Nick at the door. "I'm sure it's just one of the neighbors. You go ahead and work. I'll get the door."

He eyes me a moment, then says, "Okay. I'll be in my office."

The way he was looking at me just now makes me think he suspects something's going on with me. Even if he did have suspicions, he'd never guess the truth. He thinks I'm the perfect wife, someone who would never be unfaithful. And I plan to keep it that way.

# CHAPTER EIGHT

"You're home," Jane says with a smile as I open the door. "Renee thought she saw you leaving with Dave."

Renee lives across the street. She's married to an attorney and has two young boys. She's always taking them places so she's rarely home.

"We were gone this morning, but we're back now," I say. "I was just about to make lunch."

"What great timing! I was going to invite you over. I made the most wonderful chicken salad. You just have to try it!"

Jane is always making recipes and always says they're wonderful even when they're not. Last year, she made a creamy vegetable soup that was the most terrible thing I've ever tasted. I choked down a few bites, then told her I wasn't feeling well and couldn't finish it.

Dave said I should've just told her I didn't like it, but Jane doesn't take criticism well. One time her husband told her he didn't like the dress she was wearing and she didn't speak to him for a week. And she's no longer friends with the people down the street after they asked her to turn off the music coming out of the inflatable Santa she had on her lawn last Christmas. She purposely bought the Santa because it played music, thinking the neighbors would find it festive and fun. She took it personally when the Steinhowsers complained about the noise.

"Chicken salad sounds great," I say, knowing I have almost nothing to eat here. Dave and I are so busy we rarely have time to make it to the store. We usually end up eating out or having something delivered. "Let me just go tell Dave. He's in his office."

"Let him be. If he's working, he won't even notice you're gone." She turns back. "Renee, are you coming?"

"Be there in a minute!" I hear her say.

"Renee's coming?" I ask. "With the kids?"

"No, the kids are with their grandma today," Jane says, turning back to me. She lowers her voice to a whisper. "Renee's having some problems in her marriage. I thought maybe you could offer her some advice. Just don't make it too obvious. And don't tell her I told you."

"Jane, I can't be getting involved in Renee's marriage. I'm not a therapist, and even if I was, I wouldn't counsel her unless she asked me to."

"Don't think of it as counseling. Think of it as being her friend." Jane glances behind her. "Here she comes. Act normal."

*Act normal?* How does she think I'm going to act?

I wish Jane would stay out of everyone's business. She thinks she's helping people, but unless they ask for it, they don't want her help.

"Hi, Iris," Renee says, coming up behind Jane. She looks

flawless as always, with perfectly done makeup and hair, wearing wide-legged jeans and a fitted black sweater. I don't know how she manages to look that good and also take care of two little ones.

"Hi, Renee," I say. "I heard you got the day off."

She laughs. "Yes, Trent's mother has the kids for the day. It's her first time having them without me. I keep expecting her to call and ask me to pick them up."

"Well, until she does, you can enjoy some time with us," Jane says, smiling at her. "Shall we go?"

As the three of us walk over to Jane's house, I text Dave, letting him know Jane invited me over for lunch. He texts right back, saying he hopes she's not serving the creamy vegetable soup. I smile at his response, surprised he remembered the soup since that incident happened over a year ago. A lot of husbands wouldn't have even listened to the story, but Dave listened and remembered. I really lucked out with him. He's such a loving and attentive husband. We struggled early on in our marriage, but we're in a really good place now and I'm determined to not let anything change that. Or anyone.

"Iris?" Jane says. "Are you coming?"

As she says it, I realize I'm standing outside while Jane and Renee are already in the house.

"Oh, sorry. My mind wandered." I join them in the living room.

"Lunch is right through here," Jane says, leading Renee and me to the dining room.

The table is already set with place settings for three people. I wonder how long Jane's been planning this, and if Renee is really having marriage issues or if Jane made it up. I'm not saying Jane lies, but she does exaggerate the truth to create drama. All it would take is Renee mentioning some small complaint about her husband and Jane would turn that into Renee's marriage being in trouble.

"You girls have a seat," Jane says. "I'll be right back with the sandwiches."

"Are you sure you don't need some help?" I ask.

"I've got it," Jane says. "You go ahead and sit down."

As Renee and I take our seats, I hear Jane humming to herself in the kitchen, as if she's trying to let us know we can talk without her listening. This is so ridiculous. I barely know Renee. I'm not going to give her marriage advice.

"So how are the kids?" I ask.

"Great!" She smiles. "But I have to admit it's nice to get a little break from them. How's everything with you?"

"Good. Dave and I have been doing more events."

"Yeah, I heard. Jane said your business is really taking off."

Jane returns with a platter of chicken salad sandwiches and a bowl of fruit. "Let me know what you think! I got the recipe from a woman online."

"Thanks for doing all this," Renee says. "It looks wonderful."

"My pleasure," Jane says, sitting down. "So what were you girls talking about?"

"I was asking Iris about her business," Renee says, putting her napkin on her lap.

"Isn't it amazing?" Jane says. "She's saving so many marriages." She smiles at me. "Tell us, Iris, what's the number one secret to a happy marriage?"

Renee was about to bite into her sandwich, but stops and looks over at me.

"Actually, there isn't just one thing," I say. "It's the combination of a lot of things that makes a happy marriage."

"Yes, but if you had to pick one," Jane says, "what would it be?"

"I'd probably say honesty. Honesty builds trust, and without trust, you're going to have issues."

"Are you saying you've never lied to Dave?" Renee asks.

"When we were first together I did, which is one of the reasons we had problems. But when we committed to repairing our marriage, we decided we'd be honest with each other from that point forward."

"I find it hard to believe you two have gone that whole time without telling a lie," Jane says, her mouth full and mayonnaise sticking to the corner of her lips.

"I agree," Renee says. "Everyone lies. Even if it's something small, like your husband telling you that you look great when you really don't. Or just the other day, Trent asked if I thought he was losing his hair and I told him no, even though he is definitely losing his hair."

"How are things going with you two?" Jane asks, wiping her mouth with her napkin. Here she goes, bringing up Renee's marriage in the hopes that I'll give her advice.

"It's not the same as before we had kids, but that's to be expected. Kids can be hard on a marriage."

"What do you mean?" Jane asks with a frown. "Are you two having issues?"

"I'm sure she doesn't want to talk about that," I say. "Why don't we talk about something else? Like the chicken salad." I hold up my sandwich. "It's very good. You should definitely make this again."

"Actually, if you wouldn't mind," Renee says to me. "Could I ask for some advice?"

"Of course," I say, setting my sandwich down. I guess Jane was right and Renee really is having marital problems. Maybe Trent's having an affair. He's a rich, successful lawyer and very good-looking. I'm sure women come on to him.

Renee scoots her chair back and looks down at her lap. "I can't believe I'm telling you this. I feel so ashamed. I never wanted anyone to know."

"Go ahead, dear," Jane says. "We won't judge, will we, Iris?"

"No, of course not," I say, but I can only speak for myself. Jane judges people all the time. She also gossips. If I were Renee, I'd ask Jane to leave before saying whatever it is she's about to say.

"After I had Austin," Renee says, referring to her oldest son, "I was feeling really down about myself. I didn't like how I looked. I felt like I wasn't attractive anymore. Trent was working a lot, and when he was home, he didn't have any interest in..." She glances up at me. "In being with me. In the bedroom."

"That's fairly normal with first-time parents. They're so exhausted that being intimate is the last thing on their mind."

"I understand that now, but back then I assumed he'd lost interest in me because of how I looked after having the baby." She looks down. "I needed to feel wanted again so I..."

"You what?" Jane asks in an eager tone, like this is a story in a book and not someone's actual life.

"I had an affair," she says, her eyes rising to mine. "I didn't mean for it to happen. We were just talking online and then we met in person and... it just happened."

"You met him online?"

She nods. "In a parent group. He told me his wife lost interest in him after their first child was born. We bonded over thinking our spouses didn't want us anymore. We used that as an excuse for the affair."

That was my excuse too. When I cheated with Nick, I justified it by convincing myself my marriage was over. That Dave didn't want me anymore. All we did was fight, and I was sure we were going to get a divorce.

"How long did it go on?" I ask Renee.

"Two months. But we didn't see each other much. As a new mom, I rarely had time to myself. Friends would offer to watch the baby so I could have an hour or two to go out and get a haircut or a manicure. But instead, I'd go see Joel." She sighs. "I feel sick about it. Even now, years later, I feel so ashamed that I can barely look at Trent." She swallows. "I guess what I'm asking is, how do I get past this? Carrying this secret is hurting my marriage. I don't feel as close to Trent as I used to, and I know it's because of this secret."

"Would you ever consider telling him?" Jane asks.

"No. Never. Trent would never forgive me. We'd end up getting divorced. And I wouldn't want Trent confronting Joel and ruining his marriage. He's still with his wife, and last I heard, they're doing better. Trent and I are doing better too, but I can't stop thinking about what I did." She looks at me. "I really need some advice. I don't want this ruining my marriage."

"This is really more about you than your marriage," I say. "You need to figure out the reason you had the affair. There was a deeper reason than not feeling attractive, something you may not even realize until you spend time thinking about it. I suggest you do the journaling exercises on my website. They can help you uncover what was behind your decision to have the affair so you can understand it and then forgive yourself. Only then will you be able to get rid of the shame and move on."

"That's it?" Jane says to me. "You think writing in a journal is going to fix this?"

"Writing down your thoughts can be very powerful," I tell her. "And it can help release the guilt and shame she's feeling."

"I'll try it," Renee says. "I'll try anything at this point. I already feel better just saying it out loud. But I need both of you to promise you'll never tell anyone."

Jane and I assure her we'll keep quiet about it.

"How about you, Iris?" Jane turns to me. "As long as we're telling secrets, do you have any you'd like to share?"

"I don't," I tell her, picking up my glass of iced tea. "Do you?"

"I once kissed Richard's friend at a party, but it was years ago, before we were married. If I told him now, he wouldn't care." She pauses, eyeing me, a grin on her face. "Come on, Iris. I know you have secrets. Give us one. Renee and I promise not to tell."

"I really don't have any," I say. "I live a rather dull life."

"Nonsense," Jane scoffs. "You're a celebrity. You've got all those events. A book coming out. You're getting interviewed by the media."

"I'm not a celebrity," I say with a laugh. "And I don't have a book coming out."

"Oh, Iris, you don't need to deny it. I already know. I overheard your husband talking about it on the phone."

"When?" I ask, thinking she must've misheard him. Dave never mentioned us writing a book.

Jane shrugs. "Last week sometime. I was having a cocktail

on the patio when I heard him talking about it to someone on the phone."

"You heard him saying we're writing a book?"

"Yes. Why do you ask? Did you really not know?"

"I didn't. He never mentioned it."

Jane smiles a little. "Sounds like your husband isn't as honest as you think."

# CHAPTER NINE

"DAVE?" I call out when I'm back at the house. I go down to his office, but it's empty. I walk back to the living room. "Honey, where are you?"

"He's not here," a voice says, startling me.

I turn and see a man standing there. A tall, muscular man with a snake tattoo that wraps around his neck.

"Who are you?" I ask, panicking, because this man should not be in my house.

"The lawn guy." He folds his arms over his chest. "Are you the wife?"

"We don't have a lawn guy."

"You do now, or you will after your husband signs the agreement."

"What agreement? What are you talking about?"

"He didn't tell you?"

"No."

The guy laughs to himself.

"Why is that funny?" I ask.

"Aren't you two those marriage experts I'm always seeing on

ads?" He shrugs. "I think it's funny your husband didn't tell you. Seems like you two need to work on your communication." He laughs again.

"We communicate just fine," I say, annoyed with the guy. "My husband mentioned hiring a lawn service. He just didn't tell me he'd done it." I look around. "He's really not here?"

"He's out back, talking on the phone." The man looks me up and down. "You look a lot better in person than you do on those ads."

I take a step back. "I think you should wait outside."

"Your husband told me to wait here."

"Yes, well—"

"Iris, I thought you were having lunch with Jane," Dave says, coming up behind me.

"I was, but we finished up and I came home."

Dave puts his arm around me. "I see you met Zach."

"It's more like I ran into him." I look up at Dave. "I wasn't aware you'd hired someone."

"I haven't yet. I still need to sign the agreement."

"I've got it right here." Zach yanks a sheet of paper from his back pocket, unfolds it, and hands it to Dave.

Dave signs the agreement and hands it to Zach. "You said you can start this weekend?"

"Sure, whatever you want."

"Great!" Dave walks him to the door. "We'll see you on Saturday."

When he's gone, I say to Dave, "Why didn't you talk to me about this?"

Dave gives me a confused look. "I did, and we agreed I'd hire someone. With everything we have going on, you know I don't have time to care for the yard."

"Yes, but I thought you'd include me when deciding who to hire."

"I didn't know I needed to." He pulls me into his arms. "I'm sorry, honey. I wasn't intentionally excluding you. I just didn't think you wanted to be bothered with something like this. I thought I was helping by taking care of it."

"You were," I say as he lets me go. "And I appreciate you doing it. I just wish you'd told me he was coming over. It frightened me to find a strange man in my house."

"You're right. I should've told you."

I pause, thinking back to what Jane said about Dave and a possible book deal. "Is there anything else you haven't told me?"

"No. Why do you ask?"

"It's nothing," I say, shaking my head. "Jane thought she overheard something, but you know how she is. She's always coming up with things that aren't true."

Dave's forehead wrinkles as his brows draw together. "What did she overhear?"

"Something about us writing a book, but if that were true, you would've told me."

He looks down, rubbing his jaw.

My pulse races as I realize what Jane overheard might have been true. If it wasn't, Dave would've immediately denied it. "Dave, say something."

He sighs, his eyes meeting up with mine. "I wanted it to be a surprise. I was going to take you to dinner and—"

"Wait, so it's true? You accepted a book deal? Without telling me?"

"There isn't a deal. Not yet. We're still working out the details. Honey, I was going to tell you this week. I was just waiting to see what the final number was. How much we'd be getting for an advance."

I go to the couch to sit down, my stomach in knots, my mind racing as I try to figure out if I should be upset about this or believe Dave was only keeping this from me so he could surprise me with the news. If that really was his intention, I shouldn't be mad, but I am because it goes against our agreement to be honest with each other.

"You should've told me," I say, looking over at Dave. "We agreed not to keep things from each other."

"I understand that, but Iris, you're always saying how much you dislike the business side of things. You enjoy interacting with people, solving their problems, helping them find love again. You have no interest in contracts and negotiations. You've told me that many times."

"That doesn't mean I want to be excluded from the discussion."

Dave comes over and sits beside me. "I wasn't trying to exclude you. I was trying to take care of a job I know you don't like, and I was hoping to surprise you with the news and enjoy a celebratory dinner."

I want to believe him, but I feel like he purposely kept this from me so he wouldn't have to consider my input.

I turn to Dave. "Just because I don't like doing something doesn't mean I want you to take it over. I need to be involved in decisions about our business, and our home. Like with the lawn care. I would've liked to be involved in who we hire. I don't like Zach, but you hired him and now we're stuck with him."

"Why don't you like Zach?"

"I didn't get a good feeling from him. The way he was

looking at me made me very uncomfortable and then he made this comment saying I was prettier in person than in our ads."

Dave smiles. "Honey, you're beautiful. You can't blame a man for noticing your looks and commenting on them."

"It was inappropriate. He's our employee. I'm paying him for a service. And I'm married. If it were up to me, I never would've hired him."

"Why don't we see how it goes? I don't want to spend time finding someone else. And chances are, you'll never see him. He'll be outside doing the work and then he'll leave." Dave's phone rings and he silences it.

"Who is it?" I ask.

"Allen. He wants to discuss the ads now that Jeremy's gone. Would you like to be involved?"

"Yes," I blurt out, but then I remember how meetings with Allen can go on for hours as he goes over research and data and shows us spreadsheets. It's tedious, and most of it goes over my head. Dave loves numbers and research, but it gives me a headache. "Actually, no. I'm going to let you handle the ad discussion with Allen."

"Are you sure?" Dave asks. "You just lectured me on how I need to include you."

"I didn't lecture you," I say, irritated he used that term to describe what I would consider expressing a need. "I simply let you know that I want to be considered in all decisions."

"But not this one."

"No. I think you and Allen can handle the ad discussion without me."

"Then I'm going to go call him back," Dave says, getting up. "The ads can't wait. We need to run promotions for our next event."

"Before you go, tell me about this book we're writing."

"There isn't much to tell," he says, sitting back down. "It's basically our program in a book format."

"That's it? That's not enough for an entire book."

"It will be once we add in examples of how the program has worked for people. I've come up with some other things to add, but I'd love to get your input as well. I'll send you the outline and you can add your ideas." He smiles. "How does that sound?"

"Good, but I really wish you'd included me earlier. It almost feels like you intentionally kept this from me, like you wanted to keep it a secret."

"Iris, you know I wouldn't do that. No secrets. That was our agreement."

"And yet you didn't tell me about Zach or this book or—"

"Honey, stop." He holds my hand. "You're letting your mind turn this into something it isn't. What do we always say to our clients?"

"That actions aren't necessarily intentions."

"Exactly. Just because I did something doesn't mean there was an intention behind it to harm you or harm our marriage. I was simply trying to get things done." He rubs my hand. "You're always saying how exhausted you are, so I was trying to handle things without having to involve you. I'm sorry if you thought that meant I was trying to exclude you or hide things from you, because I promise you, that was not my intention."

I nod, but I'm not sure I believe him.

He gives me a kiss. "I'm going to go call Allen."

As he gets up to leave, I have this uneasy feeling that he's not being truthful. That there's still something he's not telling me.

# CHAPTER TEN

"You never said how your lunch went," Dave says at dinner that night. He took me to my favorite restaurant, probably hoping it'd make me get over my anger at him for keeping things from me.

I'm not really angry at Dave. It's more a feeling of disappointment. Our marriage is supposed to be built on a foundation of honesty and trust, and yet the past week, I've felt like that foundation is starting to crumble.

"It was fine," I say, taking a sip of my wine.

"Fine?" Dave chuckles. "That's all you have to say? Surely, Jane had some interesting stories to tell. Complaints about her husband. Gossip about the neighbors."

"She didn't talk as much as usual, probably because Renee was there."

"Renee from across the street?" Dave asks, cutting into his steak.

"Yes, she joined us for lunch. I guess I forgot to tell you that."

"Did she bring the kids?"

"No, they were with Trent's mother. Renee seemed relieved to have a few hours without them. I'm sure it's exhausting having two young children to care for."

"So what's new with Renee?" he asks.

I instantly think of what she told us about her affair and how it's affecting her marriage. I desperately want to tell Dave, knowing he'd probably have advice for her that I didn't think of. As a man, he'd see the situation differently than I would. That's why we work so well together. We address marital issues from different perspectives, creating a more well-rounded approach to dealing with them. It's the reason we're so successful, and why we appeal to both men and women.

"Iris?" Dave says. "Did you hear me?"

"Yes, sorry." I smile at him. "I was trying to think of what to tell you."

"About Renee?"

"Yes. She told me something I'm not supposed to share. But I feel like I could help her more if I told you."

"Help her with what?"

I lean toward him and lower my voice. "If I tell you this, you have to promise you won't tell anyone."

"Iris, you know I don't gossip about people."

"Just promise me you'll keep this between us. And if you see Renee or Trent, you have to pretend you know nothing about this."

"I won't say anything. So what's going on?"

I tell him about Renee's affair with a man she met online. Dave seems shocked at first, like I was, then concerned as I tell him how it's affecting her marriage.

"And Trent has no idea this happened?" Dave asks.

"No. Renee's kept it a secret all these years."

Dave picks up his wine and leans back in his chair. "I never would've guessed Renee would do that, especially after just having their first child."

"I can understand why she felt that way."

"You can?" Dave asks, cocking his head to the side.

"I don't mean as a mother. I mean as a woman, feeling like you're not as attractive or desirable as you once were. I felt that way when you and I were having problems."

"You felt undesirable?" Dave reaches across the table and puts his hand over mine. "Honey, I've always wanted to be with you, even when we were having problems. If you felt that way, you should've told me."

"But I couldn't back then. Just like Renee couldn't tell Trent how she was feeling. She was supposed to feel happy about being a new mother and not care how she looked or if her husband desired her. She felt ashamed for even thinking about herself when she had a new baby to care for."

"So she had an affair," Dave says, sounding disgusted with her. "To make herself feel better."

"No, she had an affair because this man allowed her to say things she couldn't say to her husband." I hear the defensiveness in my tone and scold myself for it. I'm letting my feelings about my own affair get mixed up in Renee's. I don't want Dave wondering why I'm getting my emotions involved in a situation that has nothing to do with me.

"She could've told Trent how she was feeling," Dave says. "I'm sure he would've done whatever he could to support her in what she was going through."

"How could he? He's never home. He's always at work, and I'm sure back then, he'd come home and want to spend time with the baby. Renee said he showed no interest in her, even when they were in the bedroom."

"It's still not a reason to cheat," Dave says, going back to eating his steak.

"I agree cheating wasn't the answer, but it's over now and she needs to find a way to get past it."

"She needs to tell him. That's the only way to fix this. Honesty builds trust, and trust is the foundation of a good marriage."

I'm annoyed he's quoting our marriage program. I was hoping he'd give me advice I hadn't considered, not just say what I already know.

"She can't tell Trent. He'd never forgive her. They'd end up divorcing."

"Maybe that's for the best," Dave says, taking a bite of his steak.

"They have two little boys. Do you really think divorcing is the best thing for their family?"

"If the trust is gone, there's no foundation for their marriage. It's eventually going to fail unless she tells him the truth and they work through it."

"But telling him the truth isn't an option."

"Then it's not going to work. By keeping this secret from Trent, she's lying to him, and lies lead to divorce. I feel bad for the kids, but in this case, divorce might be the best option."

"I'm really surprised to hear you say that. Our whole program is about keeping couples together, no matter what."

"But it only works if the couple agrees to be honest. If they can't do that, their marriage will fail. That's what the data shows. I'm not just making this up."

"I know what the data shows," I say, not liking his

patronizing tone. "But in this case, being honest will end their marriage. I was hoping to find a way for Renee to stay with Trent without having to tell him what happened. It was a mistake, and she regrets it. Now she just wants to move on."

"I don't know how she can when she's keeping this huge secret from her husband." He picks up the wine bottle. "Would you like some more?"

I shake my head. I'm really disappointed he's not putting more thought into this. I know we're not really friends with Renee and Trent, but they're our neighbors, and they're a couple in need of marriage help, which is what we do for a living. I assumed Dave would have better advice than to get a divorce.

For the remainder of dinner, Dave talks about our book and asks for my input, like how I think we should organize each chapter. I'm glad he's finally including me in the book project, but I'm still annoyed with him for not showing more compassion for Renee and her situation.

"I really enjoyed tonight," Dave says when we get home. "I've missed you."

"You're with me every day." I smile at him as his arms go around me.

"Yes, but we're always racing to get things done. Tonight we were able to have a nice relaxing dinner. Linger at the table. Share a bottle of wine. It was nice."

"We could have more nights like this if we cut back on our events."

"Is that what you'd like?" he asks, tucking a strand of hair behind my ear.

"Maybe. I know the events are helping a lot of people, but I don't want it to be at the expense of our marriage."

"Honey, that would never happen. Nothing will ever come between us. I wouldn't let it. And neither would you."

"Yes, but sometimes couples drift apart without even realizing it. With the events, and the podcast, and everything else, I'm starting to feel more like your coworker than your wife."

"Then perhaps we need to cut back."

"Would you really do that?" I ask, knowing he'd rather do more events than less.

"If it would make you happy, then yes. Unfortunately, we've already booked events for the next few months and can't cancel at this point, but we can certainly schedule fewer events going forward as we plan out our year."

I'm surprised he's being so agreeable. I didn't even want to bring this up, knowing how much he loves doing the events. But if we keep going at this pace, we'll have no time to relax and enjoy time together as a couple.

"You're really okay with this?" I ask.

"Of course. You and our marriage come before anything else." He gives me a kiss. "Now, could I make a request?"

"Go ahead."

"I'd like to continue our evening in the bedroom." He smiles. "You look gorgeous in that dress, but I'd really like to take it off."

I smile back. "I'd like that too."

We go into the bedroom, and as we make love, I realize I feel closer to Dave than I have in weeks. We needed this night to reconnect and reignite our love for each other. Even though we discussed the book during dinner, it didn't feel like we were focused on work. It felt like we were connecting over our shared passion for helping other couples find happiness. The past few months, as we've become consumed with growing the business, I feel like we've lost that passion, but tonight I felt it coming back. And I'm thrilled Dave agreed to cut back on our events. It proves how committed he is to our marriage.

"That was amazing," he says, holding me in his arms. He kisses my forehead. "We should do that more often."

I look at him. "We should plan a trip. Get away from here. Away from work."

"I'd love to, but we can't. We have something scheduled almost every day for the next few months."

"We could cancel some of our media appearances."

"That's free promotion. We can't turn those down." He rubs my arm. "But I promise I'll talk to Allen tomorrow and tell him to stop booking us for so many things."

"I appreciate you doing that. I know it's not what you want."

"What I want is to make my wife happy." He gives me a kiss.

Now I feel foolish for being angry with him earlier. Dave is an amazing husband. Better than I ever could've imagined. He has his faults, and we don't always agree on things, but he loves me no matter what and would do most anything for me. I need to stop finding fault with him and be grateful to have found such a wonderful man.

# CHAPTER ELEVEN

"I'M AT THE GROCERY STORE," I say, answering Dave's call as I wait in line at the checkout.

"I wish you'd waited for me. I would've gone with you."

"I didn't want to wait. I just wanted to get it done." I move over as a woman reaches past me to get a pack of gum from the rack. "So you're home now?"

"Yes, but I was going to head to the studio unless you need me to stay here."

"No, you can go. What are you doing at the studio?"

"Editing the new ads since we don't have anyone to do it now."

"Okay. Then I'll guess I'll see you when you get home. Bye!" I end the call and push my cart up in line.

"Excuse me," the woman behind me says. She's older, with short blond hair, wearing lots of makeup and well-dressed. "Are you Iris, the marriage guru?"

I smile. "I'm not sure I'd call myself a guru, but yes, I do marriage coaching."

"You have that podcast, right? The one with your husband?"

"Yes. Have you listened to it?"

Her face lights up. "Are you kidding? I listen to it all the time! I've heard every episode. I can't believe it's really you! Standing in front of me in the grocery store line! I tell everyone about your podcast. I bet I've gotten at least fifty people to subscribe to it. Probably more than that. I sell real estate, so I'm always meeting new people. I get lots of newly married couples, and I swear most of them are headed for divorce. Constant arguing. Giving each other dirty looks. I always tell them about your podcast, hoping it'll save their marriage."

"That's very nice of you. Thank you." I move forward in the line.

"Can I make a suggestion? About the podcast?"

"Sure. I always like to hear feedback from listeners."

"Ditch the husband," she says. "You don't need him. You'd be better off doing it alone."

"The premise of the show is that we're a married couple giving advice. It has to include Dave."

"Trust me, it'd be better without him. When you give advice, it sounds sincere, like you really care about couples getting help. When Dave talks, it sounds fake, like he's reading off a script."

"Next," the cashier says, and when I look over at her, I see she's waiting for me to unload my cart.

"I'm not saying your husband isn't a great guy," the woman says as I put my grocery items on the belt. "He just doesn't have the right personality to be doing the podcast. He can't relate to people like you can."

"Yes, well, thank you for your input," I say, smiling at her. "It was nice meeting you."

"You too. And hey, I didn't mean to offend you. I was just being honest."

I smile but don't say anything, thinking if I stop talking to her she'll get the hint to leave me alone. I'm sure she thinks she's being helpful, but I really don't like hearing her say bad things about my husband.

The cashier finishes up and I pay for my groceries.

"Have a good day!" the woman yells as I'm leaving.

"You too!" I say as I leave the store.

When I get to my car, I hurry to put the groceries in the trunk. I don't want that woman finding me out here and wanting to chat some more. Luckily, by the time I finish up, she's still in the store.

I get in my car and notice a note on the windshield tucked under the wiper blade. Assuming it's some kind of ad, I yank it from the wiper and am about to toss it in the back seat when I notice my name on it. Turning it over, I see a note that reads, *Dear Iris. You and I are meant to be together. He doesn't love you like I would. Why can't you see that? I need you, Iris, more than I need air or food or anything else. Be with me and I promise I'll make you happy. Love you always. Your forever love.*

I get in my car, shut the door, and lock it. I search the parking lot for whoever left the note. Is it from Nick? He's not the type of man who writes love notes, but maybe this is part of his plan. Instead of just calling me, telling me what he's up to, he's decided to play some kind of ridiculous game in which he drops hints that he's back. First the roses, then the card, and now this.

Reading the note again, it doesn't sound like something

Nick would write, especially the part about needing me more than air or food. That's a little creepy. I can't imagine him coming up with something like that. Then again, I really didn't know him that well. Other than our little meetups, we didn't see each other, and we never talked on the phone. Our only communication was by text, to arrange when we'd meet again.

What if Nick isn't mentally well and made up a story in his head that we're in love and need to be together? Would he do something to Dave? To get rid of him?

No, he'd never do that. What am I thinking? Nick isn't dangerous. I'm being paranoid, like Jane said at lunch the other day. If she noticed that, Dave might too. I can't let myself get worked up about this. I need to end it before Nick takes this any further.

Getting out of the car, I search the parking lot for him. I'm sure he's gone, but if there's even a tiny chance he's still here, I'm going to find him.

"Looking for something?" a woman asks as I go down one of the lanes. "I'd be happy to help."

"I'm fine," I say, and when I glance up I see it's the woman who was behind me in line.

"Are you sure?" she asks, stopping with her shopping cart. "You seem upset. Did you lose your keys?"

"No, I, um..." I pause to think of an excuse. "There was a cat. It was running under the cars. I didn't want it getting hurt so I was going to try to catch it and bring it inside the store to a manager. In case someone lost it."

"Aww, aren't you sweet?" the woman says. "I knew you were as nice as you come across on the podcast." She nods at her shopping cart. "Let me put these away and I'll help you search for the cat."

"Oh, no, you don't have to do that. I'm pretty sure he ran off."

She scrunches up her face. "Then why are you still looking?"

"You're right. I'm not going to find him if he's not here." I laugh. "I'm going to head back to my car." I hurry across the parking lot.

When I finally reach the car, I see the woman watching me as I get in. She'll probably post this on social media and soon I'll get messages with people either praising me for trying to save a cat or hating me for not finding it and bringing it inside.

Everything you do these days is picked apart and judged. That's another reason why I can't let anyone find out about my affair. If it became public, people would say horrible things about me online. They wouldn't care why I did it, or what my marriage was like when it happened. All they'd care about is punishing me and making me the villain.

As I'm driving home, my phone rings. It's Dave calling.

"Hey, how's it going?" I answer.

"Slow. I probably won't be home until late."

"Oh. I was planning to make dinner."

"I won't be home in time. Go ahead and eat without me."

"Why don't I bring dinner to the studio? Then I could stay and help with the ads."

"This isn't something you can help with. I'm working on the technical stuff. There's something off with the audio."

"I could still bring dinner."

"There's leftover pizza in the office fridge. I'll just have that."

"Okay, but if you change your mind, I'd be happy to bring you something."

"That's very sweet, but I don't need anything. I'll see you tonight."

"Yeah, okay."

I was hoping he'd be home with me tonight, but maybe it's best if he's not. I'm really on edge about Nick. I need to calm down before being around Dave. I don't want him asking me what's wrong and then having to lie to him.

Lying to my husband is not something I ever wanted to do. But I had no choice. When Dave committed to saving our marriage, I had to hide what I'd done. If I'd told him the truth, Dave would've left me.

I promised myself he'd never find out, and I'm keeping that promise. I'll do anything to keep Dave from knowing about Nick.

# CHAPTER TWELVE

IT'S BEEN two days since I got that note on my car and I'm still distraught about it. I've barely slept, and I keep checking out the window to make sure he's not out there, watching me.

"Iris?" Dave says, getting my attention.

I turn away from the window. "Did you need something?"

"Yes." He walks up to me. "I need you to stop checking out the window. He's not there."

"Who?" I ask, panicking, thinking Dave knows about Nick. I know he doesn't, but that's where my mind goes.

"That man. The one from the event. He's not going to show up here. In fact, I'm guessing by now he's given up on you and moved on to someone else."

"You're probably right," I say, playing along. "I don't know why I'm letting him get to me."

"Honey, it's normal. I completely understand. His actions frightened you and now you feel like you can't relax." He takes my hand. "But I'm right here, and I would never let anything happen to you."

"I know," I say, smiling at him.

"Let's go sit down," he says, bringing me to the couch. "I want to ask you something."

"Go ahead." I turn to face him.

"I was thinking about that card you got, the one with the hearts on it. And those roses."

I tense up, my pulse going faster. "What about them?"

"Do you think they could be from someone you know? Maybe someone from your past? An ex-boyfriend? Or some guy who showed an interest in you that you rejected?"

My mind immediately goes to Nick. I rejected him by ending our affair, but he knew it wouldn't last. He knew I wasn't leaving Dave. He can't possibly think this little game of his would make me change my mind. Nick was a fling. I didn't love him. Even if Dave and I had divorced, I didn't see myself having a future with Nick.

"What do you think?" Dave asks, since I haven't responded. "Is there someone from your past who might be doing this?"

"No." I shake my head. "I can't think of anyone."

"What about someone from college? Or a co-worker from one of your old jobs? Can you think of anyone who might've had a crush on you or asked you out and you turned him down?"

"No. Even if there was someone like that, he would've forgotten about me by now."

"Unless he saw you on TV or on one of our ads. We've been doing a lot more promotion the past few months. It's possible this guy saw you and it reignited old feelings."

"I don't think so. I'm sure it's like you said. It's someone who listens to the podcast and developed a little crush on me."

Dave's phone rings. He checks it and sets it down. "It's Allen. I told him I'd meet him at the studio to go over the edits I did on the ads. I can't believe how long that took. I should've had Jeremy teach me how to do it before I fired him." Dave pauses. "You don't think it's him, do you?"

"What are you talking about?"

"The person who sent you that card. Do you think it could be Jeremy?"

"No," I say, like the very idea is comical. "Just because he thought I was attractive doesn't mean he was in love with me."

"I wasn't saying that. What I'm thinking is that he might've done it to get back at us for firing him. He knew we had concerns about that man at our event coming after you once he was let out of jail. Maybe Jeremy sent that card to scare us. Make us think that man is still obsessed with you."

It's not Jeremy. It's Nick. He sent the card. I'm sure of it. But I can't tell Dave that.

"If Jeremy wanted revenge," I say, "he'd target his efforts on you, not me. He had nothing against me. And I'm not the one who fired him."

"Yes, you're right." Dave's phone rings. "It's Allen calling again. He wants to know when I'll be there. Do you mind if I go, or do you want me to stay here with you? Or you could come with me."

"I think I'll stay here. I've got Jane next door if I decide I don't want to be alone."

"Have you told her about this? About the card and the flowers?"

"No, and I don't plan to. I don't want her telling the neighbors, which I know she'll do even if I tell her not to."

Dave texts someone on his phone. "I told Allen I'm heading

to the studio." He gives me a kiss, then stands up. "I shouldn't be gone long. Maybe a couple of hours." He walks to the door and when he opens it, something drops on his feet. He picks it up and looks at it. "You want this?"

"What is it?"

"A menu for some Indian restaurant."

I jump up from the couch and go over to him. "Let me see it."

He hands it to me. "Maybe we should try it sometime." He goes out the door. "I'll see you soon."

"Bye," I mutter, staring at the menu. It's from the place Nick and I used to go to. It was down the street from the hotel we went to. Nick loved Indian food, and since the restaurant was nowhere near where I live, there was little chance anyone I knew would see us there.

Why was this menu left at my door? The restaurants that leave us menus are usually close by, within a few miles, not downtown. I look across the street at Renee's door. I don't see a menu sticking out of it, although it's possible she brought it inside.

Did Nick do this? Is this another message from him, letting me know he's back? Why doesn't he just call me? Why play this silly game of dropping hints that he's here? It doesn't make sense.

I close the door and make sure it's locked, then get my phone out and call Jane.

"Iris, how funny you called," she says when she answers. "I was just about to invite you over to try my lavender scones. You must've read my mind."

"Actually, I found this menu outside my door and I was

wondering if you got one too. It's from an Indian restaurant downtown."

"I don't think so, but let me go check." I hear her shoes clicking on the wood floor as she walks to the door. "Why are you asking?"

"I thought it was odd they'd advertise out here. It's a good thirty-minute drive, longer in traffic."

"Okay, I'm checking. There's nothing here. No menu. So are you coming over? I'd love for you to try the scones. I can't decide if they're too dry. I need another opinion."

"I can't today. I have some things I need to get done around the house."

"It won't take long, and I really need another opinion. I wanted to make them for my women's auxiliary group, but if they're no good, I'll have to bring something else."

"Okay, I'll be over," I say, deciding it might be good to not be alone right now.

If Jane didn't get a menu, either the person dropping them off missed her house or it was meant only for me. Going outside, I look at everyone's front door and don't see a menu, which makes me think it was only for me.

It had to have come from Nick. There's no other explanation. Some random person wouldn't leave a menu at my door, especially not for the place I used to go to with my former lover.

"I made tea to go with the scones," Jane says when I arrive at her house. "I got the recipe from this woman online who owns a bed and breakfast." She walks in front of me, leading me to the kitchen. "It seems to be a thing at those places. Tea and scones. Or that's what I've heard. Richard refuses to stay at one so I've never actually been. Have you?"

"Have I what?"

Jane laughs. "Stayed at a bed and breakfast."

"Um, no, I don't think I have."

"Richard thinks the very idea of them is so unappealing." She picks up the teapot and pours us each some tea. "He said it's like paying to stay at your great aunt's musty old house with strangers you're forced to interact with." She hands me a cup of tea. "But I'd still love to stay at one, at least once. Maybe I'll go with my sister." She sips her tea. "Let's go have a seat."

There's a small nook off the kitchen with a table and chairs. I see the scones arranged on a platter along with little ramekins of butter and honey. I could see Jane having a bed and breakfast. She loves cooking and entertaining guests. She'd ask all about their lives and then gossip about them when they left.

"They're good," I say, trying a scone. "Maybe cut back on the lavender."

"I thought so too. You don't think they're too dry?"

"Not at all."

"I do," she says, slathering hers with butter. "So have you talked to Renee?"

"No. Have you?"

Jane shakes her head. "I was hoping you'd follow up with her. The poor girl desperately needs someone to talk to, someone who knows what it's like to carry such a huge secret. You're the perfect person for her to confide in."

"Why me?"

"Because you know what she's going through." Jane licks a glob of butter from her fingers.

"I don't know what you mean."

She laughs. "Oh, Iris, I know about your little tryst."

"What... what are you talking about?"

"You and that man." She breaks off a piece of scone and pops it in her mouth.

My heart's pounding, but I try to remain calm. There's no way she knows. She couldn't. It's not possible.

But then what is she talking about? What man?

# CHAPTER THIRTEEN

"These are really good," I say, holding up my scone. I need to direct the conversation to a different topic. I don't know what Jane was referring to just now and I'm not going to ask. "You should definitely make these for your women's group."

"Iris, you don't have to pretend with me," Jane says, drizzling honey on her scone. "I'm not going to tell."

"There's nothing to tell." I set my scone down, suddenly feeling sick to my stomach.

"I saw you with him," she says. "Coming out of that hotel."

"You must be confusing me with someone else," I say with a laugh. "I wasn't at a hotel with some strange man."

"He definitely wasn't a stranger." She picks up her cup of tea. "The way you two were carrying on, I assumed it'd been going on for some time."

I clear my throat. "Jane, I don't like what you're implying. It's not true, and honestly, I find it very offensive. I thought we were friends."

"So did I, which is why I was hurt when you didn't think

you could tell me." She rearranges the scones on the platter so they're evenly lined up. "You know I'd never tell Dave. I'll always choose my girlfriends over some man. For all I know, Dave has been unfaithful as well. He's very handsome and he has access to all those women."

"What women?"

"The ones at your events."

"They're all married."

"As were you, and look what happened," she says with a wink. "I'm just saying, those events of yours are filled with unhappy wives stuck with men who don't want to be there and they're listening to this handsome man on stage telling them how wonderful marriage can be. It's their dream to have a man like him." She glances at me. "You don't think any of them might try to make that dream come true?"

"They come to our events to make their own husbands fulfill that dream, not mine."

"How many men actually want to work on their marriage?" She sips her tea. "They go to your events because their wives make them. Then they get home and nothing changes."

"That's not true. A lot of couples have success with the program. We get letters from them all the time."

"And what about the ones who don't have success? What about the woman who sees a man like Dave and decides she wants him rather than her husband?"

"Then she's out of luck because Dave would never be unfaithful."

Jane shrugs. "Whatever you say." She points to my cup. "Would you like some more?"

"I think I should go." I push my chair back.

"Oh, Iris, don't be like this," Jane says, reaching over to grip my arm. "Stay. Let's talk about this."

"There's nothing to talk about. I'm not going to sit here and listen to you tell me lies about my husband."

"You're right," she says, letting go of my arm. "I shouldn't have said those things about Dave. I have no evidence of him being with another woman." Her eyes rise to mine. "But I do have evidence of *you* being unfaithful. I saw you at that hotel with a man. And yes, it was definitely you. It wasn't someone else."

"When?" I swallow. "When do you think you saw me?"

"It was years ago, before you and Dave started your podcast."

The timing is right. Back then, we didn't know we'd even be doing a podcast. It was a horrible time. We were deep in debt and struggling to pay our bills. Dave kept switching jobs, not sure what he wanted to do. We were both under a lot of stress and it caused our marriage to have problems. Small fights turned into big ones, and there were times when we'd go days without speaking. I sensed the end was near when we decided to sleep in separate rooms. I didn't want a divorce, but I felt like it was inevitable.

When I met Nick, I was instantly attracted to him. He was extremely handsome, taller than Dave, and more muscular. He knew I was married, but I told him Dave and I were as good as over. At the time, I really believed that.

The affair only lasted a few months, and during that time, Dave became committed to our marriage. I don't know what sparked the change in him, but he was like a new man. He was kind and attentive and more loving than ever before. I fell for him all over again and decided to fight for our marriage.

I ended the affair and told Nick to never contact me again. From that moment on, I fully committed myself to Dave and our marriage, never even tempted by another man.

"It wasn't me," I say, sitting up straighter. "It had to have been someone else."

"It was definitely you," Jane says, licking the crumbs off her fingers. "You had on that blue dress. The one you wore to my garden party last summer."

She's right. I wore that dress with Nick, so I guess Jane is telling the truth. She saw me with him. But that doesn't prove anything.

"You know what?" I smile. "You're right. I was at that hotel. That man you saw was a friend of mine from college. He was in town for business and asked if I wanted to have dinner."

Her brows rise. "Is it common for your friends to put their hands all over you and kiss you in the lobby?"

I can't believe she caught us. Nick and I always tried to be discreet and not show any affection until we got to the room. But there were a few instances when we'd had way too much to drink and weren't as careful as we should've been.

"Nothing happened," I say.

Jane smiles. "Of course it didn't. You wouldn't be unfaithful to Dave."

Why is she doing this? Why is she bringing this up? Why now? It happened years ago. She could've pretended it never happened, that she never saw me. She didn't have to tell me.

"I don't know what's happening here," I say. "Do you want something? Is that what this is about?"

"Of course not." She frowns. "You know I wouldn't use this against you. I can't believe you'd even think that about me."

"Then why bring it up? Why are you talking about this?"

"Because I want you to help Renee. It'd be a shame if her marriage ended. She has such a beautiful family."

"I would've talked to Renee. You didn't need to bring up what I did. There has to be something else. Some other reason you felt the need to tell me this."

She sighs. "Fine. I mentioned it because I didn't like you keeping this secret from me. I thought we were friends, Iris, and here you are, hiding things from me."

"This isn't something I wanted anyone to know," I say, staring back at her.

"But don't you see what holding a secret like that does to you? Look at poor Renee. The woman was suffering in silence until she finally told us what she'd been hiding for all those years. That's what friends are for, Iris." She gives me a sad smile. "I consider you one of my closest friends, which is why I was hurt when you wouldn't tell me about this man."

I'm not one of her closest friends. We're neighbors who do things together now and then simply because it's convenient. She's a friend because she lives next door, although now I'm wishing I'd stayed away from her.

"Even if we'd been best friends since childhood, I wouldn't have told you," I say. "What I did is shameful and I feel terrible about it. The last thing I wanted was for someone to find out."

"Well, now that you're aware that I know, you can talk freely about it. Perhaps it'll help you move on."

"I already have, which is why I don't want to talk about this. It's the past, and it was a mistake. I just want to forget it ever happened."

She sips her tea. "Do you ever talk to him?"

"No! It's over. And after it ended, he moved away."

"How long did it go on?"

"I just told you I don't want to discuss this." I get up. "I need to go. I'm not feeling well."

"Was it the scones?" She hurries up from her chair. "I can't imagine they'd make you ill."

She knows what's making me feel sick, so why is she pretending not to?

"Maybe the lavender didn't agree with your stomach," she says, walking me to the door.

"I don't think that was it," I say as I leave.

"Iris, wait."

I turn back. "What?"

"I'm truly sorry," she says, a hurt look on her face. "I didn't mean to upset you. I really did think opening up to me would help you. When I saw how distraught Renee was, I realized you may be suffering as well. I only wanted to help."

"Yes, well, I'd appreciate it if you didn't speak of this again. To anyone."

"I understand." She winks at me and smiles. "It'll be our little secret."

A secret she was never supposed to know.

"Goodbye, Jane."

"Bye!" She waves at me as I leave. "Tell Dave I said hello!"

I don't respond. I'm so angry at her, pretending we're friends when we're clearly not. That whole story about wanting to relieve my suffering was a complete and utter lie. She's going to use this against me. I don't know how or why, but I know she's going to do something. The sly grin on her face when she told me she knew my secret was a giant neon sign that she'd be using this to her advantage.

What does she want? Is she going to try to destroy my business? Tell the media I cheated on Dave and claim I'm a fraud and shouldn't be giving marital advice? But why would she do that? Is she jealous of me? Jealous of all the attention I'm getting?

I went to her house thinking it would get my mind off all my concerns about Nick, but I left with yet another concern. Jane, and what she's going to do with this secret she knows about me.

# CHAPTER FOURTEEN

"Iris, where are you?" Dave calls out when he gets home later that afternoon.

"I'm upstairs," I call back.

"Could you come down here? Allen wants to talk to you about something."

*Allen?* Why is Allen here? And why didn't Dave tell me he'd be coming over?

I run down the stairs, smiling when I see Allen. "I wasn't expecting to see you today."

"Sorry to intrude like this, but I needed to discuss something with you and it couldn't wait."

"What do you need to discuss?"

"Why don't we sit down?" Dave says, motioning to the couch.

I'm getting concerned. What is this about?

"I got a call from Linda," Allen says once we're all seated. "The woman interviewing you next week for the morning news?"

"Yes?" I say. "What about her?"

"She'd like to discuss infidelity and wants to make sure you're comfortable talking about it."

I glance at Dave. "Why wouldn't I be?"

Allen shrugs. "It's a sensitive issue. People get emotional about it. You'll probably receive a lot of comments after the segment airs and not all will be positive."

"That's nothing new. I'm used to that."

"You should also be prepared for her to ask about your own experience."

"Experience with what?" I ask, my pulse going faster.

"With infidelity."

I nervously laugh. "Why would she ask me that? She knows Dave and I are happily married. I've never even considered being with someone else."

Allen glances at Dave, then back at me. "I was referring to your relationships prior to Dave. And I wasn't implying you were the one who was unfaithful. I was referring to a previous partner."

"Oh." I laugh again. "Of course. Well, fortunately, I haven't experienced that."

I feel Dave staring at me, but don't look at him. How could I be so stupid, assuming Allen was talking about me? I hope Dave doesn't think my assumption meant anything.

"So I can tell her you're good with the infidelity focus?" Allen asks.

"Yes, that's fine."

"She also plans to ask you about the man who was arrested, the one who interrupted your event."

"Why? That was weeks ago and he hasn't bothered me since."

"Yes, but Dave said you've had other disturbing things happen."

"I'm not sure if I'd describe it as disturbing. It's only been a card with a note inside."

I haven't told Dave about the note that was left on my car, and I'm not going to. Telling him would cause him to ask more questions. Ones I can't answer.

"And the roses," Dave says.

"Well, yes, but it's possible they were from someone we know."

"Honey, we've checked with everyone we can think of that could've sent them and they've all told us the roses weren't from them. I think it's safe to assume they were from a stranger. An admirer of yours."

I look at Allen. "Why would I talk about this in a story about relationships?"

"It's not for the interview. This would be for a feature story Linda's doing on women who've experienced unwanted attention from men. She was hoping to include you."

"Tell her no. It doesn't make sense for me to be included. That man at the event made a scene, but he wasn't harassing me or threatening me."

"What about the man who sent the flowers?" Dave says. "Or the card?"

"I thought we decided we weren't going to be concerned about that," I say.

"Listen, Iris," Allen says, leaning back in his chair. "I know these guys are probably harmless, but talking about this will help other women. Linda said a lot of women feel threatened by men following them or making unwanted advances, but they brush it off, not wanting to make a big deal out of it. But in some cases, it *does* become a big deal. Women suffer emotionally and physically, and in some cases end up dead."

"That's not what's going on here," I say. "It was one card and some roses, and we don't know who they were from."

"And yet look what this has done to you," Dave says. "You aren't sleeping. You can't concentrate. You haven't had an appetite."

That's because of Nick. I'm worried he's going to show up and try to ruin my life. It has nothing to do with mysterious strangers threatening me. There are no mysterious strangers. It's Nick. He's the one doing this, and I'm not going to draw attention to it by being featured in a special news story.

"The men sending you these things are clearly affecting you in a negative way," Allen says. "Sharing that with an audience of women who know you and look up to you could be quite powerful."

Dave reaches over and holds my hand. "Honey, I really think you should do this. You'd be helping other women."

"I'm sorry, but I can't. I wouldn't feel right about it. My situation is different. I'd feel like I'm deceiving people."

"Okay, I'll tell Linda." Allen gets up. "I should get going."

Dave walks him to the door. "I've found some possible candidates for the ad position."

"You need to find someone soon. You can't keep doing it on your own with everything else you have going on."

"I agree. We'll see you later."

Allen leaves and Dave shuts the door.

"Do you think I should be doing this?" I ask as Dave comes back beside me. "Our brand is based on hope and love. Having my interview focused on infidelity is going against our message."

"It's not going against it. It's part of it. Infidelity happens all the time. We can't ignore it, and we don't. We address it all the time."

"Yes, but the people watching the interview don't know that. I don't want them thinking this is the type of thing we focus on during our podcast or events."

"You're overthinking it. You're going on there as a marriage coach, and infidelity is an issue that happens in marriages. I think it'll be good. It shows we're not afraid of tackling difficult issues."

"I guess that's true."

My phone rings and I see my mother's name on the screen. "It's my mom."

"Go ahead and talk to her. I'll start dinner."

As he goes to the kitchen, I answer the call. "Hey, Mom."

"How's my celebrity daughter?" she says.

I smile. "I'm not a celebrity."

"Then why is everyone talking about you?"

"What do you mean?"

"I was at the beauty salon yesterday and overheard some women talking about your podcast, saying what good advice you have and how you're so relatable."

"Do you know these women?" I ask, assuming she's talking about her friends.

"No, I'd never met them. But, of course, I had to tell them you're my daughter. I couldn't stay quiet after hearing that. They think you should have your own talk show! They said you have the looks and the personality for it, and I had to agree. You have so much talent, honey. I'm happy people are finally recognizing that. So when's your next event?"

"Tomorrow night. We have three events this week and some media appearances."

"How's David?"

I keep telling her to call him Dave, but she insists on using his full name.

"He's good." I look back at him in the kitchen. "He's making dinner."

"Oh, how nice. You're lucky to have a man who will cook for you. Did you two have a nice weekend?"

"We spent most of it working. Or Dave did. He was working on ads. Oh, we got a book deal!"

"That's not final yet," Dave calls out from the kitchen.

"It's not final, but it's in the works. And we're going to have branded products. Things that will support our program, like a relationship game where couples ask each other questions."

"That's great, honey. It sounds like your business is really expanding."

"That's mainly because of Dave," I say. "He's the deal maker. And Allen. The two of them are always finding new opportunities."

"But you're the reason the podcast is doing so well."

"As my mom, I think you have to say that," I say with a laugh.

"No, really. If you heard those women at the salon today, they had nothing but good things to say about you. They weren't as complimentary to Dave."

"Why? What did they say?"

"They thought he came across as a little arrogant. I assured them he's not like that. He just has strong feelings about his opinions, which can come across as arrogant to some people. They noticed it more in the newer episodes than the old ones."

"I might need some help over here," Dave says. "How do you want these seasoned?"

Looking back, I see him holding up a chicken breast.

"Mom, I need to help Dave with dinner."

"Sure, we'll talk soon. Bye! Love you!"

"Love you too!"

"What's new with your mom?" Dave asks as I join him in the kitchen.

"Not much. She was at the hair salon and overheard these women talking about us."

"What'd they say?"

"That they love the podcast. They think I should have a talk show." I laugh. "Like I can just snap my fingers and have a TV show." I grab a spice blend from the cupboard and hand it to Dave. "Try this."

He sprinkles it over the chicken. "Would you ever consider that?"

"What?"

"A talk show. One where you talk about relationships and interact with the audience. It'd be like our events but more structured and scripted."

I turn to Dave. "It sounds like you've thought about this."

"I have. In fact, I was thinking we might put together a proposal. Something we could pitch to a studio."

"Like locally?"

"No. In Hollywood."

I smile. "This is a joke, right?"

"Why would I joke about that?"

"Because it's ridiculous." I playfully shove his arm. "We're not moving to Hollywood. Our life is here. We have a house. Friends. A business."

"We could have all that in LA."

"Dave, come on." I turn to him. "Nobody's giving us a TV show. It'd be a waste of time to come up with a proposal for something that's never going to happen."

He wipes his hands on a towel. "Okay, I'm just going to tell you."

"Tell me what?"

"Allen got a call the other day from a production company in LA. They asked if we'd ever consider doing a show, like the kind I just mentioned where we discuss relationship issues with people in the audience."

"And you're just telling me this now?"

"I assumed your answer would be no, so I wasn't even going to mention it to you. I almost told Allen to tell them to forget it, but then I thought I should talk to you first."

I shake my head. "I don't want a show. We're already doing too much. I don't want to add more, and I definitely don't want to move to LA."

"Iris, think about this. Think about all the people we could help if we had a show on national TV. And we'd make more money. We could cut back on our events."

"But the events are what I like most. I didn't at first, but now I really enjoy them."

"The show would be set up like our events. They'd just be recorded and put on TV."

"Why would some LA production company want *us* to do this? There are so many other relationship experts out there."

"But they don't have the program we developed. That's what makes us unique. We've created a whole new approach to relationship counseling that's new and fresh. Even just calling ourselves coaches instead of counselors sets us apart and makes people want to hear what we have to say."

"I'm still not interested in having a show."

"Would you at least think about it before saying no?"

I sigh. "Fine. I'll think about it, but I don't see myself changing my mind. I like our life the way it is. I don't want to change it."

"Sometimes change can be good."

"And sometimes it's not."

He gives me a kiss on the cheek. "Just think about it. That's all I'm asking."

As we finish making dinner, I try to imagine us living in California, having our own TV show. I can see Dave liking that, but it's not for me. I like what we're doing now. I don't need to do more. Honestly, I don't even want to do the book, but I know Dave does so I'm trying to be excited about it, along with the branded products Dave wants us to do.

Our business is growing faster than I would like, and although Dave thinks that's a good thing, he wouldn't if he knew my secret. If people found out about my affair, the business Dave's working so hard to build would crumble and disintegrate. No one would want to take marriage advice from us. I wish I could tell Dave the truth so he'd know that all his efforts might be for nothing if this secret gets out.

But I can't tell him about Nick. I need to deal with this on my own.

# CHAPTER FIFTEEN

"It's a pleasure having you here today," Linda says, giving me her fake newscaster smile.

"Thank you, Linda," I say. "It's a pleasure being here."

It's Wednesday, the day of my interview at the local news station. I'm tired from the event last night and really don't want to do this. I don't feel like I'm prepared. I asked Linda to send me the questions beforehand, but she never did, which has me concerned about what she's going to ask.

"Let's get right to it," she says. "Our focus today is on infidelity. Tell us some of the reasons why a person would risk their marriage to be with someone else."

"Falling out of love. Not feeling seen or heard by their partner. Boredom. Lack of desire. Anger and resentment toward their partner. Revenge. There are many reasons, but those are some of the main ones."

"What can couples do to prevent this from happening?" Linda asks.

These are easy questions with straightforward answers. If

this is how the interview is going to go, I have nothing to worry about.

"Honest communication is the best thing couples can do to prevent infidelity," I say. "If there's an issue in the marriage, it needs to be discussed right away, and partners need to feel safe to express themselves without fear of being attacked or judged. The program my husband and I developed guides couples through the process of learning how to communicate effectively so that issues like infidelity never come up."

Linda leans back and crosses her legs. "Let's get personal for a moment. Tell me about your own marital issues which led you and your husband to develop your program."

That's another easy question. I've told the story so many times I've memorized it. I don't go into details, but just highlight the main issues which coincide with the issues addressed in our marriage-saving program. It's brilliant marketing when I think about it. Using our own marriage as the blueprint for our program makes it more appealing and relatable than some plan created by a psychologist based on theories and academic studies.

"Those years when you two were struggling sound like a very difficult time," Linda says when I finish the story. "I assume you felt alone, like you had no one to talk to about this?"

"I did sometimes feel like that, but I got through it." I smile at her, wondering where she's taking this.

"And during that difficult time, did you ever consider seeking comfort in someone else?" Her brows rise. "Another man?"

My heart beats faster, but I force myself to remain calm. "No. Never. I was committed to Dave. I just needed to learn how to communicate with him, which I did by using the steps outlined in our program."

"I understand that, but going back to my question, when your marriage was struggling, did you ever consider Dave might not be the right man for you?"

"No, never," I say, sitting up straighter. "I'm not sure what you're getting at here."

She shrugs. "I'm simply asking if you ever thought about being with someone else. Or maybe testing the waters by—"

"No," I blurt out, getting angry. "That didn't happen. I'd like to move to a different question."

"Why is that?" She cocks her head to the side. "Why does that question bother you?"

"It's not relevant. And frankly, I find it inappropriate. You're basically asking if I cheated on my husband."

"And you're saying you didn't?"

"Of course not. I was fully committed to Dave. Being with someone else never even crossed my mind. Dave has been, and always will be, the only man for me."

"And what about Dave?"

"What about him?"

"Is there any truth to the rumors?"

"I'm not sure what you're referring to," I say, suddenly feeling very warm. It's either because of the hot lights beating down on me or the stress I'm feeling from how this conversation is going.

Linda picks up a piece of paper from the table next to her. "It says here that Dave has been seen having dinner and drinks with a much younger woman. Mid-twenties. Blond hair."

I try to think of who that might be. An image of Heather immediately comes to mind.

"She's a business associate," I say. "Dave is working with her on something I can't yet talk about, but I think our audience will be very excited when we announce what's coming."

"Does your husband typically hold hands with a business associate?" Linda asks.

*They were holding hands?* When? And who saw them doing this?

"It's right here if you'd like to see it." Linda gives me the piece of paper. It's a printout of comments written online about Dave and the woman who may or may not be Heather.

"You can't believe what you read online," I say, setting the piece of paper down. "I would think most journalists would know this."

I shouldn't have insulted her like that, especially on TV, but my anger took over and I blurted it out without thinking.

"I realize it's just a rumor," she calmly says, "but sometimes rumors are true. I thought you might like to take this opportunity to set people straight."

"I don't feel the need to address a rumor that's completely false. I don't believe in giving attention to lies or the people who spread them."

She smiles. "Let's move on and talk about the man who attacked you at one of your live events."

He didn't attack me, but I'm not surprised she described it that way. The media is always trying to create drama where there isn't any. I understand why they do it, but I don't want any part of it. It's why I don't like doing interviews.

After I address her question about the man at the event, I notice the producer giving the cue that our time is up.

"It was so nice having you here today," Linda says with her fake smile. "I look forward to having you back."

I'm not coming back. Linda deceived me. This wasn't an interview meant to help people avoid infidelity. It was an interview about me and my marriage and the rumors about Dave.

As they go to a commercial, Linda pops up from her chair. "I need to run back to the news desk, but thanks so much for being here! Great job!"

She runs off as the producer motions me off the set. Dave is waiting for me at the back of the studio. I go up to him and he pulls me in for a hug.

"You did a wonderful job," he says.

"Are you kidding? It was horrible." I push away from him. "Let's get out of here. Do you have my things? My makeup bag and my extra clothes?"

"They're already in the car." He takes my hand as we walk out of the studio. "Iris, don't be so hard on yourself. You did great."

"I'm not upset about how I did," I say as we leave the building. "I'm upset about Linda and the way she attacked me."

"Attacked you?" Dave says, like he has no idea what I'm talking about.

We get to the car and I stop and turn to Dave. "Didn't you hear how she kept asking if I'd been unfaithful? And when I told her no, she wouldn't let it go. It was completely inappropriate. She was supposed to ask about infidelity as it relates to our program, not go after me personally."

"Honey, she's a reporter. They always ask questions like that."

"No. They don't. I've done plenty of interviews the past few months and not a single person asked if I've cheated on you." I get in the car, slamming the door shut, still furious with

Linda, and angry at Dave for not agreeing with me that what she did was wrong.

Dave goes around to the driver's side and gets in. "It was a story about infidelity. Of course she's going to ask if you've ever been unfaithful. Allen told you that the other day when he came to the house. He told you to be prepared to answer questions about your own experience with the topic."

"Yes, well, I thought she'd focus on our program and how we help couples deal with infidelity. I didn't expect the focus to be on me. And you." I look at Dave. "Are you telling me you were okay with her asking about you and some other woman?"

"I didn't like it, but it didn't surprise me."

"It wasn't even true. It was a rumor. That piece of paper she gave me was just a list of comments people made online."

He doesn't say anything. My anxiety rises as his silence continues.

"It's not true, right?" I say. "The comments about you and this woman?"

"What you said is correct," he says, flipping his visor down to block the sun. "The woman people saw me with was Heather. She took me to dinner to discuss a possible deal. It was months ago, when I first met her."

I'm concerned he had dinner with her without telling me.

"Why wasn't I invited to this dinner?"

"I didn't think you'd want to go. You kept telling me we were doing too much and that you wanted to slow down, so I decided to handle this on my own."

"I wish you'd told me you had dinner with her so I wasn't finding this out during an interview."

"I'm sorry, honey. I didn't even think about it. It was so long ago."

"And that was it? You only had dinner with her one time?"

The comments online said he'd been seen with her several times, but I want to hear his side of the story.

"We had dinner again a few weeks later," he says. "Allen was supposed to be there, but he didn't show up. We also met a couple of times for drinks. Heather's boss was supposed to join us, but things came up and he never did."

"And you didn't think I needed to know about any of this?"

"Iris, you knew I was meeting with her," Dave says, glancing at me. "After those first initial meetings, I told you we might be doing a deal with them and asked you to come with me to meet Heather for drinks. You chose to stay home."

"I don't remember that."

"Probably because you were so exhausted back then. You weren't used to doing the events. You'd come home and want to go straight to bed."

That might be true, but I still don't remember it. I think if Dave told me he was meeting a beautiful young woman for drinks, I'd want to go with him, even if I was tired.

"People said they saw you holding her hand," I say. "Did they make that up?"

"I wasn't holding her hand. I put my hand over hers after she told me her boyfriend had broken up with her. It wasn't anything romantic. I was trying to comfort her."

Was that really all it was, or is he just telling me what I want to hear? What else happened? Did he take her somewhere after they had drinks? Did they go back to her place? Or to a hotel?

"Iris, nothing happened," Dave says, as though he was reading my mind. "I swear to you, my interactions with Heather have been strictly professional."

"And yet she talked to you about her boyfriend. And you comforted her by holding her hand."

"I was not holding her hand. And yes, we did discuss some personal matters, but only because we got to know each other while working on the deal. She considers me a friend, but she knows nothing would ever happen between us."

I'd like to believe that, but the fact that Dave didn't tell me about having dinner with Heather has me concerned. And I swear he never told me they had drinks. That's something I would remember.

I've been so worried about Dave finding out about my affair, but maybe I should've been putting my focus on him. What if he's been having an affair this entire time and I didn't know?

# CHAPTER SIXTEEN

"When we get home, I have some things to do in the office," Dave says. "Maybe you should rest. You haven't been sleeping well."

Because I'm so on edge about Nick. And now, with my suspicions about Dave, I have something new to worry about.

"I'd like to be included the next time you meet with Heather," I say.

"Of course. I think it's important you're involved as we get closer to having a deal. I'd definitely like your input on the products."

"And once we have a deal, you won't need to meet with Heather anymore?"

"I'll still be working with her. She's our main contact if we need anything or have questions."

"There's no one else we could work with?"

"Why are you asking?" Dave pulls into the driveway. "Do you not like Heather?"

"I don't like that she's confiding in you about her personal life," I say, thinking that's how my affair with Nick started. "A person in her position shouldn't be doing that. It's not appropriate."

Dave turns off the car. "She confided in me because she considers me a friend. People can be friends and still do business together."

"Not when it's a beautiful woman who has a crush on you."

Dave laughs. "Heather does not have a crush on me. I'm too old for her. She's only 26."

"I saw how she looked at you. She's definitely attracted to you."

"Iris, this whole conversation is ridiculous," Dave says as we go into the house. "There's nothing going on with Heather and me, and there never will be." He gives me a kiss on the cheek. "I'll be in my office."

I go to the bedroom to put away my makeup and hang up the extra dresses I brought to the studio. I'm still upset about how the interview went. I'm sure there are already hundreds of comments online about it, saying Dave is having an affair and that we're frauds who shouldn't be giving out marriage advice.

My phone rings and I see Jane's name on the screen. I ignore her call and change out of my dress, putting on jeans and a sweater. I'd like to take a nap, but I'm too worked up after the interview.

My phone stops ringing, then starts up again. It's Jane calling again. I've been avoiding her since she told me she saw me with Nick. I still don't know why she told me that. She didn't have to, which makes me think there's a motive behind it.

"Hi, Jane," I say, deciding to answer her call.

"Oh, good, I caught you!" she says in an excited tone. "When you didn't answer, I thought you might still be at the news station. How did your interview go?"

"It was okay," I say, not wanting to tell her what happened. She'll find out when she watches it. "Did you need something?"

"Yes, I wanted to know if you and Dave could be here at six instead of seven."

"I'm not sure what you mean."

"Dave didn't tell you?"

"Tell me what?"

"That I invited you two for dinner. I'm making this fabulous new recipe for shrimp scampi. I've made it twice now and both times it turned out perfectly."

"When did you talk to Dave about us going there for dinner?"

"This morning, when he was out getting the mail. I saw him and thought I'd ask if you two were free tonight. I was thrilled when he said yes. It seems like forever since we've had you two over. Anyway, does six work?"

"Um, yes, that should work," I say, thinking the sooner we get there, the sooner we can leave.

"Dave eats shrimp, right? I probably should've asked him that before planning the menu. I assumed he did, but with so many people having food allergies these days, you never know."

"Yes, he eats shrimp. Can I bring something? Maybe some wine?"

"No. Richard will take some from the wine cellar. He's very particular about wine. Whenever someone brings us some, he won't drink it."

Why has she never told me that? I've brought wine to her house at least ten times. Maybe she drinks it herself.

"See you in a few hours!" She ends the call.

I'm not feeling good about this. Why is Jane having us over?

Does it have something to do with her knowing my secret? Is she planning to tell Dave?

She wouldn't do that. Jane and I have been friends for years. She wouldn't try to ruin my marriage. Would she?

Going to Dave's office, I stop outside the door when I hear him talking.

"I'm hoping next week," he says. "I'm still trying to figure out the best spot. It needs to be a hotel Iris would never think of going to."

Who is he on the phone with? And why is he talking about a hotel? One I wouldn't think of going to? Is he planning to meet some woman at a hotel? Is it Heather? Are they having an affair? Is the rumor true?

"Yes, we'll talk tomorrow," he says. "Bye."

I knock, then open the door. "Hey, are you busy?"

"Not too busy for my beautiful wife."

Dave's sitting at his desk, a big smile on his face. Is the smile for me, or because he just talked to his mistress?

"Were you talking to someone? I thought I heard you on the phone."

"I was talking to Allen. I told him how upset you were about the interview. He's going to call the program manager and let him know we weren't pleased with Linda and the questions she asked. I doubt it'll make a difference, but at least they'll know how we felt about it."

That was Allen on the phone? Then maybe Dave's not having an affair, but why was he talking to Allen about a hotel?

"I thought you were going to rest," Dave says, leaning back in his chair.

"I don't feel like it." I walk up to his desk. "Jane just called. She said we're having dinner over there tonight?"

He sighs. "I forgot to tell you. I was so focused on your interview that I forgot to mention that Jane invited us to dinner. How'd you find out?"

"She just called. She wants us over there at six instead of seven."

"Then I better hurry up and finish what I need to get done."

"What are you working on?"

"Some ideas for the talk show." He smiles. "Just in case your answer is yes."

"Dave, I told you, I'm not interested."

"You said you'd think about it."

"And I did. I decided I don't want to do it."

"That's your final answer?" He closes his laptop. "Then I guess I'm done. I don't need to keep working on it."

"Are you mad at me? For not agreeing to this?"

"Not at all." He gets up and comes over to me. "I admit I was excited we were being considered for a possible talk show, but honestly, the likelihood of it actually happening was pretty low."

"But you still wanted to try."

He shrugs. "You know how I am. If there's a chance, I'm going to go for it."

Dave and I are different that way. He's a risk taker, while I'm more cautious. He'll pursue an opportunity even if there's little chance it'll turn into anything, while I'm more realistic.

"We could make a show ourselves," I tell him. "We could do videos of us working with couples and put them online."

"We already do that."

"Yes, but we could make it look like a talk show with an actual set."

“That would look amateurish, to the point it might hurt our brand.”

“It was just an idea. I was trying to come up with something that would make you feel better about not pursuing this.”

“I appreciate that, but really, I’m fine.” He checks his watch. “We have some time before we need to be at Jane’s house.” He gives me a sexy smile. “Would you like to go to the bedroom?”

I’m not in the mood to be with him that way, not after hearing what he said to whoever was on the phone. Was it really Allen? Or was Dave lying?

“I’m not feeling up to it,” I say. “Maybe later.”

“Then would you care if I did a quick workout at the gym?”

“No, go ahead.”

For years, Dave belonged to a gym but never went. Then a few months ago, he starting going there several times a week. I thought it was great he was so devoted to improving his health, but now I’m wondering if he’s getting in shape for Heather.

That can’t possibly be true. Can it? Dave wouldn’t have an affair. We have a thriving business that we enjoy and that makes us a lot of money. He wouldn’t risk giving all that up to have an affair.

So what’s going on with him? Or is nothing going on and I’m making up stories about him that aren’t true? Am I trying to relieve my guilt over my own affair by creating a story in which Dave is being unfaithful? If so, I need to stop that right now. It’s not fair to Dave. He told me there’s nothing going on with Heather, and if I trust him, I need to believe he’s telling the truth.

But part of me isn’t sure I trust him.

# CHAPTER SEVENTEEN

"Please, have a seat," Jane says as Dave and I join her and Richard in the dining room.

The last time I was in here, I was talking to Renee about her marriage after Jane nearly forced me to. It was uncomfortable to hear Renee talk about cheating on her husband, knowing I'd done the same thing. And that whole time, Jane knew it. She knew what I'd done but didn't tell me until later.

"The table looks wonderful, Jane," Dave says as we sit down. The table's covered in a plum-colored cloth and along the center are candles lined up on a long wooden tray with a floral centerpiece in the middle. It's probably an idea Jane found online. In addition to finding new recipes, Jane spends her days searching for decorating ideas.

"Thank you, Dave," Jane says, beaming with pride. I'm sure Richard didn't even notice the table. She's always complaining that he never notices how hard she works to make him a nice home.

"It's good you could join us," Richard says. "You haven't been over in what... about a year?"

"It was six months, dear," Jane says, standing beside the table. "Last April, I believe."

"That's right," Dave says. "I didn't realize it'd been that long."

"Richard, why don't you pour the wine?" Jane says. "I'll go get the appetizers." She takes off for the kitchen.

She didn't mention we'd be having appetizers. I thought we'd only be having the main course, but I should've known Jane would make this dinner into a huge production. I'm sure she included a dessert course as well. We're going to be here all night.

"It isn't much," Jane says, bringing a platter into the dining room. "Just some stuffed mushrooms, bruschetta with goat cheese, and these cute little cheese puffs I found a recipe for yesterday." She sets down the tray, a huge grin on her face as she passes out appetizer plates and napkins.

"You didn't need to do all this," I say, but what I mean is, I wish she hadn't. This was supposed to be a simple dinner, but when it comes to entertaining, Jane doesn't do simple.

"Everything is great," Dave says after he's sampled all the appetizers. "Although I think I like the cheese puffs the best."

"Aren't they wonderful?" Jane's eyes light up. "I'll be sure to give Iris the recipe."

I'm not making cheese puffs. I barely have time to make dinner.

"So how's the marriage coaching business?" Richard asks with a slight grin. That's as close to a smile as you get with him. He's very serious.

"It's good," Dave says. "Did Jane tell you about our book deal?"

"I don't believe she did," Richard says as Jane brings out the main course, individually portioned out in shallow bowls. "When's the book coming out?"

"Not for at least a year. We're still negotiating the deal."

"I assume the book is based on your program?"

Dave nods. "It'll include the basics of the program, but not everything. We have to save a few things for our events to entice people to show up."

"Are you having trouble selling tickets?"

"No, we're usually sold out," Dave says. "But as time goes on, that could change. We need to come up with ways to keep people coming back."

"That shouldn't be an issue," Richard says with that slight grin of his. "Marriages are always having problems. You'll never run out of customers."

"Richard, that's a cynical thing to say," Jane scoffs. "Not every marriage has problems."

"I'd like to see one that doesn't," he says, picking up his wineglass.

"Ours doesn't," I say, smiling at Dave.

"You never argue?" Richard asks. "I find that hard to believe."

"We disagree on some things," Dave says, "but we talk it out before it turns into an actual argument. Open and honest communication is the key to a good marriage."

"Does anyone need anything before I sit down?" Jane asks, placing a basket of rolls on the table.

No one answers her.

She smiles. "Then I guess we can go ahead and eat."

Jane sits at the end of the table, directly across from Richard, while Dave and I sit between them, facing each other.

It's a very long table. It feels awkward to have everyone spaced so far apart.

"This is excellent," Dave says to Jane after taking a bite of the shrimp scampi.

Jane's beaming. "You really think so?"

"It's very good," I tell her.

"Better than you'd get at a restaurant," Dave says.

"Did you hear that, Richard?" Jane says to him. "He gave me a compliment. Several, actually. Why can't you do that?"

"Not now, Jane," he says, glaring at her from the end of the table. "We have guests."

She clears her throat. "So, Iris, how was your interview this morning?"

"It was fine," I say, not wanting to talk about it.

"I thought you looked beautiful in that dress," Jane says. "The blue really brought out the blue in your eyes."

"You saw the interview?" I ask, wondering why she asked how it went if she already watched it.

"I hadn't planned to see it, but I turned on the TV when I was doing the dishes and there you were."

"What did you think?" Dave asks, which annoys me because I really don't want to discuss it. I was trying to forget about it.

"I thought Iris was rather hostile to Linda," Jane says, taking a bite of the scampi.

"You thought *I* was hostile?" I huff. "Linda was the one who was hostile. I can't believe you'd take her side on this, Jane."

"Am I missing something?" Richard says. "What happened during the interview?"

"Linda, the woman from the news," I explain, "was asking me about rumors people posted online as if they were fact."

"Rumors about what?" he asks.

"It doesn't matter. The point is, a journalist should know better than to treat a rumor as fact."

"Many rumors are based on fact," Jane says. "I'm not saying that's true in this instance. I'm just saying that may be the reason Linda chose to address them."

"There was no need to address them," I say, getting angry with Jane. "I was there to talk about our marriage program and our events. I wasn't there to talk about myself."

"But isn't that why you're so successful? Because you talk about your own personal marriage struggles?" Jane gives me a smug grin that infuriates me.

What is she up to? Ever since she told me she knows about Nick, she's been acting strange, even a little mean.

"She has a point," Dave says, taking Jane's side. "Maybe you should've been more open about it."

"Open about what?" I snap, my anger now directed at my husband. "There's nothing to tell. Linda was asking if I ever had an affair. And she accused *you* of having an affair. Did you want me to lie and say those things were true?"

"No, of course not. What I'm saying is you could've said something like it's normal for couples to be attracted to someone other than their spouse, but that neither of us have ever acted on that attraction. But instead, you became defensive, which could make people think you're hiding something."

"I completely agree," Jane says. "In fact, if I didn't know you, I'd think you were guilty of having an affair."

I'm so shocked by her words that I drop my fork in the bowl, causing it to splatter butter sauce all over the tablecloth.

"Oh, goodness!" Jane says, hurrying up from her chair. "Let me get something to clean that up." She races to the kitchen.

"I didn't mean to upset you, honey," Dave says, his eyes meeting up with mine across the table. "We'll talk about something else."

"I think that's a good idea," I say with a tight smile.

"You see what I mean?" Richard smirks. "Every marriage has problems."

Jane returns with a damp dishcloth and reaches across me to blot the stains. "I'm not sure this will do the trick, but I'll give it a try."

"Sorry about that," I say. "I can get you a new tablecloth."

"That's not necessary. I have plenty." She stops blotting and assesses the mess I made. It looks even worse now that it's wet from the dishcloth. "I'm sure it'll clean up in the wash."

"Jane, stop worrying about it and sit down," Richard says.

She goes back to the kitchen to dispose of the dishcloth, then returns to her seat, out of breath from all the racing around.

"Where were we?" she asks, smiling at Dave and me. "Oh, yes, we were talking about the interview."

"We're moving past that," I say. "I think we can all agree it wasn't the best topic for conversation."

"Why is that?" she asks, as though she can't imagine why I'd be upset after she just made that comment about me having an affair. "I thought you enjoyed talking about your work."

"I do, but I don't want to talk about the interview."

"Just out of curiosity," Richard says, "what was the interview supposed to be about?"

"Infidelity," Jane says. "Iris listed off all the reasons spouses are unfaithful. I found it very interesting."

"One of the nurses in my office recently discovered her

husband is cheating," Richard says, pouring himself more wine. He holds up the bottle. "Would anyone like more?"

"I would," Dave says, holding up his glass.

"Who was it?" Jane asks, looking at Richard. "Which nurse?"

"Annie, the one who got married last year." He refills Dave's glass, then sets the bottle of wine down.

Jane frowns. "What a shame. Annie is such a sweet girl. Do you know how she found out?"

"I believe she found him with the woman," Richard says. "I doubt her husband told her."

"Actually, research shows many people tell their spouse," Dave says.

"Do you have actual numbers to back that up?" Richard asks.

"Percentages," Dave says. "Over half of people tell their spouse about their affair, mainly out of guilt."

"And of the ones that don't," Richard says, "how many get caught?"

"It varies. Women are caught more often than men."

Talking about this is making me sick to my stomach, and the smell of the shrimp is making me feel worse. I can't eat any more. I set my fork down, gently this time, and take a sip of my wine.

"That's not good news for Renee," Jane mutters.

My eyes dart to Jane. Why did she say that? Renee made us promise to keep her affair a secret. I told Dave, but I regret it. I should've kept quiet about it. And so should Jane.

"What was that about Renee?" Richard asks.

"Nothing," I say. "Jane was just—"

"Oh, Iris, it's just us. Dave isn't going to tell and Richard wouldn't either."

"What are we talking about?" Richard asks.

"Renee had an affair," Jane says. "After her first son was born."

"Jane, stop," I say. "She asked us not to tell anyone."

"That doesn't include our husbands," she says, like it's obvious. "You really weren't going to tell Dave? What happened to always telling him the truth?"

"She already told me," Dave says, before taking a drink of his wine.

"You told your husband and you're scolding me for telling Richard?" Jane says to me.

"It was a mistake," I say. "I shouldn't have told him."

"Why wouldn't you?" Dave says. "Like Jane said, the promise not to tell anyone doesn't include your spouse."

Why does Dave keep taking Jane's side? And why does she keep taking his? She's supposed to be friends with me, not my husband.

"Are we talking about our neighbor Renee?" Richard asks.

"Yes," Jane says. "Can you believe it? She's the last person I would have thought would cheat, but I guess you never know."

"Is it still going on?" Richard asks.

"No, or that's what she told us. She said it only lasted a few months."

"When did you find out?" he asks.

"When I had Iris and her over for lunch."

I look at Jane. "Renee made us promise not to tell anyone."

"And yet you did," Jane says with a smug grin.

"Only because I thought Dave might have some advice. Something I hadn't thought of."

“And what did you say?” Jane asks Dave. “What do you think Renee should do?”

“I think she needs to tell Trent. If she doesn’t, she’ll be living a lie which will eventually destroy her marriage.”

“I agree,” Jane says. “I think the best thing is to be honest.”

She’s talking about me, not Renee. She wants me to tell Dave, but why? Why can’t she leave this alone? It’s not her marriage, it’s mine.

I’m becoming very concerned about Jane. It might be time to end my friendship with her.

# CHAPTER EIGHTEEN

"IF TRENT FINDS OUT, it'll be devastating for Renee," Richard says. "The woman has no job and two young children. She'll end up a single mother living in some tiny apartment instead of that mansion across the street."

"It's hardly a mansion," Jane scoffs, although it is one of the biggest houses on the block. She looks down the table at Richard. "Why are you so worried about Renee? Trent's the one who's been betrayed. If anything, Renee should be punished, not given sympathy."

"Trent finding out would be punishment enough for her," Richard says in a stern tone, staring back at Jane. "The man's a lawyer. He'll make sure Renee receives as little as possible in the divorce."

"Maybe Trent could get past it," I say. "Some men would."

"Not Trent," Richard says. "He's not the type."

"What about you, Dave?" Jane asks. "Would you forgive her? Assuming you were Trent."

Dave pauses, tapping his hand on the table. "No. I don't think I would."

I shove my chair back. "I'm going to use the bathroom."

"Are you okay?" Jane asks as I get up from the table. "You don't look well. And you barely ate anything."

"I think the butter sauce was too rich for my stomach. I'll be right back."

I hurry out of the dining room and go down the hall to the guest bathroom. I shut the door and take some deep breaths.

"Iris?" Jane knocks on the door. "Is everything okay?"

"Yes, I'm fine."

"I could get you some ginger tablets. They help with stomach upset."

Does she really think this is about my stomach? She can't possibly be that clueless.

"Do you want the ginger?" she asks. "Or I might have some antacids upstairs. I'd have to check."

I fling open the door. "Get in here."

"In the bathroom?"

"Yes. I need to talk to you. Get in here."

"If you want to talk, let's go back to the table."

"We need to talk in private." I grab her arm and pull her into the tiny room.

"What is going on with you?" she says. "You're acting very strange tonight."

"Because you won't stop talking about..." I glance at the closed door, worried someone will hear. "About the thing you're not supposed to talk about."

"You mean Renee? Iris, I don't know why you're—"

"Not Renee. I'm talking about me!" I say in a hushed tone. "Why would you bring up the topic of affairs, knowing what you know about me? Are you trying to break up my marriage?"

"No! Of course not. I was just making conversation. It had nothing to do with you."

"That's a lie, and you know it." I huff. "I can't believe you. I thought we were friends."

"We are."

"A friend doesn't do this. You purposely brought up infidelity and kept talking about it because of what I did. The question is... why? What were you hoping to accomplish? Did you think I'd break down and tell Dave the truth?"

"Iris, I was helping you." She grips my arm. "I wasn't trying to upset you."

"How was that helping me?" I say, yanking my arm from her.

"I was trying to find out how Dave would react if he found out the truth."

"By telling my husband you thought I was guilty of having an affair?"

"I never said you were guilty," she says. "I said I would've assumed you were if I didn't know you based on how you acted in the interview today."

"Just saying that put the idea in Dave's head that I might've done something wrong. That's all it takes to make him suspicious."

"You're being paranoid. He doesn't suspect a thing. If he had, he would've said something."

"Not here. At your dinner party. He'd wait until we got home."

"Perhaps it's time you two have an honest conversation about this. Get it out in the open." She turns to the mirror and smooths her hair. "Or you could continue to lie to him. It's up to you."

"Yes. It *is* up to me. So stop interfering."

She turns to face me. "I don't know why you're being this way. I really am trying to help."

"I don't need your help. I'll deal with this on my own." I go to open the door, but then stop and turn to Jane. "You didn't tell anyone, did you?"

"About Nick?"

"How do you know his name?" I ask, my pulse racing.

"I asked the bartender. I saw Nick getting a drink at the bar before you arrived."

"Why would you ask the bartender for his name? Why would you care?"

"He looked familiar. I thought he might be someone I know. But it turns out I remembered him because I'd seen him there before." She smiles. "With you."

"You saw us more than once?"

"I believe it was three times. My women's auxiliary meetings used to be held there every month. Sometimes we'd meet twice a month if we had an event coming up."

If only I'd known that. I would've met Nick at a different hotel. It's a small boutique hotel tucked away on a side street downtown. I doubt many people have even heard of it, so why would Jane's group decide to meet there? There are hundreds of other hotel options in Chicago.

"Promise me you'll never say his name again."

"I can't promise that," Jane says. "It's a common name."

"Then at least promise you won't talk about this again. To anyone. That includes Richard." I pause, eyeing Jane. "You didn't already tell him, did you?"

"Iris, he's my husband."

I sigh. "You told him."

"Yes, but I didn't say it was you who had the affair. I said it was a friend of ours."

"I'm sure he'll figure it out. The man's a surgeon. He's not stupid. And you practically told him it was me just now at dinner."

"You're getting worked up over nothing. You know Richard. Half the time he's not even listening. Even if he figured it out, what's he going to do? Tell Dave?"

"Maybe."

She shakes her head. "He'd never do that. Richard stays out of these types of things." She opens the door. "Let's go, before the men come looking for us."

"Feeling better?" Dave asks when I return to the table.

"A little."

"I gave her a ginger tablet to settle her stomach," Jane says, in such a convincing way I almost believed her. "Would anyone like more shrimp?"

"None for me," Dave says. "But it really was excellent, Jane."

"I'm so glad you enjoyed it." She takes his bowl, then goes past him to get Richard's. "We're having amaretto cheesecake for dessert. I tried a little and was very pleased with how it came out."

"Maybe we could take a piece to go," I say. "I'm still not feeling well."

"Perhaps you're coming down with something," Richard says. "We're entering flu season. The receptionist in my office is sick with it right now."

"It's not the flu," I tell him. "I'm sure it's something minor, but I do think I need to go home and lie down."

"She hasn't been sleeping," Dave says to Richard. "I'm sure that's part of the reason she isn't feeling well."

"Why aren't you sleeping?" Richard asks me.

"I'm guessing it's stress from all the events we're doing." I look over at Dave. "Honey, are you ready to go?"

"You want to leave right now?"

"Yes," I say, giving him a look to not argue with me about this.

"Dave, you're welcome to stay," Jane says. "If it's okay with Iris."

Why is she encouraging him to be here without me? So she can tell him about my affair?

"Insomnia can be a sign of something else," Richard says to me in his serious doctor's voice. "When's the last time you had a physical?"

"Maybe a year ago? I'm not sure." I get up from my chair. "Dave, let's go."

"If you're leaving," Jane says, "let me pack you up some cheesecake. It'll just take a minute." She hurries to the kitchen.

"It was nice seeing you both," Richard says. "Maybe six months from now we'll do this again."

Dave laughs at his joke. "Hopefully, it won't be that long. Iris and I need to host next time, although neither of us is much of a cook."

Jane returns with the cheesecake. "Just take the whole thing. Richard and I don't need it."

"Thank you," Dave says, taking it from her. "And thank you for dinner. I'm sorry we have to take off early."

"Don't be." She smiles at him. "You go home and take care of your wife."

"The dinner was wonderful," I tell Jane. "I'm sorry it didn't agree with me. Or maybe Richard is right and I'm coming down with something."

"Hopefully, you'll feel better tomorrow," she says. "Let me walk you two out."

When we're finally out of there, I feel like I can breathe again. I was so tense sitting at the table, wondering what Jane was going to say next, that I had to leave. I couldn't wait until after dessert.

"Should I make you some tea?" Dave asks as we go into the house. "That usually helps when you're not feeling well."

"I think I'll just go to bed." I head to our room.

"Iris, wait." Dave comes over to me. "What was going on with you tonight?"

"What do you mean?"

"You seemed angry at Jane. You were being very argumentative with her. Did something happen between you two?"

"No, I just didn't like that she kept bringing up the interview. She could tell it upset me, but she wouldn't let it go."

"I think she was just trying to make conversation. She wasn't trying to upset you."

I put my hands on my hips. "Why do you keep taking her side? You did it all through dinner. You should be supporting me, your wife, not our neighbor."

"I wasn't taking her side. I don't know why you're being this way. Jane is your friend."

"Yes, well, I think our friendship is coming to an end."

"Because of tonight?"

"Because I don't trust her. Just look at how open she was

about Renee's affair. Renee made it clear she didn't want anyone knowing, and then Jane goes and tells Richard."

"You told *me*."

"Because I thought you might be able to help, but as soon as I said it, I regretted it. Renee was very clear that Jane and I weren't to tell anyone."

"Spouses don't count. That's one of those unspoken rules."

"I really don't think Renee wanted us telling our husbands. You and Richard both talk to Trent. What if one of you accidentally told him? It would ruin Renee's marriage."

Dave puts his hands on my shoulders. "We're done talking about this. It's clearly upsetting you, and if we keep discussing it, you're only going to get more upset. Why don't you take a hot bath? Try to relax? I'm going to run over to the gas station and fill the car up. I forgot to do it this morning and it's on empty."

"Would you fill mine up too?"

"Sure." He kisses me. "Try to rest. I'll be back soon."

I go into the bedroom and lie down on the bed. I didn't think I'd be able to sleep, but I find myself drifting off.

When I wake up, I hear the TV on in the other room. I check the time. It's after ten. Dave is usually in bed by now.

Getting up, I go to the living room and find Dave sitting on the couch. I'm sure he heard me come in here, but he doesn't look over at me.

"Dave?" I walk up to him. "Aren't you going to bed?"

He stares straight ahead at the TV. "Why didn't you tell me?"

He knows. He knows about the affair. But how? Was it Jane? Did she come over while I was asleep and tell him about Nick?

I stand there, shocked and confused, not sure how to respond. My heart's racing so fast I feel like I can't catch my breath.

"Iris, say something." Dave finally looks at me. "Why didn't you tell me?"

# CHAPTER NINETEEN

"DAVE, I..." I sit down beside him. "I didn't know how to tell you."

"You didn't know how? What does that even mean?"

"It means I—" I shake my head. "I don't know. I don't know how to explain myself. It was a mistake."

"Then why not just tell me that? And why continue to keep it a secret?"

I can't look at him. I don't even want to imagine what he thinks of me right now.

"We need to talk about this," Dave says. "I need to know why you hid this from me."

Isn't that obvious? Does he really need to ask?

"Iris, say something," he says, getting angry.

I look down at the floor. "I don't know what to say. I know I should've told you, but I couldn't."

"Why? You didn't think I should know about it? Iris, this involves both of us. You should've told me."

I nod, still not wanting to look at him.

Why would Jane tell him? Why would she do that to me? It

had to be her. But when did she do it? How long has Dave been sitting here, knowing this, and waiting for me to wake up?

"When did you find out?" I ask.

"When I went to get gas."

My eyes rise to his. "What did you say?"

"When I got gas for your car."

"I don't understand. Jane was at the gas station?"

"Jane? What does Jane have to do with this?"

I'm really confused. What is going on here? What is he talking about?

"You said you found out at the gas station?" I ask.

"Yes. That's when I found it."

"Found what?"

"The note. The one you hid in the glove compartment. I was looking to see if I left my sunglasses in there and that's when I found the note."

He's talking about the note that was left on my car. I relax a little, relieved he wasn't referring to my affair.

"How long have you had it?" Dave asks. "And where did you find it?"

"Someone left it on my windshield when I was at the grocery store. It was last week sometime."

"And you didn't think I should know about this? Iris, whoever left you that note could be dangerous."

"I'm sure he's not dangerous. He's just another one of our fans that seems to have a little crush on me."

"A little crush?" Dave picks up the note, which I hadn't noticed was on the couch cushion next to him. "You and I are meant to be? I need you more than I need air or food?" He holds the note up. "You don't think this person could be dangerous?"

"If he was, he would've waited for me at my car, not taken off."

"Unless he has something else planned and this was just a warning." Dave turns to me. "I think we need to show this note to the police."

"They're not going to do anything. Look what they did with the man who interrupted our event. He spent a few hours in jail and then they let him go."

"We can't just do nothing. This man thinks you're meant to be with him. What if he really believes that and tries to take you?"

"That's not going to happen."

"Why aren't you more upset about this? I would've thought you'd want to contact the police the moment you got the note."

"I knew they wouldn't do anything. And I decided I can't panic every time I get a note like that. The more we put ourselves out there, the more things like this will happen. I just have to get used to it." I take Dave's hand. "And the reason I didn't tell you is because I didn't want you worrying about me."

"I'll always worry about you. You're my wife. I love you."

I smile. "I love you too. And I'm sorry I didn't tell you. Honestly, I haven't thought about it since it happened."

"If you get another one of those notes, I want to know."

"Then I'll be sure to tell you. Now can we go to bed? It's late, and I'm really tired."

"You go ahead. I'm going to try some of Jane's cheesecake."

He goes to the kitchen while I go back to bed.

That was close. I thought for sure Dave knew my secret. Good thing I didn't give too much away. If I'd said just a little more, I might've accidentally told him the truth.

WHEN I WAKE UP, it's morning and I find I'm alone in bed. I hear noise coming from the kitchen and smell bacon cooking. I didn't even know we had bacon.

"Dave?" I call out.

He appears at the door to the bedroom, already dressed and ready for the day.

"Stay there," he says, coming over to give me a kiss. "I'm bringing you breakfast."

"I'm getting breakfast in bed? Is it my birthday?"

"I wanted to do something special for you. You've been so stressed lately and I feel like part of that is my fault. Because I keep scheduling you for things."

"That's more Allen's fault than yours, and he schedules you for things as well."

"Yes, but you do far more media appearances than I do. Our fans clearly prefer you over me." He smiles. "Breakfast is almost done. Don't get up. I'll be right back."

He's being very sweet. Maybe he felt bad about getting so upset last night about that note.

A few minutes later, he returns with a tray. "Okay, I've got scrambled eggs, bacon, toast, and some grapes. That's the best I could do. I hope you like it!"

"It looks wonderful," I say as he gives me the tray. "Did you go buy all this?"

"Just the bacon. We had everything else."

"I didn't hear you leave."

"I tried to be very quiet. Enjoy your breakfast. I have a call with Allen in a few minutes. I'm going to take it in my office."

"What's the call about?"

"The candidates I'm considering for the ad manager job. I can go over their resumes with you later if you'd like."

"Thanks, but I'm going to let you handle that."

Dave's phone rings. "That's Allen." He takes off for his office.

As I'm having breakfast, I look through my phone and see several messages from Jane saying she's sorry last night didn't go well and asking if we're still friends. I'm not as angry at her today, but I'm not ready to talk to her, and I'm not sure if I want us to remain friends.

When I'm done eating, I take a long shower and get dressed. It's been an hour since Allen called Dave. I didn't think they'd talk this long. We need to get to the studio soon to record our podcast. We always record the shorter podcast on Friday, which is today, so we can end our work day early.

"Sorry it took so long," Dave says, coming into the bedroom as I'm putting on my earrings. "Allen and I were arguing."

"About who you want to hire?"

"No, about this weekend."

"You mean the bridal show?" I ask, knowing we're scheduled to spend all day there tomorrow, promoting our events and the podcast.

"Yes. I told him we're not doing it."

"Why? We already paid for the booth."

"Someone else can stand there all day. I told him to hire someone from the promo company we've used in the past. Anyone can hand out materials. It doesn't need to be us."

"So what are we doing instead?"

He smiles as he comes up to me. "We're having a romantic

weekend, just the two of us, with no work and no interruptions."

"You just decided this? Like today?"

"I've been thinking about it for weeks, but I wasn't sure where to take you. We can't go very far since we have an event on Sunday, so I found a place downtown."

"You mean a hotel?"

"A very nice hotel. It's already booked. We'll go there tonight and come back on Sunday." He wraps his arms around me. "I'm really looking forward to this. I hope you are too."

"I am. I just wasn't expecting it."

"I wanted it to be a surprise."

"Where are we staying? Is it a place we've been to before?"

"No, it's actually a place I've never heard of. I saw a brochure for it on that table outside our office, the one by the mailboxes." He reaches into his back pocket and pulls something out. "Here. Take a look."

My jaw drops when I see it. It's the hotel I used to go to with Nick.

And now I'm going there with Dave.

That can't be a coincidence. Someone set this up.

# CHAPTER TWENTY

"DON'T you want to look at it?" Dave says, holding up the brochure.

I take it, my stomach knotting up as I open the brochure and see a photo of a room that looks just like the one I stayed in with Nick.

"What do you think?" Dave's beaming, like he's proud of himself for booking the perfect hotel for our romantic weekend getaway. "It's one of those small boutique hotels you love. And on weekends they have wine tastings in the lobby."

I know all that. I've been there. Many times.

"We'll go to a nice restaurant tonight for dinner, and then maybe tomorrow we could go to one of the museums."

"Sounds nice," I say, trying to show some enthusiasm. If he'd booked us at any other hotel, I'd be thrilled about this little surprise trip, but knowing we'll be at the hotel I was at with Nick makes me feel sick.

"Honey, what's wrong?" Dave asks.

"Nothing." I force out a smile. "So when are we leaving?"

"I thought we'd drive down there this afternoon." He

takes the brochure from me and sets it on the dresser. "Why do I feel like I did something wrong? Do you not want to go?"

"Honey, of course I want to go. I'm just surprised. You don't usually do things like this."

"But I should." He puts his arms around me. "Romantic gestures are important in a marriage. Making your wife breakfast. Planning romantic getaways. I haven't been doing as much for you because I've been so preoccupied with growing the business, but you and our marriage come first. I don't want to ever forget that."

"That's very sweet, but you didn't have to do all this. I really don't need it."

"Maybe not, but I still wanted to do it. And we could use some time away. I know we're not going far, but it's good for us to get out of the house where we're not having to think about chores that need to be done and things that need to be fixed. Our focus can be on each other." He smiles. "Doesn't that sound nice?"

I nod. "It does."

And I'd be looking forward to it if he hadn't picked that hotel.

"Where did you say you got that brochure?" I ask.

"At our office building. You know that table by the mailboxes where restaurants leave takeout menus?"

"Yes, but it's usually only menus. I've never seen a hotel brochure there."

"I haven't either. That's probably why it caught my eye. As soon as I saw it, I took it as a sign we should go away for the weekend. Actually, I've been wanting to do that for weeks. I just wasn't sure where to take you. Then I saw the brochure and that was my answer. I know it's last minute, but sometimes it's good to be spontaneous."

"How many brochures were there?"

He gives me a confused look. "For the hotel?"

"Yes, was there a whole stack or just one?"

"I think just one. I wasn't paying attention to how many were there. Why do you ask?"

"I just wondered."

It's odd the hotel would only leave one brochure. Wouldn't they leave a whole stack so people could take them? And why would they advertise to an office building?

I don't think the hotel did it. I think Nick put the brochure there. It had to be him. It's another message, telling me he's back. But instead of me finding it, Dave did, and now he's making us stay there.

This weekend is going to be a nightmare. All I'll be able to think about is Nick and what we did in that hotel. The guilt will overwhelm me, making me unable to be with Dave the way he expects. How could I possibly be intimate with my husband at the place where I was intimate with another man? I feel sick just thinking about it.

The doorbell rings.

"I'll get it," Dave says, taking off to get the door.

I remain in the bedroom, still frozen in shock. I can't believe this is happening. I was sure Nick wouldn't come back. He'd moved on, and moved away. It's been years since I saw him. Why would he come back now?

"Iris," Dave calls out. "Jane's here."

*Jane's here?* Why? What does she want? I thought ignoring all her text messages would've clued her into the fact that I wasn't ready to talk to her. But Jane can be very persistent.

"Hello, Jane," I say in a formal tone as I join her and Dave in the living room.

"Jane brought us some homemade cinnamon rolls," Dave says, holding up a plate covered with foil.

"That's very nice," I say. "Thank you, Jane."

"It's my pleasure." She smiles at me. "Are you feeling better today?"

"Much. I got a good night's sleep."

"I'm glad." Jane glances at Dave. "Your husband was just telling me that you two are going to have a romantic weekend in the city."

Why did he tell her that? She doesn't need to know what we're doing.

"Jane said she's been to the hotel we're staying at," Dave says.

He told her about the hotel? Or maybe she asked. She's very nosy. But I wish he hadn't told her.

"My women's auxiliary group used to have meetings there," she says, like I don't already know this. "It's a beautiful hotel." She looks at Dave. "You've never been there?"

"No. I've never heard of it. Iris hasn't either." He glances at me. "Have you? I guess I didn't ask."

"No, I've never heard of it."

"I think you'll really enjoy it," Jane says. "It's very romantic. Perfect for couples."

She continues talking, saying something about the hotel's history, but I tune her out as an idea pops into my head. What if Jane did this? What if she was the one who left the brochure? Maybe she thought going there with Dave would cause me to feel so much guilt that I'd break down and tell him about the affair. I don't understand why she keeps insisting I tell him. She needs to stay out of it.

"That's very interesting," Dave says when Jane finishes talking. "I didn't realize that hotel had such rich history."

"Honey, could I talk to Jane a minute?" I say to Dave.

"Sure." He holds up the plate. "I'll go put these in the kitchen."

When he's gone, I lower my voice and say to Jane, "Did you plan this?"

"Plan what?" she asks.

"The hotel. Did you leave that brochure at our office building?"

"What brochure? I don't know what you mean."

She genuinely seems to have no idea what I'm talking about. So I guess it wasn't her who left the brochure. It was Nick. Of course it was Nick. Why did I think it could be anyone else? Because I didn't want it to be him. That's why. My mind keeps trying to find ways to make this not about him. But the card, the notes, the roses, the menu, the brochure. I'm almost certain they're all from him.

"Never mind," I say. "I was confused for a moment."

"Are you okay?" Jane puts her hand on my arm. "I'm worried about you."

"I'm fine." I take a step back and fold my arms over my chest. "You should go. Dave and I have to get to the studio."

"About last night. I'm sorry for how it went. I hope we're still friends."

Dave comes back before I can answer. "Jane, those cinnamon rolls are delicious. I only had a few bites, but I could've easily eaten the whole thing."

"Go ahead." She smiles. "That's what they're for."

"I already had breakfast." He puts his arm around my shoulder. "And I have to watch what I eat. I want to stay fit and trim for my wife."

"I'm sure she'd love you at any size," Jane says with a laugh. "Well, I'll let you two get on with your day." She walks to the door. "Have a wonderful time this weekend! I can't wait to hear all about it!"

There's not going to be anything to tell. I'm going to make sure it's uneventful. I'll bury my guilt so far down that Dave will have no idea anything's wrong. I've done that for years now, so I'm certain I can do it for a weekend, despite that hotel being full of memories.

Nothing is going to go wrong. I just need to keep telling myself that.

There's just one thing that could ruin it. Or one person.

I don't think he'd do it, but what if he did? What if Nick shows up at the hotel?

# CHAPTER TWENTY-ONE

"It's beautiful," Dave says, as we enter the hotel lobby. "Don't you think?"

It's exactly like I remember, like nothing's changed since I came here with Nick. I can picture him sitting on the red velvet sofa in the lobby, waiting for me. He'd give me a slight smile as I approached him and then we'd head to the bar for a drink.

"Iris," Dave says, waking me from the memory. "What do you think?"

"It's lovely. Looks just like the brochure."

"I think it looks better. Check out those pillars." He points to the carved wood pillars in the lobby. I remember Nick pulling me behind one of them and sneaking a kiss. I scolded him for it, but I secretly liked that he did it. Even though I was worried someone might see us, it also gave me a thrill, knowing we might be caught.

Back then, I wouldn't have cared if I'd been caught because I assumed my marriage was ending and I just wanted it to be over. I was tired of all the fighting and yelling and sleeping in separate beds. But then things changed. My marriage got better, and the affair was no longer thrilling but shameful. It had to end.

"Let's go check in," Dave says, taking my hand as he heads to the check-in desk.

"Good afternoon," the woman at the desk says, smiling at Dave. "Checking in?"

"Yes. Dave Larson."

She clicks on her keyboard, then stops and looks at us. "Are you two those marriage experts?"

"I'm not sure we're experts," Dave says with a laugh. "We prefer to call ourselves marriage coaches. We help people have winning marriages."

He's quoting our branding. Next, he'll give her our business card. He said we wouldn't talk about the business this weekend, yet here we are, at the hotel less than five minutes, and he's telling this woman about our events.

"We have one this Sunday," he says. "But unfortunately it's sold out." He hands her a business card. "If you go to our website, you can see all the event dates we have coming up. I'm sure some of them still have tickets available."

"Thanks! I'll check it out." She sets the card down and goes back to typing on her keyboard. "I have you down for two nights. Is that correct?"

"Yes." Dave puts his arm around me. "We're looking forward to it. It's a beautiful hotel."

"You've never been here?" She finishes typing and looks at Dave.

"We haven't," he says. "I only know about it because I found one of your brochures."

"Well, I'm glad you found us." She hands us the key cards.

"Your room is upstairs on the fourth floor. Oh, and at six tonight we have a wine tasting in the lobby. Enjoy your stay!"

*The fourth floor.* Nick would always reserve a room for us on the fourth floor. I don't know why. Four was his lucky number, so maybe that was the reason. He never told me, and I didn't ask. After he'd take me up to the room, we didn't do much talking.

"Iris?" Dave says. "Are you coming?"

I wake from my thoughts and notice I'm still standing inside the elevator while he's outside of it.

I join him in the hallway, plastering a smile on my face. "What's the room number?"

He checks the little envelope the key cards are in. "It looks like we're in 404."

No. Not that room. Any room but that one. Room 404 is where I had my last encounter with Nick. It's where I told him it was over and that I'd decided to stay with Dave. That room has too many memories, ones I'd like to forget.

"Looks like this is it," Dave says, stopping in front of room 404. He gets out the key and opens the door, then smiles at me. "Ladies first."

I go inside and the memories come flooding back. Everywhere I look, I see Nick and what we did in this room.

"It's smaller than I thought it'd be," Dave says, coming up behind me. "But we don't need a lot of room." He leans down and kisses the side of my neck. "I'm hoping we'll be spending most of our time in bed."

*In bed?* The same bed I was in with Nick?

"I can't stay here," I blurt out.

"What do you mean? At the hotel?"

I turn to Dave. "This room. I don't like it. It, um, smells. Like mold."

He sniffs the air. "I don't smell anything."

"I'm more sensitive to smells than you are. Dave, I'm telling you, it definitely smells moldy in here. I can't stay in a room that has mold."

"Honey, if this one does, they probably all do."

"Not necessarily." I head to the door. "Let's go see if we can get a different one."

We return to the lobby and have to wait in line. When we reach the check-in desk, the woman who assisted us before says, "Can I help you?"

Dave answers. "Yes, my wife is very sensitive to mold and she thinks the room we're in might have a mold issue."

The woman frowns. "Oh, that's not good. Let me see if we have something else." As she types on her keyboard, she says, "We've never had anyone tell us that. I wonder if it's something new. Maybe the shower curtain needs to be replaced?"

"I think it's more than that," I say. "I'm not sure. I just know I won't feel good if I stay there."

"It looks like we have a room open on the first floor. Would you like to try that one?"

"Yes," I say, glancing at Dave.

My poor husband. He was trying to do something romantic, planning this special weekend for us, and it's already turning into a disaster. I thought I could play along and pretend I've never been here, but the memories are too strong. Everywhere I look reminds me of Nick.

"What do you think?" Dave asks as we go into our new room. "Any mold issues?"

"No, I don't think so," I say, but the room's layout is the same, bringing my mind back to Nick.

"Good," Dave says. "I'll put our bags over here." He sets them by the window, then comes over to me. "What should we do first?" He glances at the bed. That's the last thing I want to do, especially when all I can think about is Nick.

"Maybe we could walk around."

"Outside? It just started raining."

"It did? I guess I didn't notice."

"Why don't we go to the bar? Have a drink?"

"That sounds good."

Maybe a drink will help me relax. I'm very tense, and if I don't calm down Dave will notice and ask what's wrong.

The bar is just off the lobby. It's dimly lit, with dark furnishings and low ceilings. Nick said it reminded him of a speakeasy. He used to read a lot and knew all about speakeasies along with lots of other things. I enjoyed listening to him talk while I sipped my wine. Nick always got bourbon. Top shelf. Neat.

"What can I get you?" the bartender asks as Dave and I sit down at the bar.

I glance up and see it's him. The same bartender that was serving drinks when I came here with Nick. He couldn't possibly remember me, could he? It's been years.

"I'll have a glass of chardonnay," I say.

"Your best, please," Dave says to the guy. "And I'll have a Manhattan."

"Got it," he says, going to get our drinks.

"I didn't need the best they have," I say to Dave.

"You deserve the best." He kisses me. "And why shouldn't you have it? We're making good money. Why not enjoy it?"

My gaze keeps going to the bartender, wondering if he remembers me. It's more likely he'd remember Nick. He'd come here on his own sometimes, just to sit at the bar and have a drink. His office was close to here. Sometimes I wondered if I wasn't the only one. If he brought other women here. I never asked. I didn't want to know.

"We should do this more often," Dave says.

"Do what?"

"These little getaways. Weekends away from home."

I turn to him. "Where would we go?"

"I don't know. I'd have to give it some thought. I just think it's good for us to get away."

"Chardonnay and a Manhattan," the bartender says, setting our drinks down. "Need anything else?"

"I think we're good," Dave says. "Thank you."

The bartender looks at me. "You've been here before, haven't you?"

"Me?" I smile at him. "No. Never. This is my first time."

"Really? Because you look like this woman who used to come here a lot. And she always ordered chardonnay."

"You must be thinking of someone else," Dave says.

"Guess so." He continues to stare at me. "But I swear I've seen you before."

"Probably on television," Dave says. "Or maybe one of our ads. My wife and I run a marriage-coaching business. We're fairly well-known in the area. We're in the media a lot. In fact, Iris did an interview for one of the local news stations just last week. Perhaps you saw it."

"I doubt it. I don't watch the news." He motions to our drinks. "Let me know when you're ready for another." He walks off.

"That was odd," Dave says. "That guy seemed convinced he'd seen you before."

"I must have a twin," I joke.

"You sure you've never been here?"

I swirl the wine around in my glass, staring down at it. "Why would I come here? I rarely come into the city, and when I do, I'm with you."

He shrugs. "Maybe it was a long time ago. Before we met. You used to come to the city more when you were single."

"I'd remember if I had been here. And I doubt the bartender's been working here that long."

"Then he must recognize you from our ads."

"I'm sure that's it."

"Let's toast." Dave holds up his glass. "To us."

"That's it?" I smile. "We're toasting to us?"

"Isn't that enough?"

"It is." I lift my glass. "To us."

We clink our glasses and sip our drinks, then Dave leans over and gives me a kiss.

"I love you," he says. "Marrying you was the best decision I ever made."

His words should make me happy, but instead I feel sick inside. How could I do it? How could I cheat on Dave? I know we've had our problems, but he's always loved me, even during our rough patch. He's the one who got our marriage back on track. If it weren't for him, we probably wouldn't still be together. We wouldn't have our business. Wouldn't live in such a beautiful house.

So why wasn't I happy? Why wasn't Dave enough? Why didn't I fight for our marriage instead of being with someone else?

# CHAPTER TWENTY-TWO

"I CAN'T BELIEVE we have to leave today," Dave says, turning toward me in bed.

It's Sunday morning. I made it to the end of this surprise weekend away without Dave becoming suspicious. I pretended to be thrilled that he took me here. I let him make love to me multiple times even though I had zero desire. And I went along with his endless comments about how great the hotel is and how we need to come back.

We're never coming back. I never want to step foot in this hotel again. Even now, with Dave lying next to me in bed, I'm imagining Nick being there. It's like he's haunting the place and I can't get away from him.

"Should we order room service?" Dave asks. "Or would you like to do something else?" He moves so his body is over mine.

Not again. We've already done it more times than we did on our honeymoon. Hasn't he had enough?

"Why don't we head out?" I say.

"Like go home?"

"Yes. We need to get ready for the event."

"That's not until tonight."

"I know, but I have things I need to get done at home."

He moves off me and lies on his side, facing me. "You don't want to order breakfast?"

"No, I'd like to get home."

"Then that's what we'll do."

I start to get up, but Dave grabs my arm. "Hold on."

"I was going to take a shower," I tell him.

"Before you do, did you like this?"

"Like what?"

"Coming here. Getting away for a few days."

"Yes. Honey, I told you I liked it. Several times."

"I wasn't sure you meant it. It kind of felt like you were just saying it to please me."

"That's not why I said it. I had a good time."

"Then is something else going on? Because you've seemed really distracted this weekend, like there's something on your mind."

"The only thing on my mind was you." I smile at him. "And you can be very distracting."

"Iris, I'm serious. You kept looking away, tuning me out, like you were in your own world. I kept having to get your attention and repeat myself."

"I'm just tired. I didn't sleep well in this bed. And I think the mold is bothering me. I didn't want to say anything, but I can smell the mold in here, just like the first room."

"You should've told me. We could've gone to a different hotel."

"We'd already paid for the room, and I could tell how much you enjoyed being here."

"Yes, but not if your health is suffering."

"Don't worry about it. I'm fine." I kiss him. "I'm going to go get in the shower."

By ten o'clock, we're on our way home. A huge wave of relief came over me the moment we left the hotel. The whole time we were there, I kept expecting Nick to show up.

"You've been quiet the whole way home," Dave says as he turns down our street. "You aren't mad at me, are you?"

"Of course not. I'm just in my head, preparing for the event tonight."

"Honey, we've done this enough times now. We really don't need to prepare."

"I still like to run through it in my head. It keeps me from getting nervous."

"Speaking of preparing, I need to prepare for an interview I'm doing tomorrow for the ad position. I left my notes at the studio. Would you mind if I ran over there and got them?"

"Go ahead. I'll go inside and get the laundry started."

"I'll carry in our things." He leaves the car running as he gets out and takes our overnight bags from the trunk. He brings them into the house, then gives me a kiss goodbye before he leaves.

As he drives off, I go out to get the mail. I'm walking back to the house when Jane appears.

"Iris!" She waves at me as she hurries over.

"This isn't a good time, Jane. I just got home, and I have a lot to do before the event tonight."

She follows me into the house. "I have to know how it went." She glances around. "Dave isn't here, right? I thought I just saw him leave."

"He's gone, but he'll be back soon," I say, going to the

kitchen and setting the mail down. "He just had to run to the studio."

"So?" She races up beside me. "What happened? Did he suspect anything?"

"No. He has no reason to."

"But it was the same hotel that you and—"

"Yes, I know," I say, not needing her to tell me.

"Didn't you feel odd being there with Dave?"

I hesitate, wanting to tell her about my weekend, but not sure I trust her, not after how she's been acting lately. But she's one of my only friends, and I really need to get this off my chest.

"It was horrible," I say. "Everywhere I looked, I saw him."

She gasps. "He was there? At the hotel?"

"No, I mean he was in my head. I couldn't stop thinking about him, and thinking about all the memories we had there."

"Did Dave notice?"

"No, fortunately. But he did notice that I was distracted. He said I kept looking away and that he had to keep repeating things. I told him it was because I was tired."

"And he bought it?"

"I think so." I sit down on the stool next to the center island. "It was awful. The whole weekend. I couldn't wait to leave."

"If only he could've picked a different hotel. Out of all the places..." Her voice drifts off.

"It was because of that brochure. The one Dave picked up outside our office. That's what gave him the idea to do this." I pause, trying to decide if I should tell her. Before I can stop myself, I blurt out, "I think it was him."

"Who?" Jane asks. "What are we talking about?"

"Nick," I whisper, even though Dave isn't around to hear us.

"What about him?"

"I think he's the one who left the brochure at our office."

"I don't understand. Didn't you say he moved away?"

"Yes, but I think he's back."

She pulls out a stool and sits beside me. "He moved back to Chicago?"

"I don't know if he moved or if he's just here for a short time. But I know he's back." I turn to Jane. "He's been leaving me messages."

"He's been calling you?"

"No, not phone messages. Other messages. The card. The roses. That hotel brochure."

"You said you didn't know who sent the roses."

"I think it was Nick. I can't prove it, but they were yellow and he grew up in Texas and there's that song about yellow roses and Texas, so it had to be him."

"That's a bit of a stretch. Anyone could've sent you yellow roses."

"And they just happen to show up at the same time as the notes?"

"What notes?"

I tell her about the card with the heart on it and the note I found on my windshield.

"Those came from one of your fans," Jane says, like she's sure of it. "Like that strange man who got arrested at your event. He's probably the one who sent you those things."

"It's possible, but I'm almost certain they're from Nick. And what about the menu? The one left at my door? Nick and I went to that restaurant all the time."

"You think he left you a menu," she says, like she's confirming what I said.

"Yes, to tell me he's back in town. Same for the hotel brochure. He's sending me messages to tell me he's here. Jane, what am I going to do? I can't have him show up here and—"

"Okay, slow down." She puts her hand on my arm. "Take a breath."

I try, but I can only take a shallow one because my chest is so tight.

"I think you might be reading too much into this," she says. "I don't think Nick is the person doing this."

"Jane, I'm telling you. It's him."

"If that's true, then he sounds like a very disturbed man. Is that how he was before?" Her brows rise. "When you two were..."

"No. He wasn't that way at all. But I didn't know him that well. We didn't spend much time together. It's possible he was like this and I just didn't know."

"Anyone could've sent you that card. Same for the roses. And the menu and brochure could've just been a coincidence."

"You really think that? After everything I just told you?"

"I'm sorry, Iris, but I can't imagine some man you were with for only a few months would show up out of the blue and leave you messages that he's back in town. Why wouldn't he just call? Or come to the house?"

"I don't know. That's why I'm concerned. I don't understand what's happening. Why is he doing this? What does he want?"

"Call him. Ask him if he's the one doing these things."

"I tried, but he doesn't have the same number."

She shakes her head. "I think you're making something out

of nothing. I think your guilt has you imagining things that aren't real and you're driving yourself crazy."

"What about the menu? Who else would put it there? And why did I get one but nobody else did?"

"You checked with everyone in the neighborhood?"

"Well, no, but I looked at all the houses on the street and didn't see a menu at anyone else's door."

"Maybe the person delivering them put one in your door, then realized he was in the wrong neighborhood."

"That's never happened for as long as I've lived here."

"That you know of, and that doesn't mean it isn't possible."

"And the hotel brochure? How do you explain that?"

"Maybe someone in the building left it there. Someone from one of the other offices."

"Maybe, but don't you think it's odd that it was for *that* hotel, out of all the ones in Chicago?"

"Iris, you need to stop this. You're worrying yourself sick about something that's likely not even true. If you keep this up, Dave is going to notice and then you'll have no choice but to tell him the truth."

"It won't come to that." I pause. "I just need to find a way to contact Nick and tell him to stop this."

"Assuming he has something to do with it. My advice is to leave it alone."

"You mean do nothing?"

"Why in the world would you contact him? You're only creating more problems for yourself. Do you really want to bring this man back into your life?"

"That's not what I'm doing. I'm just going to find his number, call him, and ask what he wants."

"What if it's you? What if he wants to start something with you again?"

"Then I'll make it clear that's not going to happen."

"What if Dave finds out? What if he finds out you contacted this man? How are you going to explain that?"

The door opens and I hear Dave's voice. "I'm home! And I have a surprise!"

I get up as Dave comes into the kitchen. He's holding a large bouquet of flowers.

"Jane." He smiles at her. "I didn't know you were here."

She smiles back at him. "I came over to ask Iris about your romantic weekend."

"It was wonderful." He walks up to me and gives me a kiss. "And it's not over." He hands me the flowers. "These are for you."

"They're beautiful. Thank you."

"She's so lucky to have you," Jane says to Dave. "Richard hasn't brought me flowers since before we were married."

"Perhaps I need to have a talk with him," Dave says in a kidding tone.

"It wouldn't do any good," Jane says, getting up. "Richard's not the romantic type. I'll leave you two lovebirds to enjoy your Sunday." She starts to leave, then turns back. "Oh, and Iris, call me if you want to finish our little discussion." She winks at me, then glances at Dave.

Why did she do that? Now Dave's going to wonder what's going on. I swear she does things for the sole purpose of stirring up drama. I shouldn't have told her about Nick, but I was desperate to talk to someone. I wanted someone else's opinion, and Jane's the only person I could talk to, the only person who knows about Nick.

Maybe she's right. Maybe all these messages I've been getting aren't messages at all. Maybe I'm making them mean something when they really don't. I thought for sure Nick was back, but what if he's not? What if I've been worried about something that's not even true?

# CHAPTER TWENTY-THREE

"What were you two talking about?" Dave asks after Jane leaves.

"I was just telling her about our weekend." I set the flowers next to the sink. "Could you get the vase?"

He takes it from the cupboard and hands it to me. "What did you tell her?"

"I said we had a nice time." I put the vase in the sink and fill it with water. "It was really sweet of you to get me flowers. And such a nice surprise."

"What else did you tell her?" Dave asks, watching as I arrange the flowers in the vase.

"Not much." I glance at him and smile. "We spent most of yesterday in bed. I didn't want to tell Jane that."

"She made it sound like you were talking about something else. Something you didn't want me to hear."

"That's not it at all," I say with a laugh. "We were talking about remodeling projects. I mentioned wanting to update the kitchen and Jane got all excited, wanting to discuss all the different ways we could change things up in here. You know how much she loves decorating."

His brows draw together. "You want to remodel the kitchen?"

I shrug. "It was just a thought. We don't actually have to do it."

"We can. I'm just surprised you'd want to. Neither one of us likes to cook. I'd rather remodel a room we actually use."

We're not remodeling any rooms. I just said that so he'd stop asking what Jane and I were discussing. I need to get myself out of this before Dave takes this any further.

"It's actually a terrible idea," I say with a laugh, setting the vase on the counter. "A remodeling project is the last thing we need with everything else we have going on. Speaking of that, did you get what you needed at the studio?"

"No, I got there and my notes were gone. Allen took them home to look over." Dave's phone rings and he checks to see who's calling. "It's Allen. I can call him back later."

"Go ahead and talk to him."

"You sure? I was thinking we'd do something together." He smiles. "Our romantic weekend doesn't have to end yet."

"It's fine. I have some things to get done."

He takes the call and goes down to his office while I go into the bedroom. I shut the door and get out my phone and search online for Nick. I've already done this, but I need to check again.

Unfortunately, I can't find anything. He has nothing on social media, not even a profile. I search for his phone number but can't find it. Nick's one of those people who doesn't like being tracked online or having his personal information made public, so I'm not surprised I'm struggling to find a way to contact him.

---

THAT NIGHT, Dave and I have our event and it's one of our best ones yet. We had a lot of participation from the audience and some great questions. It's nights like this that I really love what I do. It's energizing to see people excited about saving their marriage. We're able to give them hope, which is often what they need most when their marriage is in trouble.

I didn't have hope back when Dave and I were struggling and it led to me being unfaithful. If I can save other couples from going down that path, that's enough for me. The money doesn't matter. In fact, I've suggested Dave and I do some free events for people who can't afford to attend the paid ones, but he wouldn't agree to it. He said it would make our program seem less valuable and harm our brand.

As Dave and I exit the stage, people clap for us while the music plays. Dave's beaming, as he always is after these events. I think he loves them even more than I do.

"Tonight was great," he says as we walk down the hall. "I think it was our best one yet."

"I thought the same thing. People seemed to really like our new skit."

We tried out a new role-playing exercise showing how to resolve conflict in a marriage.

"We need to do it for the podcast," Dave says. "And then make it into a video for social media."

Dave's constantly thinking of ways to promote us. I don't

think his mind ever shuts down. He even comes up with ideas while he sleeps.

"Dave," someone yells. We look back and see Neal, the guy we pay to video record our events.

"What do you need?" Dave asks.

"I've got a problem with the video. You got a minute to come look at it?"

"Sure." Dave follows Neal down the hall.

I continue to the dressing room. When I get there, I notice something in front of the door. It's a tall, narrow box with a ribbon wrapped around it. Is it another gift from Dave? I thought our romantic weekend was over, but maybe he decided it's not. Maybe this is another surprise gift.

Bringing the box into the dressing room, I shut the door and set the box on the table. I undo the ribbon and open the box to find a bottle of champagne. But not just any champagne. It's the exact same kind Nick used to have delivered to our room at the hotel.

"He did this," I mutter, picking up the bottle. I look around the room, searching for him, but he's not here. He's probably not even in the building. I'm guessing he dropped this off and left.

It's another message. It has to be. Jane would say it's a coincidence, that it's a common champagne and anyone could've left it, but I don't believe that. One coincidence? Maybe. But the restaurant menu, the hotel brochure, and now this? That can't all be a coincidence.

Setting the bottle down, I notice a note inside the box. There's something printed on it. I pick it up and read it.

*Congratulations! Wonderful performance tonight,*

*pretending to have the perfect marriage. If only it were real. But as you told your audience, a good marriage is based on honesty. And you're living a lie. How long before you tell him the truth? How long before he finds out?*

"I'm back," Dave says.

I whip around and see him coming into the room.

"The video's fine," he says. "Neal and I figured out the issue."

"That's great!" I say, crumpling up the note and hiding it in my hand.

Dave points to the box. "What's that?"

"Champagne. Someone left it for us."

"Do we know who?"

"No, there wasn't a note. I guess they want to remain anonymous."

He picks up the bottle. "I wish we knew who gave it to us so we could thank them. You sure there's not a note?" He searches the box.

"I already looked. There's nothing there."

"It could be from Heather. She was in the audience tonight."

"She was?"

"Yes, I thought I told you."

"I don't think you mentioned it. Did she bring someone?"

"No, she wanted to see how we do our events so I sent her a ticket."

I walk away from him, being careful to hide my hand so he doesn't notice the note in it.

"This was a great night," Dave says. "The perfect way to end a perfect weekend."

This weekend was far from perfect. It was a nightmare, at least for me. As for tonight, I agree it was great... until I found the champagne and the note from Nick.

Why won't he end this? What is he waiting for?

# CHAPTER TWENTY-FOUR

It's been three days since I found that note with the champagne. When I got home Sunday night, I put the note in the garbage disposal and ground it up so Dave wouldn't find it. He insisted we drink the champagne last night to celebrate signing the deal to create our branded products. Heather wanted to take us to dinner, but Dave suggested we do it some other night, which was good because I wasn't in the mood to celebrate. But Dave still wanted to open the champagne. I only had a few sips, then told Dave it was giving me a headache.

"I'm heading to the studio," Dave says, coming over to give me a kiss as I put our breakfast dishes in the sink.

"I'll be there soon," I tell him, wishing he'd hurry up and leave. I purposely didn't get myself ready this morning so I'd have an excuse to stay behind.

"I have some news to share when you get there," Dave says, a big smile on his face. He's been in a really good mood this week, probably because we signed the product deal and are close to signing the book deal. I'd be in a good mood too if I didn't have the Nick problem to deal with.

"What's the news?" I ask.

"I'll tell you when you get to the studio."

"Why not just tell me now? Is this about the book? Are we ready to sign the deal?"

"No, it's not that exciting. But it's still good news. I'll see you later."

"Yeah, bye."

When he's gone and I see his car turn down the street, I race over to Jane's house.

She answers the door wearing an apron with fall leaves printed all over it. She has an apron for every season and holiday.

"I made apple-cinnamon muffins for our little chat. I found the recipe on—"

"Sorry, Jane, I can't talk about recipes," I say, going past her into the house. "It happened again."

"What are we talking about?" she asks, closing the door.

"I got another message. Or sign, clue, whatever you want to call it. From Nick."

"Oh," she says in a concerned tone. "Why don't we go sit down?" She takes my arm and guides me to the kitchen like she thinks I might be losing my mind.

"Jane, I'm not crazy," I tell her, stopping before we get to the kitchen table. "I'm telling you, it's him. Sunday night, I found a bottle of champagne outside my dressing room. It was the same kind he'd order when we were together."

"You realize anyone could've bought that champagne," she says. "Just because it's the same kind you had with—"

"There was a note. He called me a liar for pretending to have a perfect marriage while keeping this secret from Dave."

"Did he actually say that, or are you just interpreting it that way?"

"I don't remember the exact wording, but he said something about how I was living a lie and how a good marriage is based on honesty. And then he ended it by asking how long I'd wait until I told Dave the truth. Or until he found out."

Jane walks over to the counter where the muffins are cooling. "Would you like yours with butter?"

She's asking me about muffins? After what I just told her about Nick?

"Jane, forget the muffins. I need some advice here!"

She calmly puts two muffins on two small white plates and brings them over to the table. "Sit down, Iris. You're making me anxious."

I sit at the table, concerned by her strange response. I'm starting to think she's the crazy one, not me.

"I'm not hungry," I say as she sets a dish of butter on the table.

"Would you like some coffee?" She smiles at me.

"No, I'd like you to sit down and talk to me. What is going on with you?"

"I could ask you the same thing. I don't like this version of you, Iris. It's very disturbing."

"*I'm* disturbing? You're carrying on about muffins after I just told you Nick left me a threatening note!"

"It doesn't sound threatening," she says, pouring herself some coffee. "It sounds like he told you to tell Dave the truth. And I agree. I've been telling you that for weeks." She joins me at the table. "The only way to end this is to tell your husband what you did. Then it's all out in the open and you can stop driving yourself crazy worrying that Dave will find out."

"It's not that simple. Telling Dave the truth could mean the end of our marriage. And if our marriage ends, our business ends. No more podcast. No more events. No book deal. It all goes away."

She takes a bite of her muffin, closing her eyes as she chews. "I might've added too much cinnamon." Her eyes pop open. "Try it. Let me know if it's too much."

"I'm leaving." I get up from the table. "I thought you would help me, but this is a waste of time."

"Oh, Iris, stop being so dramatic." She follows me to the door. "What do you want me to say? I gave you advice and you chose to disregard it."

I turn to her. "Tell Dave? That's your advice?"

"Honestly, Iris, I don't know why you're even asking me. You're the one who's supposed to be the marriage expert. And aren't you always telling people to be honest with their spouse?"

"Yes, but—" I stop, because she's right. I just can't bring myself to follow my own advice. What I did with Nick was wrong, but it's the past and telling Dave will only harm our marriage. Even if we don't divorce, our marriage will never be the same. Dave may tell me he forgives me, but he won't. He's someone who holds a grudge.

"Okay," Jane says. "Here's another approach. Let's say Nick shows up and tells Dave about the affair. You simply deny it. Dave's going to believe you over some strange man who appears out of nowhere making ridiculous claims about his wife. He'll think Nick is just another fan who believes he's in love with you."

"Yes, I've considered that."

She shrugs. "There you go. Problem solved."

"It's not solved, but that's an option." My phone dings with a text. "That's Dave. I told him I'd meet him at the studio."

"You want to bring him some muffins?"

"No. I need to go." I walk quickly down the sidewalk from her house to mine.

Talking to her didn't make me feel better. I don't know why I went to her for advice. I already knew what she'd say.

When I get to the studio, I find Dave in the office.

"What are you working on?" I ask.

"Hi, honey." He smiles and gets up from his chair. "I didn't hear you come in." He gives me a hug. "I was just looking over the new ads."

"New ads?"

"I had each of the candidates for the ad manager position write a couple online ads based on material from our podcast, just to see what they'd come up with. One of the candidates did such a good job I decided to use his ads. I thought we'd record them today, see how they sound."

"Sure. So how are the interviews going?"

"They're done. I hired a guy. It's the guy who wrote the ads I was just telling you about. That's the good news I was talking about earlier. Now that I've hired someone, I won't have to be here as much, which means I'll have more time with you." He takes my hand. "Let's go to the studio so you can meet him."

"He's here?"

"Yes, and he wants to meet you. Allen was going to stop by to meet him, but he hasn't shown up yet."

We go into the studio and I see a man with his back to us. He hears us come in and turns around.

No. No, no, no, no!

I'm going to be sick. This can't be happening.

"Nick," Dave says, walking up to him. "I want you to meet my wife. Iris, this is Nick, our new online ad manager."

# CHAPTER TWENTY-FIVE

"Hello, Iris," Nick says, walking up to me.

He's just as handsome as I remember. He has a few more lines around his eyes, but it somehow makes him look better, not worse. He's dressed casually, in jeans and a white button-up shirt with a black leather jacket over it.

"It's nice to meet you." He extends his hand.

"Hello, Nick," I say in a business-like tone, my heart pounding as I shake his hand. He keeps hold of it, locking his eyes on mine before letting me go.

"Your husband's told me a lot about you."

"He's told me nothing about you," I say.

Dave walks over to us and says to Nick, "Iris didn't want to be part of the interview process so I didn't tell her about any of the candidates." He looks at me. "Nick used to live in the area, but moved away a few years ago."

"And now you've moved back?" I ask.

"Temporarily. I'll see how it goes. I left because I was tired of being in a big city. I needed a break so I moved to a small town. But I've been feeling the need for a little more excitement." He smirks, but he did it so fast I doubt Dave even noticed.

Is working for my husband the excitement Nick's talking about? Is he getting a thrill from mentally torturing me? He clearly has a reason for taking this job, but what is it? Why is he doing this?

"Nick has his own company," Dave says. "He's a technology expert, specializing in helping small businesses. He'll be working for us as an independent contractor."

When Nick and I had our affair, he was in charge of online security at a company downtown. I was impressed with both him and his job, which was one of the reasons I fell for him. He was successful and driven, the opposite of Dave at the time, who couldn't keep a job and didn't seem to care. His lack of employment was one of the many things we fought about.

"If you're a tech guy and own a company," I say to Nick, "why would you want the ad manager job? It's an entry-level position. It doesn't seem to fit someone with your experience."

"Honey, don't talk him out of this," Dave says with a laugh. "I just hired him."

Nick looks me in the eye. "I'm overqualified from a tech standpoint, but as for online marketing, I'm still learning. I have some experience with it, but I could certainly get better. This job will give me a chance to improve my skills, and in return, you and your husband will benefit from having a tech expert on staff."

"His contract's only for six months," Dave explains. "And he won't be working for us full time, at least not to start. We'll see how things go, and when his contract is up, we'll discuss what happens next."

"Why would you choose to work *here*?" I ask, continuing to

fire questions at Nick. "You'd learn a lot more doing online marketing for a big company."

Nick smiles at Dave. "Your wife is a much tougher interviewer than you were. She likes to ask the hard questions."

"Iris, he's answered enough," Dave says. "Why don't we move on to the ads?"

"I'd like to know," I say, keeping my eyes on Nick. "Why us, and not some other company?"

"Because I believe in what you're doing. Fixing relationships. Saving marriages. It's important work. I'd like to see you two succeed."

"He's listened to our podcast for years," Dave says. "He's one of our biggest fans."

"It's odd you would listen to it since you're not married," I say to Nick. I glance at his hand. "Or do you not wear a ring?"

"I'm not married, but I still enjoy your podcast. It's taught me a lot about how to be a good partner."

"I wish I'd learned that when I met Iris," Dave says. "If I had, we wouldn't have struggled so much early on in our marriage."

"But you worked through it," Nick says. "And turned it into a thriving company."

"We did, but it wasn't easy." Dave puts his arm around me. "As you know from listening to the podcast, Iris and I went through a very difficult time. We almost divorced."

"And look at you now," Nick says. "The perfect couple. Happy and in love. It's proof your program works."

"Sorry I'm late," Allen says, joining us in the recording studio. He walks up to Nick. "I'm Allen. I'm assuming you're Nick? The new ad manager?"

"I am." He shakes Allen's hand. "It's a pleasure to meet you."

"Allen's the reason we're growing so fast," Dave says. "He's always finding us new opportunities. Making new deals."

"I'd have them doing events every night if they'd agree to it," Allen says, smiling at Nick. "Their audience can't seem to get enough of them."

"That's a good problem to have," Nick says, glancing at me. "Assuming you want to grow your audience, which I assume you do or I wouldn't be here."

"We absolutely want to grow it," Allen says. "I'm hoping by the end of the year, these two will be known all around the country, not just the Midwest. I want to get them scheduled for some events in New York and LA."

"Is that really happening?" I ask Dave. "I thought we said—"

"We can talk about it later," Dave says, brushing me off. "Allen, I want to show you the mock-up for the relationship game we're developing. Heather just sent it over. It's in my office."

"Great! I'd love to see it."

Allen and Dave walk out of the studio, leaving me alone with Nick.

"So, Iris," Nick says with a slight smile. "How have you been?"

I storm up to him. "I don't know what kind of game you're playing, but it needs to stop! You are *not* doing this. I will not let you—"

"Iris, enough," he says. "You're letting your imagination run wild. I'm not here to cause any trouble."

"Yeah, right," I huff. "Just tell me what you're up to. Why you're doing this."

"I want to help your business. Like I told your husband, I believe in what you're doing. Saving marriages from divorce? It's noble work."

"Stop with the sarcasm and just tell me what you want. Is it money? Did you see our success and—"

"Do you really think I'm here for money?" He steps closer to me. Too close. "You know me, Iris. You know I'm not the type of person who would do that."

"Actually, I don't. We didn't talk much when we were..." I glance back at the door, making sure Dave isn't there.

"We talked enough for you to know I'm not the type of person you're describing."

"You're exactly that type of person. Cunning. Manipulative. Playing those ridiculous mind games."

"Mind games?" He laughs. "I don't know what you mean."

"See? You're doing it again! Acting like you don't know what I'm talking about in order to confuse me."

"No, Iris, I honestly have no idea what you're referring to."

I put my hands on my hips. "The note you left on my car? The card you sent? The roses?"

"I didn't do any of those things." He smiles. "Maybe you have a secret admirer."

"This isn't funny! I know you were the one doing it. Who else would send me yellow roses?"

"I'm not getting the significance." He folds his arms over his chest. "What does that have to do with me?"

"Yellow roses? Texas?"

"What about it?"

"You grew up in Texas." I check the door again. "And you talked about moving back there."

"A lot of people grew up in Texas. And I didn't move back there. I moved a few hours south of here. To a small town where I could get some peace and quiet. Like I told your husband, I needed a break from the city."

"What about the card? I know it was from you. It said we'll be together soon, and here you are."

"I didn't send you a card. I honestly have no idea what you're talking about."

Is he lying or telling the truth? I can't tell. I don't know him well enough to sense if he's making this up.

"What about the hotel brochure?" I ask. "That couldn't have just been a coincidence."

"Again, I don't know what you mean."

"Are you two getting to know each other?" Dave asks, coming into the studio.

"We are," Nick says, smiling at my husband. "Your wife was telling me about all the fan mail and gifts she receives."

Why is Nick telling Dave that? Knowing he was the one who sent them? It had to be him. Who else would it be?

"Unfortunately, some of it's rather unsettling," Dave says, coming up beside me. "Notes telling Iris they love her and want to be with her. I'm sure whoever's behind it is harmless, but then again, you never know. There's a lot of disturbed people out there."

"That's for sure," Nick says, glancing at me.

"Dave, I need to head out," Allen says, appearing at the door to the studio. "I need to take my wife to her doctor's appointment."

"I hope it's nothing serious," Dave says.

"It's a cosmetic procedure. Nothing serious, but I need to go with her since she won't be able to drive herself home." He waves at Nick. "Nice meeting you. From what Dave's told me, you sound like a perfect fit for the job."

"Thank you, Allen," Nick says. "Nice meeting you too."

"Let's schedule lunch next week. I'll have my assistant call you and set something up."

"Sounds good," Nick says.

"See you later, Dave. Iris."

"Bye, Allen," Dave says as he leaves.

"Should we get started?" Nick asks. "I'm looking forward to hearing you two perform the ads I came up with."

Dave smiles at me. "Ready, honey?"

No, I'm not ready. I feel sick. I don't want to be here.

None of this makes sense. Why is Nick writing ad copy? He's not a writer. And this job is beneath him. I don't care what he says about wanting to gain experience or wanting to help our business. It's all lies.

So what's he really up to? Why is he doing this?

# CHAPTER TWENTY-SIX

"Iris, what a pleasant surprise," Jane says, answering the door.

"I need to talk to you," I say, looking behind her. "Are you alone? Is Richard here?"

"On a Thursday morning?" She laughs. "No, he's at work. Why are you acting so strange?"

"Something happened. Something bad. Can I come in?"

"Yes, of course." She steps aside. "Would you like some coffee? It's fresh. I just made it."

"No, I can't have caffeine. I'm already too wired. I need to calm down."

"Iris, what is this about?" She shuts the door, looking at me with concern. "You look terrible. No offense. I'm just worried you might be ill."

"I'm not ill. I'm stressed, and I didn't get any sleep last night."

"Come sit down," she says, taking my arm and leading me to the couch.

"I didn't know who else to talk to," I say, sitting beside Jane. "You're the only one who knows."

"Knows what?"

"About Nick." I turn to Jane, my foot nervously tapping the floor. "He's back. Nick is back."

"What do you mean he's back? You saw him?"

"I saw him. Talked to him." I grip Jane's arm. "You're never going to believe this."

"What? What is it?"

"Dave hired him. He hired him to work for us."

"I don't understand. Why would he hire your ex-lover?"

"Because he doesn't know he's my—" I pause, not wanting to call Nick my lover. "Dave doesn't know. He just thinks Nick is some guy who applied for the job."

"What job?"

"The online ad manager job. Dave revised it to be an online marketing position, but it's basically the job Jeremy used to have."

"I'm still confused. Why would Nick even apply for a job like that? I'd imagine someone his age would be overqualified. Wasn't it an entry level position?"

"Jane, you're not getting it. It isn't about the job. It's about me. And him. Nick is playing some kind of game with me. That's why he applied for the job."

"Why would Dave hire Nick over someone else? Someone who's a better fit for the job?"

"Because Dave wanted someone with experience. He didn't want another kid straight out of college. And Nick made up a story about wanting to get more experience in online marketing and how he specifically wanted to work for Dave and me because he believes in our business. It's all lies, but he said it as though it were the truth."

"Did you ask Nick what he's up to?"

"Of course I asked him. I demanded he tell me why he's here and what he wants."

"And what did he say?"

"Nothing. He wouldn't tell me anything." I sit back on the couch, staring at the wall in front of me as my mind tries to process this. "How did he even find out about the job?"

"Maybe he had an alert set up on one of those job sites. I've never done it, but I've heard it's a thing. You tell the job site what company you want to work for and they let you know when the company posts an opening."

"I'm guessing that's what he did, but why? That's what I need to find out." I look at Jane. "I have to get him alone so I can talk to him. Yesterday, at the studio, we only had a few minutes together and then Dave showed up. He wanted to take Nick to dinner to celebrate his new job, but luckily Nick declined."

"Well, at least now this will finally be over," Jane says.

"What will be over?"

"This secret you've been keeping from your husband." She pauses. "You're telling him about Nick, aren't you?"

"No! If I told him, it could be the end of our marriage."

"Iris, you have to tell him. Nick is working for you. You can't just pretend he's not there."

"I'll make him quit. Or I'll convince Dave to fire him."

"He's not going to fire a man he just hired because his wife told him to. And if you tell him to fire Nick, he's going to wonder why. How are you going to answer him?"

"I don't know, but I'll figure it out."

"Iris, you're making this much harder than it needs to be. Just tell Dave the truth. Once he knows your history with Nick, he'll fire him and Nick will leave you alone. He'll stop sending you notes. Stop sending flowers. This mess with Nick will all be over and you and Dave can work on repairing whatever damage this has caused to your marriage."

"You don't get it. Dave isn't someone who forgives and forgets. He won't be able to get past this, especially when he finds out I kept it a secret for so long. Maybe if I'd told him right after it happened he would've forgiven me. But now? It's too late. I not only cheated, but also lied about it. For years."

"If you don't tell Dave," Jane says, "there's a very good chance Nick will. You said yourself that's why he's here."

"I assume that's the reason, but I really don't know. He won't tell me anything."

"What other reason would he have for doing this?"

I shrug. "It's possible it's like you said and he wants to start something with me again."

"You wouldn't..." Her brows rise.

"No! Absolutely not. Things were different when I was with Nick. I thought my marriage was over. I really believed Dave and I were headed for a divorce. If I had thought my marriage could be saved, I never would've been with Nick."

"Did he explain all the little clues he left you?" Jane asks.

"He claims he didn't send the flowers, or the card, or any of the other stuff. He denied it all, but it had to have been him."

"Or it was from one of your fans, like I tried to tell you before."

"A fan wouldn't leave me a menu or a hotel brochure." I lean forward, rubbing my head. "I'm so confused, Jane. I don't know what's happening here. Or what to do about it."

"I've given you my advice. If you'd just told Dave years ago, you wouldn't be in this mess."

I sit up straight. "That is not at all helpful."

"Honestly, Iris, what do you want me to say?" she scoffs. "Do you want me to feel sorry for you? Tell you what you did was okay, given the condition of your marriage at the time?"

"No, that's not what I want. I just..." I take a breath. "You're right. Nothing you say will make this better. I just needed to talk it out. Keeping it all inside was making my head feel like it was about to explode. I couldn't sleep last night and now I'm exhausted and can't focus. I don't know how I'm going to get through the event tomorrow night."

"You should take something to help you sleep. Do you need a prescription? I'm sure Richard could give you one."

"No, and don't tell him about this. Please, Jane, I don't want Richard to know."

"How did Nick look? Has he changed at all?"

"He looked the same except for a few more wrinkles around the eyes." My phone rings. "It's Dave. I need to get this."

She smiles. "Go ahead."

"Hi, honey," I answer, getting up from the couch. "Are you home?"

"Yes, I just got here. Where are you?"

"I'm over at Jane's." I glance at her. "She wanted me to try her apple strudel. It's a new recipe."

"See if you could bring some home for me. I love apple strudel. My mother used to make it."

There's no apple strudel. Why did I tell him that?

"I'm not sure Jane has any left, but I'll ask."

"Are you coming home soon, or do you and Jane have plans?"

"We don't have plans. Why do you ask?"

"I'm taking Nick out for lunch. I thought you might want to join us."

"Maybe," I say, biting my lip. "What time are you leaving?"

"In a few minutes. Honey, I'd really like you to go. I think Nick would like it too. He really wants to get to know you."

He already does. He knows me quite well, at least certain parts of me.

"Sure, I'll join you. I'll be home shortly." I end the call, my stomach knotting up, my heart racing.

"You look like you're about to be sick," Jane says.

"I feel like I might."

She gets up and comes over to me. "What happened?"

"Dave's taking Nick to lunch. He wants me to go with them. I said I would, but I don't feel up to it. I'm so on edge I feel like I can't breathe."

"Just calm down. Getting all worked up about this isn't going to help."

"I don't think I can go to this lunch. I'm not ready. I haven't figured out how to handle Nick."

"You have to go. Do you really want Dave being alone with Nick? What if he says something? Something you don't want him saying?"

I nod. "You're right. I'll go." I hurry to the door.

"Iris, what were you saying about apple strudel?"

"Oh, I told Dave that's why I was over here. To taste your apple strudel. He wanted me to bring him some, but I told him you're out."

Her face lights up. "Tell him I'll make him some! I haven't made strudel in years. I have just the perfect recipe!"

I'm annoyed she's getting excited about baking when I'm

going through a crisis. But that's Jane. She has a short attention span. She can only talk about something for so long before she needs to move on to something else.

I knew I'd feel frustrated talking to her about Nick. I saw her losing interest soon after I told her he'd taken the marketing job. At least she showed some concern, but it didn't last. And I'm really getting tired of her telling me to be honest with Dave. If I could be honest with him, I would, but this isn't something I can tell him. Jane doesn't seem to understand that. She doesn't know Dave like I do.

I love my husband, and he has many good qualities. But forgiveness isn't one of them.

# CHAPTER TWENTY-SEVEN

WHEN I GET BACK to the house, Dave is sitting on the couch looking at his phone.

"I'm home," I say, getting his attention. "What time are we leaving?"

"As soon as you're ready," he says, smiling at me. "I told Nick I'd text him when we're on our way."

"I just need a few minutes to change clothes and fix my hair."

"Honey, it's just Nick. You don't need to look good for him. Why don't you go like you are?"

"I can't go like this." I glance down at my black leggings and oversized sweatshirt that I just noticed has a stain on it. "I'm a mess."

"I think you look beautiful."

"Because you're my husband." I smile at him. "You're supposed to say that."

He gets up and follows me into the bedroom. "How was Jane?"

"Good." I go into the walk-in closet and pick out a pair of

black pants and a ruby-red sweater. Yesterday, I was dressed like it was summer, but today there's a chill in the air, which is typical for this time of the year. The weather can't decide if it wants to be summer or fall.

"What's new with her?" Dave calls from the bedroom.

"Jane?" I call back. "Not much. She's excited about all the fall baking she plans to do." I leave the closet. "How's this?"

"You look great," Dave says. "I love that color on you."

Nick did too. He used to tell me I looked best in jewel tones so I'd plan my outfits accordingly when I knew I was going to be seeing him.

"Oh, Jane is making you more strudel," I say. "She felt bad that we ate it all."

"That's nice of her. She certainly didn't need to."

"You know Jane. She loves baking. I made her day when I told her you wanted some." I go into the bathroom to fix my hair and put on some makeup.

Usually, by this time of day, I'm dressed and ready to go out. Even if I'm staying home, I always do my hair and makeup. But this morning, I was so exhausted from not sleeping that I could barely drag myself out of bed. Dave asked if I wasn't feeling well so I told him I had a headache. I need to start acting normal or Dave's going to notice something is up with me.

"Okay, I'm ready," I say, after quickly applying some makeup and brushing out my hair.

Dave smiles when he sees me. "I'm not sure I want to meet Nick for lunch now."

"Why?"

His eyes move over me. "You look gorgeous. What if he tries to steal you from me?"

I tense up, thinking he knows about Nick and me, but then

relax, realizing it was just a comment. I need to stop this. I can't react to everything Dave says about Nick.

"I wouldn't allow it," I say to Dave, going up to him. "I only want you." I give him a kiss.

"And I only want you." He tucks some strands of hair behind my ear. "You're mine. I'm not giving you up."

"You'll never have to," I say, forcing out a smile.

Dave gets out his phone. "Let me text Nick that we're leaving." He texts him and I hear a message come back. "Nick says he'll head over there."

"Where are we meeting him?" I ask as we go to the garage.

"That new cafe that just opened a few miles from our studio. Does that work?"

"Yes, I've been wanting to try it."

But not with Nick. Now the place will be ruined. Every time I go there, I'll think of Nick. I have to get him out of our lives. But how?

"What do you know about him?" I ask Dave as we're driving to the restaurant.

"About Nick?"

"Yeah, we haven't really talked about him. I didn't see you last night and this morning you were at the gym."

After we left the studio yesterday, Allen called and invited Dave and some other men over to play cards and drink. Allen's wife was recovering from her procedure so Allen had to stay home with her. Since she was knocked out from the pain medication, Allen decided to host a poker night. Dave didn't get home until after midnight.

"What do you want to know?" Dave asks.

"What has Nick told you about himself?"

"Well, let's see. He said he grew up in Texas, went to college in Indiana, came to Chicago, worked a few years, then decided to leave the city, start his own business, and move to a small town."

"Does he have a girlfriend?"

"I don't believe so, but you could ask him at lunch today. I didn't ask him much about his personal life. I was more interested in his experience and what he could do for us."

"I wish you had talked to me before you made your final decision about who to hire."

"Iris, you told me you wanted to stay out of it."

"I know, but I didn't realize you were changing the position to be one that pays more. We're paying him almost as much as Allen."

"Because Nick has a lot of experience. He's not some kid straight out of college. And it's only a short-term contract. I'm hoping we'll get a lot out of him in six months. Some new ideas. A new online marketing plan. Better ads. Nick's really good at writing ad copy. I wasn't expecting that from a tech guy."

"He's not really writing them. He's using things we've said in the podcast."

"And combining it with compelling sales copy to make a very effective ad."

"We don't know if they're effective. We haven't used them yet."

"Honey, why are you being so negative?" Dave glances at me. "Are you upset with me for hiring Nick?"

"I'm not upset with you. I'm just not sure it's the right decision. I don't think Nick's the right fit for us."

"How would you know that? You just met him."

"I got a bad feeling from him."

"Bad feeling? What do you mean?"

"I can't describe it. It's just a feeling I had when we met. Like something was off with him."

"I think you need to give him another chance. I really like Nick. I think you will too once you get to know him."

For the rest of the drive, I keep quiet. Telling Dave to fire Nick isn't going to work. Nick's already managed to win Dave over, so saying I don't like him isn't going to be reason enough for Dave to let him go. I need to build a case against Nick to prove that he shouldn't be working for us.

"Sorry we're a little late," Dave says to Nick as we meet up with him at the cafe. "Iris felt the need to get herself fixed up for our lunch." He glances at me and smiles. "I told her she didn't need to, but she insisted."

Why is Dave telling him this? He's making it sound like I went out of my way to look good for Nick.

"I'm glad you could join us," Nick says to me.

He looks handsome as always with his deep blue eyes and thick dark hair. He's wearing a black polo shirt and I notice his arms seem more muscular than I remember.

Why am I looking at him this way? I'm not attracted to this man, at least not anymore. I want him gone, out of our lives. Just being in his presence has me on edge, wondering what he might say or do.

The hostess seats us at the table. Dave and I sit on one side with Nick on the other. Nick takes the seat directly across from me, which makes me very uncomfortable. He should've sat across from Dave, not me.

"How was the poker game?" Nick asks Dave.

"Good, although I left some money behind." Dave laughs. "I'm not great at poker, but I still enjoy it. We play a few times a month. You should join us sometime."

"I'd like that," Nick says.

I glare at him, trying to signal to him that I don't want him hanging out with my husband. But he doesn't seem to notice. Or more likely, he doesn't care. He clearly has an agenda and what I want doesn't matter.

"Next time we play," Dave says, "I'll make sure to invite you."

I open my menu. "We should probably order."

"Honey, there's no rush," Dave says. "We don't have anything scheduled this afternoon."

"No, but we still need to decide on next month's podcast topics. Since we have some time, today would be a good day to work on it."

"Maybe Nick could join us. We'd love to get your input," Dave says to Nick. "From the marketing side, but also as a listener."

"I'd be happy to weigh in with some suggestions," Nick says.

"Great!" Dave says. "Let's head over to the studio after lunch. I've got a list of ideas in my office to get us started."

This is turning into a nightmare. I wanted less time with Nick, not more. I was trying to find a way to hurry up this lunch to get away from Nick, but now Dave has invited him to spend all afternoon with us.

# CHAPTER TWENTY-EIGHT

The waitress comes over and asks if we're ready to order. I am, but Nick and Dave haven't even looked at their menus. The waitress says she'll come back later, and instead of figuring out what they want to eat, Dave and Nick start talking about golf and get into a debate about the best golf courses in the area.

"Honey, could you decide what you'd like?" I say to Dave when there's a break in the conversation. "The waitress will be back soon."

"Oh, yes, I keep forgetting to look." He finally opens his menu.

While Dave is busy finding something to order, Nick catches my eye and smiles at me. Is he flirting? Or is he smiling because he finds this whole situation humorous?

If I could, I'd slap that smile right off his face. This is my life he's messing with, and my marriage. What he's doing isn't the least bit funny.

The waitress returns and we finally place our order.

After she leaves, Dave says to Nick, "Iris was asking me

about your personal life. I told her I didn't know much about it."

"What would you like to know?" Nick asks, directing the question to me.

"Whatever you'd like to share," I say, staring back at him.

"She wondered if you had a girlfriend," Dave says. "I assumed you didn't or you would've mentioned it."

"I don't have a girlfriend," Nick says to me. "Why do you ask?"

"Being in a relationship is important for the job. It helps you relate to the content we put out."

"Iris, that isn't necessary," Dave says, looking at me with confusion. "Jeremy wasn't in a relationship."

"Yes, and you fired him," I point out.

"That wasn't the reason."

"What was the reason?" Nick asks. "Do you mind if I ask?"

Dave clears his throat. "I overheard him saying inappropriate things about Iris. About her appearance and... well, I don't need to get into it. The point is, I don't want someone like that working for us."

"I can assure you that won't be an issue with me," Nick says. "And as for my relationship status, although I'm not currently in a relationship, I have been in the past so I can certainly relate to your content."

"But you've never been married," I say. "Our content is for people who are married."

"Honey, I'm sure he can still relate," Dave says, in a tone that's urging me to drop this.

"Marriage is a commitment," I say. "A legal contract between two people. That changes the stakes. It's not the same as dating someone. So I highly doubt Nick could relate to our content the way a married person would."

"Yes, well, that wasn't part of the job description," Dave says with a nervous laugh. "So let's just let it go, honey."

"I don't mind if she expresses her concerns about me," Nick says, eyeing me across the table. "Tell me, Iris. What other concerns do you have?"

"It wasn't a concern but more of a comment," I say, realizing I need to stop my attack against Nick. It's too early for me to turn against him, at least in front of Dave. He'll be suspicious if I show a dislike for Nick this soon after meeting him. I need to take a step back and pretend he's a guy I just met, not someone I have a history with who I believe is out to destroy me.

"This conversation has taken a rather negative tone," Dave says. "Why don't we talk about something else?"

As he says it, the waitress returns with our drinks.

She leaves, and I say to Nick, "So where are you living?"

"I sublet a place," Nick says, squeezing the lemon into his iced tea. "A one-bedroom apartment. It's nothing great, but it's fine for a few months."

"Where's it at?" Dave asks.

After Nick tells him, Dave says, "I just took Iris to a hotel down the street from there. I surprised her with a romantic weekend."

"How nice," Nick says, smiling at me, because he knows the hotel Dave's talking about is the one he and I used to go to. It's the only one on that street. "I've been to that hotel."

My heart stops, fearing he's going to tell Dave about us.

"I got a drink in their bar the other night," Nick says, and my heart starts up again.

"It's a beautiful hotel," Dave says. "I told Iris we need to go back." He puts his arm around me. "Right, honey?"

"Yes." I force out a smile. "It was very nice."

"So who's watching your house while you're here?" Dave asks Nick.

"One of my neighbors. He's retired. He'll keep an eye on it until I'm back."

"And when is that?" I ask. "When are you moving back?"

"When I'm ready to," he says. "There's no rush. The house isn't going anywhere. I can return there any time."

"How do you like being back in the city?" Dave asks.

Nick shrugs. "I'm still getting used to the noise and the crowds, but for the most part, I like it. There were things I missed about it." He glances at me as he says it. Was that intentional? Is he trying to say he missed me? He can't possibly think we'd get back together. He can see how happy I am with Dave.

"I need to use the restroom," Dave says, getting up. "I'll be right back."

When he's gone, I lean toward Nick and say, "You need to stop this."

"Stop what?" he casually asks.

"Stop messing with my life. You shouldn't be here. Just tell me what you want so we can end this."

"I want you to leave him."

"Are you serious?" I laugh, not because it's funny, but because I can't believe Nick thinks I would leave my husband just because he told me to. "This is why you're here? To get me to leave Dave?"

"There's more to it than that, but yes, I want you to leave him."

"Why would I leave the man I love? To be with you? Is that what this is? You're here because you want us to get back together?" I shake my head. "I can't believe you're doing this. It's been years. Why now?"

"Would you just listen to me?" he says in an angry tone.

"Why would I listen to you? You're crazy! You've completely lost your mind. Moving here? Taking the marketing job? Sending me creepy notes and cards?" I sit back. "Honestly, I'm frightened by you, and I want you to go. I want you out of my life."

"I'm not going anywhere. Not until you—" He stops suddenly and I notice Dave is back, sitting down beside me.

"The bathroom was out of paper towels," he says, wiping his hands on the cloth napkin. "Don't you hate that?"

Nick and I don't answer.

"What's going on?" Dave says with a laugh. "Did I interrupt something?"

"No, nothing," Nick says. "Sorry, what were you saying? Something about paper towels?"

"Never mind," Dave says. "Anyway, I was thinking about the golf course you mentioned earlier. I'd like to check it out, maybe play a round of eighteen. You think they're still open?"

"They should be," Nick says. "They're usually open through October."

"Then what do you say? You want to go this weekend?"

"Sure, let's do it."

"Honey, shouldn't we discuss this?" I say to Dave. "We might have plans."

"Do we?"

We don't, so I try to think of something. I don't want Dave playing golf with Nick.

"We have an event on Saturday," I say to Dave.

"That's at night. Nick and I would be golfing in the morning."

"We can forget it," Nick says. "I don't want to get in the way of your plans with Iris."

"We don't have plans in the morning," Dave says. "Do we, honey?"

"I guess not," I mutter.

"Great!" Dave smiles at Nick. "Can you get us a tee time? Maybe around seven or eight?"

"I'll see what I can do."

If Nick doesn't want me being with Dave, then why is he doing this? Why is he making plans to golf with him and play poker?

Our food arrives and the waitress says, "Can I get you anything else?"

"I think we're good," Dave says, answering for us.

"If you think of anything, just let me know." She smiles at Nick as she says it.

"I think she was flirting with you," Dave says to Nick when the waitress leaves. "Maybe you should get her number."

"I'm not interested," Nick says, picking up his fork.

"You sure?" Dave looks over at the waitress. "She's very attractive."

"She is," Nick says, "but I don't want to get involved with someone right now."

"Any reason why?" Dave asks, stuffing a French fry in his mouth.

"He's leaving soon," I say, answering for Nick. "It wouldn't make sense for him to get involved with someone."

"He might stay if he met the right woman." Dave smiles at

me. "Men will do most anything to be with the woman they love."

I feel Nick's eyes on me and look back at him. "You'll have to forgive my husband. He has this habit of trying to set people up."

Dave laughs. "What are you talking about? I never do that."

"You just did."

"Only because the waitress was flirting with him."

"Sorry," I say to Nick. "We're talking about you like you're not here."

"It's fine. I'm used to people trying to set me up."

"I didn't mean to pressure you," Dave says. "Maybe Iris is right and I'm turning into a matchmaker." He looks at me. "I guess I just want people to be as happy as Iris and I are."

I really wish Dave would stop talking about our relationship and how we're so in love. He never does this, at least not when we're out with people. He saves those comments for the podcast or our events.

"You ever been close to getting married?" Dave asks Nick.

"No." Nick cuts into his steak. "I don't like being tied down. Even if I found the right woman, I don't think marriage is for me."

"Why is that?" Dave asks, squirting ketchup on his plate.

"Listening to your podcast. Hearing all the problems married people have. I don't know why someone would want to put themselves through that."

"Because the problems come and go. The love remains."

Nick shakes his head. "Not sure I believe that. A lot of marriages look good on the outside, but behind closed doors, the couple is fighting. Sleeping in separate rooms. Keeping secrets."

"If you have such a negative view of marriage," I say, "you shouldn't be working for us."

"I'm not being negative," Nick says. "I'm describing what most marriages are like."

"He has a point," Dave says to me. "A lot of marriages are just what he described. But they can be fixed. That's why our program is so popular and why Nick wanted to work for us. He believes our program works."

"Do you?" I ask Nick, challenging him.

"Absolutely. Just look at you and Dave." Nick's eyes lock on mine, like he's sending me some kind of message.

"How's your burger?" I say to Dave, in a desperate attempt to change topics.

"It's good, but the fries are overcooked."

"Maybe you should ask for new ones."

"It's okay. They're still edible."

We continue our lunch and Dave and Nick talk about golf again. It's extremely boring, but far better than talking about relationships, specifically mine.

Was Nick serious when he told me to leave Dave? He seemed like he was, but why would he say that? He knows it would never happen.

# CHAPTER TWENTY-NINE

"ANOTHER GREAT EVENT LAST NIGHT," Dave says, joining me at the table for breakfast.

He's bursting with energy while I can barely keep my eyes open. It's been several days since Nick showed up and I've barely slept. I'm amazed I was able to go on stage last night and make it through the evening without stumbling over my words.

"Yes, it was good," I mutter, staring into my coffee.

"Honey, what's wrong?" Dave puts his hand over mine. "You didn't sleep again?"

"No, I kept waking up."

"Maybe you should see a doctor. You might have some kind of condition."

"It's not that. I just have a lot on my mind."

"You want to talk about it?"

"No." I look up at him. "It's nothing important."

Just my ex-lover returning, and working for us, and telling me to leave you. That's what I'm thinking, but of course I can't say it.

"You mind if I go to the gym this morning?" Dave asks, ripping open the wrapper on his protein bar.

"Go ahead. I'm going to try to rest."

Dave takes a bite of his bar. "Did I tell you Nick joined?"

I perk up, my groggy mind suddenly alert and awake. "Nick what?"

"Joined my gym. I'm meeting him there." Dave takes a drink of his coffee. "Then we might go to an early lunch."

Nick joined Dave's gym? And is working out with him? Why? This doesn't make sense.

"You're spending a lot of time with Nick," I say.

"Is that a problem?"

"Yes. I mean, he's our employee. It's not a good idea to be friends with an employee."

"We're friends with Allen."

"Sure, but Allen can separate his personal life from his work life. When we're working, Allen is all business. He knows we're the boss and not just his friends. I'm not sure Nick will be the same way."

"He has been so far. Yesterday, I told him to have the latest ad research to me by noon and he did. He got up early to get it done."

"I still think you should consider spending less time with him. I'm sure he has friends in town. People he'd like to see."

"Actually, he doesn't. He said most of his friends moved away, and the ones that are still here have demanding jobs and young kids to care for. They don't have time to go out." Dave eats what's left of his protein bar and balls up the wrapper. "I like hanging out with Nick. We have a lot in common."

"Like what?"

"We both like golf. Going to the gym. Playing poker. And

we can talk business. He really wants to learn more about what we're doing. I'm thinking he might stick around beyond the length of his contract."

He is not sticking around. I'll make sure of it.

Dave gulps down the rest of his coffee and stands up. "I need to get going. I'll text you if Nick and I decide to go to lunch." He gives me a kiss. "Bye, honey."

"Bye," I mutter, feeling groggy again.

The doorbell rings.

"I'll get it," Dave says, heading over there. "Good morning, Jane."

Why is Jane here? We didn't make plans, did we?

"Come on in," I hear Dave say.

I get up and see Jane coming into the house, holding a plate of something.

"I made these just for you," she says to Dave, handing him the plate.

"Apple strudel?"

"Fresh from the oven," Jane says, smiling at him. "Try one. Let me know what you think."

"I would, but I'm on my way to the gym. I'm meeting someone there so I need to get going."

"I'll put them away," I say, going up to Dave and taking the plate of strudel. "You can have one when you get back."

"Thanks, Jane," Dave says to her. "I'm sure they're wonderful." He gives me a kiss. "Enjoy your morning." He heads out to the garage.

I bring the plate to the kitchen. "Thanks for making these."

"I was happy to," Jane says, sitting down at the table. "I doubled the recipe so Richard and I would have some."

"Did we have plans today?" I ask.

"No, I just thought I'd stop over."

"Okay. I couldn't remember. I didn't think we had plans, but I've been so out of it this week that I thought we might've scheduled something and I forgot." I walk over to the table. "Did you want something? Coffee? Tea?"

"I'll have coffee, but let me get it." She gets up from her chair. "You look like you're about to fall asleep."

"I'm trying to wake up." I sit down and gulp down more coffee. "I haven't been sleeping well. I keep waking up."

"Iris, you really need to take something. Let me ask Richard to prescribe you some pills. Or take one of mine. I have some in my bathroom cabinet."

"I guess I could try one."

"I'll bring some over later." She joins me at the table with her coffee mug. "So what's going on? I haven't seen you for days. I thought I'd have an update by now."

"I haven't felt like talking. And you're—" I stop before I say it, remembering how she can't tolerate criticism.

"I'm what?"

"Nothing." I smile at her. "What's new with you?"

"Iris, what were you going to say?" She sips her coffee.

"I just... I don't think I should talk to you about Nick. When I do, I end up feeling worse, not better."

"Why do you feel worse?" she says, sounding offended. I knew she'd react this way, which is why I didn't want to tell her. "Is it because you don't like my advice?"

"Basically, yes. You keep telling me to do something I can't do, making me feel even more hopeless about the situation. But it's fine. I shouldn't have told you. I caused this problem, and it's my job to fix it."

She leans toward me. "Tell me what's going on. I promise to only listen and not give you any advice."

"I don't think I should." I wrap my hands around my coffee mug, staring down at my now lukewarm coffee. "I think it's best if I keep this to myself."

"Then I'll guess." She sits back. "He wants you back."

I look at her. "What did you say?"

"Nick wants things between you two to start up again. Am I right?"

"No. He told me to leave Dave."

"So you could be with him, which means I was right. He wants you back."

"He didn't say he wanted to be with me. He just told me to leave Dave."

"He would only say that if he wanted you for himself."

"But he doesn't want that. He told us at lunch the other day that he doesn't want a relationship."

"What you and him had wasn't a relationship," she scoffs. "It was a fling. A tryst. An affair."

"I know what it was," I say, annoyed that she speaks so casually about it. "But he doesn't want that. Or if he does, he didn't tell me that. And it wouldn't happen. I would never do that again."

"Then what was his reason? Why did he tell you to leave your husband?"

"He didn't say. He just told me to leave him. He was very insistent, like he just expected me to go along with it because he told me to. Does he really think he can just show up and tell me to leave my husband and I'll do it?"

"How did it end? What did you tell him?"

"I said he was crazy and that I want him out of my life. He

told me he wasn't leaving and then Dave came back to the table, ending the conversation. This all happened the other day. He hasn't said anything to me since."

"What are you going to do?"

"I'm going to try to get Dave to fire him. The problem is, Dave's decided he likes Nick and wants to be best friends with him."

Jane laughs. "You must be joking."

"No. I'm not. And this isn't funny."

"Yes, sorry." She stops laughing. "Iris, I'm sure they won't be friends. Dave has no time. He's always working."

"And yet he's with Nick at the gym right now. And they're going golfing this weekend. And Dave invited Nick to play poker."

"Oh," Jane says, sounding concerned. "That's not good."

"No. It's not. And I can't seem to stop it. Every time I say something bad about Nick, Dave defends him. He says I need to give Nick a chance."

"Nick must be very persuasive if Dave's taking his side over yours."

"That's what worries me. Dave's never done that. He's never taken the side of one of his friends over me."

"Then why do you think he's doing it with Nick?"

"Maybe he looks up to him? Wants Nick to like him? I don't know."

"Perhaps you should plan some outings with Dave so he doesn't have time to spend with Nick."

"Knowing Dave, he'd invite Nick to join us," I say, rolling my eyes.

"You still don't have any idea what Nick is up to?"

"I thought for sure he was here to tell Dave what I did, but if that's true, then why hasn't he told him? What's he waiting for?"

"That *is* rather strange." Jane sips her coffee. "And you're sure Nick isn't trying to reignite your affair?"

"He claims he's not, but I'm not sure I believe him. He's said and done several things that seemed like flirting, although I may have misinterpreted it."

"I think Dave would notice if Nick was showing interest in you that way. He certainly wouldn't like it. It might even be enough for him to fire Nick. Didn't he fire that kid for the same reason?"

"Jeremy wasn't flirting with me. Dave overheard him saying things about me, about how I looked." I pause, getting an idea. "Maybe that's it. Maybe I tell Dave that Nick has been flirting with me and it's making me uncomfortable. Maybe that will make Dave fire him."

"You need to be careful. If you make an accusation like that and Nick finds out, he might turn against you and tell Dave about the affair."

"Then I'll deny it. That's been my plan all along if Nick told him."

"But would Dave believe you over Nick?" Jane's brows rise. "You just said Dave's been taking Nick's side over yours."

I'm not sure how to answer that. A few weeks ago, I would've had no doubt that Dave would take my side and believe whatever I told him. But now? I'm not sure.

# CHAPTER THIRTY

"WHAT DO you want to do tonight?" I ask Dave.

It's Friday, and we just got home from recording a podcast. We usually record in the morning, but Dave wanted to go to the gym so we switched the recording to the afternoon. Nick wasn't there, which was probably why it went so smoothly. I wasn't nervous and tripping over my words. I was also more alert than I have been in days. I took one of Jane's sleeping pills last night and it knocked me out. I slept for ten hours straight.

"What do you mean?" Dave asks, going into the kitchen.

I follow him in there. "We have tonight off. I thought we'd go do something. Maybe see a movie. Go out to eat."

"Honey, we have plans."

"What plans?"

He stares at me, seeming confused. "Dinner. With Nick. We invited him over."

"Here? To the house?"

"Yes. We're grilling out." He opens the fridge and takes out a package of meat. "That's why I bought the steaks."

Why don't I remember Dave telling me this? And why did I agree to it?

"Iris, you were there when I invited him," Dave says. "At the office yesterday. You really don't remember?"

"No. Are you sure I was there? Maybe I stepped out to use the restroom."

"You were definitely there. Nick asked you what kind of wine you like. He's bringing some over."

If this actually happened, I have no memory of it. Is it because of my lack of sleep? I've heard that can affect memory, but I would think I'd remember something as major as inviting Nick over for dinner. I don't want him coming to my house, knowing where I live. I guess he already knows where I live since he left that menu at my door. He claims he didn't do that, but I don't believe him.

"What time will he be here?" I ask.

"Around six," Dave says. "I'm going to leave the steaks out to warm up."

Six is a half-hour from now. I'm not ready for this. I'm not ready to have Nick at my house, around all my things. It's too personal. I don't want him knowing everything about me. During our affair, I was determined to keep my life with Dave completely separate from what I was doing with Nick. I almost felt like a different person when I was with him. Like it wasn't even me.

"What else are we having?" I ask, going into the bedroom with Dave. "Besides the steak?"

"I bought some potatoes and one of those salad blends in a bag." Dave goes into the closet to change his clothes.

I don't think I need to change. I'm wearing jeans and a nice sweater. But it's a baggy sweater and the jeans are loose. Maybe I should put on something sexier, something that will draw Nick's attention to me. If Dave sees Nick looking at me, checking me out, he might believe me when I tell him Nick has been flirting with me. But is that enough to make Dave fire him? It's worth a shot.

I change into a pair of tight-fitting jeans and a low-cut red sweater. Then I go into the bathroom, let my hair down from the messy bun it was in, and add some makeup to my face.

"Look at you," Dave says in a sexy voice when he sees me coming out of the bedroom. "Now I wish Nick wasn't coming over."

"Why is that?" I ask, slinking over to him.

"You look really hot." He puts his arms around me. "I'd like to have my way with you."

"Guess we'll have to hurry up with this dinner so Nick can leave and we can finish our evening in the bedroom."

"I'd love to, but..." He sighs. "I kind of told Nick we'd watch the game."

"What game?" I say, pulling away from him.

"The baseball game."

"Nick's staying to watch the game?" I take a step back. "It's Friday night. That's supposed to be *our* time, not time you hang out with the guys."

"I know, but Nick is new in town and doesn't have anything to do. And it's just for tonight. Tomorrow, you and I will do something."

"We have an event tomorrow night," I point out, surprised he didn't remember.

"Then we'll do something earlier. We can go out for brunch in the morning."

I go past Dave to the kitchen. "I really wish you'd asked me about this before you invited Nick to watch the game." I open the refrigerator and take out the potatoes. "How do you want to cook these?"

Dave comes over and takes the potatoes from me, setting them on the counter. "You're right. I should've discussed it with you. But I really thought you'd be okay with it. You've been saying how tired you've been. I thought you might want to go to bed early, or relax in the tub, or watch a movie in bed. I didn't think watching the game with Nick would be an issue."

"It's fine, but please don't do it again."

"Do what?"

"Invite Nick over. I don't want him coming to the house."

Dave's brows furrow. "Why don't you want him coming over?"

"It's not a good idea." I fold my arms over my chest. "He's our employee, not our friend. You shouldn't mix business with friendship. I know Allen is a friend, but even that isn't a good idea. I don't make a fuss about it because I know how much you enjoy spending time with him." I open the fridge and take out the bottle of white wine that I didn't finish the other night.

"I also like spending time with Nick. And he's younger than Allen. It's nice to have a friend who's closer to my age."

"You have other friends who are close to your age," I say, pouring the wine into a glass. "Do something with them."

"They're too busy with their careers and families. You know this, Iris. It's the same for you. People our age are either at work or raising their children. They don't have a lot of free time. But Nick is single, and I feel bad that he's alone on a Friday night with nothing to do."

"I'm sure he could find something to do. He's lived here before. He knows all the places to go." I gulp my wine, hoping it'll relax me because I'm extremely tense right now, knowing Nick's on his way here.

Dave cocks his head to the side. "Why are you arguing with me about this? You're usually supportive when I want to spend time with a friend."

"Nick isn't your friend. You just met him."

"And I would like us to be friends." Dave takes the wineglass from me. "Would you at least get to know him before you forbid me from seeing him outside the office?"

"Okay, fine." I reach for my wineglass. "Could I have that back?"

Dave hands it to me as the doorbell rings.

"I'll get it," he says, heading over there.

My heart's racing and my chest feels tight. I'm not prepared for this. It's not something I ever thought would happen. Nick coming to my house? Having dinner with us? Watching a baseball game with my husband?

"Hey, Nick," Dave says. "Come on in."

I look up and see Nick coming into the house, wearing jeans and a black sweater that fits close to his lean, muscular body. As handsome as he is, he could easily go out and find himself a date for tonight. Or he could've met up with an old friend. So why did he choose to come here?

"Sorry I'm early," Nick says. "I wasn't sure how long it would take to get here."

"Don't worry about it," Dave says. "We can have a drink before dinner."

"Hi, Nick." I walk up beside Dave, putting a fake smile on my face.

"Iris." He smiles back, his gaze moving over my body. It was quick, but obvious. Dave had to have noticed. I knew this outfit would get Nick's attention. "I hope you don't mind me watching the game with your husband. I realize it's Friday and you probably wanted him all to yourself."

Dave puts his arm around me. "She has me to herself all the time. I think she could use a break. Isn't that right, honey?"

"Actually, no." I look up at Dave. "I love spending time with you."

The truth is, I do sometimes need a break from Dave. Working together and living together can be a lot. It's normal to want some time apart now and then. But I don't want Dave's time being spent with Nick.

"I brought some wine," Nick says, holding out a bottle of cabernet. It's the same kind I used to order when Nick and I would go out for dinner. "I hope you like it."

"Thank you," I say as I take the bottle. "I've never had this kind. I look forward to trying it."

"Why don't you go open it up?" Dave says to me. "I'll give Nick a quick tour of the house."

"Let me," I say, handing Dave the wine. "I can show Nick around."

"Thank you, honey." Dave smiles at me like he's pleased I'm being nice to Nick given the argument we just had about him. "I'll meet you two in the kitchen."

As he leaves, I say to Nick, "Let's start down the hall."

He follows me down there, to the room Dave and I use as an office. I go into the room with Nick.

"Nice office," he says, looking around like we're actually doing a tour.

I grab his arm and say in a hushed tone, "What the hell are you doing?"

"Getting a tour?" He smirks.

"This isn't funny!" I whisper. I let go of his arm and move in front of him. "You shouldn't be here! Why did you agree to this?"

"Your husband was very insistent. He really wanted me to come for dinner." Nick walks over to the bookcase. "That's a lot of self-help books. Have you read all of these?" He takes one from the shelf.

I storm over to him and yank the book from his hand. "Stop it."

"Stop what?" He turns to me. "I'm not allowed to look at a book?"

"Why are you doing this?" I say, glaring at him. "When Dave invited you, you could've turned him down. Told him you were busy."

"But I wasn't. And I wanted to come. I wanted to see what your life was like..." He glances at the hallway. "With him."

"My life with Dave is none of your business." I shove the book back on the shelf and turn to Nick. "You and I are over. I thought I made that clear, but if I didn't, then I'm doing it now. Nothing is going to happen between us. Dave and I are—"

"You didn't make it very far," Dave says, coming into the office.

"Iris was showing me all your books," Nick says.

"We'll soon have one of our own," Dave says. "Did I tell you that?"

"I don't think you did." Nick glances at me. "You two are writing a book?"

"Not yet," Dave answers. "But soon. We'll probably start on it next year."

"Congratulations," Nick says. "That's great news. Having a book out will really help expand your audience."

"We should finish up the tour," I say, walking over to Dave. "Are you going to get the grill started?"

"I think I'll wait. There's no rush. We have plenty of time." He motions to Nick. "Follow me. I'll show you the bedrooms."

With Dave coming along for the tour, I won't be able to talk to Nick. I really wanted to find out what he's up to, but even if we were alone, I don't think he'd tell me. He seems determined to keep me guessing, wondering why he's playing this ridiculous game.

At least I made it clear that nothing will happen between us. But when I said it, Nick didn't seem to care, which makes me think his reason for showing up here isn't about us getting back together. So why did he send me that card saying he loves me? And leave that note on my windshield saying he wanted to be with me?

Is it possible those weren't from Nick? But if they weren't, then who were they from?

I don't know what's going on here. Who has been sending me things if it's not Nick? And if Nick's no longer interested in me, then why is he back? If he's here to tell Dave about our affair, why hasn't he done it? What is he waiting for?

I'm more confused than ever. I need answers, and I don't think Nick is going to give them to me.

# CHAPTER THIRTY-ONE

On Saturday morning, I wake up and find I'm alone in bed. I check my phone and see it's just after seven. Dave doesn't usually get up this early on the weekend.

"Dave?" I call out.

He doesn't answer.

I get out of bed and hear some noise, like pans clanking together. I leave the bedroom and make my way to the kitchen. Dave is there, cracking eggs into a skillet.

"You're up early," I say, going over to him.

"I couldn't sleep," he says, continuing to crack eggs.

"Why are you making eggs? I thought we were going to brunch."

"I can't. I need to look over that book contract."

"Today? Can't it wait until Monday?"

"I've put it off long enough. Allen said we need to get it signed or we might lose the deal." He grabs a dishtowel and wipes his hands then turns on the burner on the stove.

"Could I help with the contract? Maybe if we both look at it, we'll be done sooner and could go do something."

"How would you help with the contract?" He puts the carton of eggs in the fridge. "You wouldn't understand it."

"That's not very nice," I say, feeling like he just implied that I'm stupid.

He shrugs. "I'm just saying you struggle to understand all that legal jargon."

"Yes, but I can look up what I don't understand."

"Honey, it's fine. I don't mind doing it." He gets a spatula from the drawer and uses it to move the eggs around the pan. "You want some of these? I only made enough for myself, but I can make more."

"I'm not ready to eat yet. I'll just have some coffee." I go over to the coffeemaker and find the coffee's not made.

Dave always makes me coffee. It's the first thing he does when he wakes up. He doesn't drink it, but he still makes it. Sometimes he even brings it to me in bed.

"Are we out of coffee?" I ask.

"No, I just didn't make any," Dave says, continuing to cook the eggs. "You can make it yourself, can't you?"

"Sure," I say, but I'm surprised he didn't offer to do it. I can't remember a time when he hasn't made my coffee. It's one of those small gestures that might seem trivial to some, but to me is very sweet and thoughtful.

As I'm making the coffee, Dave doesn't say anything. He's not usually this quiet. He's acting very strange this morning. He hasn't hugged me or kissed me, and he doesn't seem to want to talk.

"Did you get to bed late?" I ask, because I was asleep by the time he came into our room.

"It was after midnight."

"The game went that late?" I ask, starting the coffeemaker.

"It ended at ten. Then Nick and I stayed up and talked." Dave pauses, and when I glance over at him, I see him staring at me, looking very serious.

My heart takes off, beating out of control as I realize what's happening. The reason why Dave is acting so strange. Why he won't talk to me or hug me or kiss me.

He knows. Nick told him. He told him about our affair. And now Dave hates me.

What do I do? What do I say? I knew this day might come and yet I'm not prepared.

"He thinks we need to improve our online security," Dave says.

*Online security?* So Nick didn't tell him about us?

"The website," Dave says. "The videos we have online. All our materials. He said it'd be easy for someone to hack in and get everything for free."

"That's what you talked about? The website?"

"Yeah, he brought it up and it turned into a two-hour conversation."

I relax a little. "I guess that's good, but it probably could've waited until Monday. It sounds like thinking about it kept you up all night."

"That's not what kept me up," he says, turning the burner off.

What does he mean? Did Nick say something else? Something about me?

Dave puts the eggs on a plate and grabs a fork from the drawer. He leans back against the counter and starts eating.

"Aren't you going to sit down?" I ask.

"No, I just want to eat and get to work."

Something is going on with him. He's being very cold, like he doesn't want to be around me.

"Did you and Nick talk about anything else?" I ask.

"He said something about you." Dave hesitates, then looks over at me. "And him."

My stomach knots and my heart's beating so fast I feel like it's about to leap out of my chest.

This is it. The moment I've been dreading. When Dave tells me he knows about the affair.

I'll deny it. That's always been my plan and I'm not changing it. I hate lying to my husband, but I don't have a choice. If I want to save my marriage, I have to deny whatever Nick told him.

"What did he say?" I ask.

"I'm not sure I want to tell you," Dave says, moving his eggs around the plate with his fork.

"Honey, come on," I say with a nervous laugh. "What did Nick say?"

Dave glances at me. "He thought you were rude."

*Rude?* That's what Nick said about me?

"Why would he say that?" I ask Dave. "I wasn't rude."

"You were. All night long, you barely talked to him. You barely even looked at him. And you wouldn't try the wine he brought."

"Because I wasn't in the mood for red. It had nothing to do with Nick."

"Really, Iris?" Dave says like he doesn't believe me. "You always have red wine with steak. I've never once seen you have white wine with red meat until last night."

"It's because I had a headache," I say, my heart rate slowly returning to normal now that I know this isn't about the affair. "Red wine always makes my headaches worse."

Dave sets his plate down and walks over to me. "Iris, I don't understand why you have something against Nick, but I'm asking you to give him a chance. He has a lot of great ideas and could really help us grow the business."

I'm so tired of hearing Dave talk about growing the business. It's already grown beyond what I ever wanted it to become.

"Do we really need that?" I ask.

"Need what?"

"To keep growing the business. We already have a thriving business that provides enough money for us to live a comfortable life. Why do we need to do more?"

"Because things change, Iris," he says like he's speaking to a child. "People could stop coming to our events. They could stop listening to our podcast. If that's all we had, we'd be done. We'd have to go back to working for someone else. Is that what you want?" he says, raising his voice. "To go back to sitting in an office all day, having some boss tell you what to do, when you have to be there, when you get to go home?"

"No, but—"

"Then this is what we have to do. It's not whether we want to or not." He's talking fast and his voice keeps getting louder. "It's how it has to be. It's survival. We have to keep growing and evolving and preparing for what's ahead!"

"Honey, calm down," I say, surprised he's getting so angry about this. "I didn't mean to upset you. I just don't think we need to keep adding things to the business. Soon we'll be working so much we won't have time to enjoy our lives."

"Are you saying you don't enjoy what we're doing?"

"I do, but what we're doing is enough. We don't need to add more. I'm fine with the book. We'll do it and it'll be done. But pitching a talk show? Making our own products? It's too much. That was never the plan."

"Because we never thought we'd be in this position. Now that we are, why would we pass on opportunities that could change our lives?"

"Our life doesn't need to be changed," I say, rubbing his arm. "I love our life. Don't you?"

"I don't understand you, Iris." He storms past me, and when I turn around, I see him on the other side of the kitchen, his back to me. "I thought we were a team. I thought we agreed to support each other."

"We did, but I can't support something I don't agree with." I walk over to him. "I know you want to grow the business, but when does it end? When is what we're doing enough?"

He turns to me, looking angry and frustrated. "If you don't grow, you die. It's as simple as that. You ask why I'm doing this? Why I'm pursuing all these opportunities? It's to make sure we're still around in five, ten, twenty years." He goes past me. "I'll be in my office."

"Dave, wait!" I catch up to him in the hall. "I don't want to fight about this. I think we both need to calm down, and then maybe we can talk about this later."

He sighs, then nods his head. "Yes. I agree."

"Good." I hold my arms out. "Can I get a hug?"

His phone rings and he takes it from his pocket and answers the call.

"Nick, hey. How's it going?" He smiles as he listens. "I'd love to. You said you already got us a spot?" He continues to smile as Nick talks. "Sounds great! I'll meet you there in a half hour. See you then." He ends the call.

"You're going somewhere with Nick?" I ask.

"We're going golfing." Dave takes off for the bedroom.

I follow him in there. "You're going now? I thought you had work to do."

"I can't do it. Not after that argument we had." Dave goes into the closet and comes out holding one of his golf polos. "Like you said, we need to calm down, and golfing is a good way to do that, at least for me."

"How long will you be gone?" I ask, watching him change shirts.

"I don't know. We'll golf eighteen holes and then maybe go to lunch."

"Is it just going to be the two of you?"

"Yes." He looks over at me. "Why?"

I shrug. "I just wondered."

But the truth is, I asked because I don't want Nick alone with Dave.

"Maybe you should invite Allen," I say. "It'd be a chance for him to get to know Nick."

"Allen is doing something with his wife this morning. I think they're painting the bedroom. I can't remember. It's something to do with the house." He walks over to me and gives me a kiss on the cheek. "Why don't you go out with Jane? Or go get a massage? Maybe it would help you sleep."

"That's a good idea." I smile at him. "Maybe I will."

"See?" He smiles back. "We don't work all the time. We take time off."

We do, but it's not enough. And I don't want Dave's free time being spent with Nick.

"I need to go," Dave says. "Enjoy your day. I'll see you this afternoon."

He hurries out of the room and I hear him going out to the garage. I look out the window and see his car pulling out, then speeding down the road.

He's acting like he couldn't wait to get away from me. To go spend time with Nick.

This needs to stop. I am not letting Dave become friends with Nick. He was never supposed to meet him. Never supposed to know he existed.

Nick knows that, so why is he doing this? Why is he trying to be friends with my husband?

# CHAPTER THIRTY-TWO

"I'M SORRY, but we don't have any openings today," the woman at the spa says when I call about a massage. "But I could get you in on Tuesday. Would that work?"

"I was really hoping to get in today," I tell her. "I don't think Tuesday will work, but thank you for checking." I end the call and consider calling another place, but then change my mind. I'm not in the mood for a massage, even though I'm very tense and could probably use one.

It's almost noon. Dave's been gone for hours and hasn't checked in with me once. He always checks in with me. It's something we do. If we're apart for more than a couple hours, we send a text with an update on where we are, what we're doing, or just to say hello. Some people would say that's excessive, but it works for us and many of the couples we coach. It's a way to connect when you're not together, enhancing your bond, letting each other know you're thinking of them.

I've sent Dave three texts and not heard anything back. I know he's golfing, but I also know his phone is on and that he could easily take a moment to text me back. The longer I go without hearing from him, the more I worry Nick is filling his mind with ideas for our business. Ideas I won't like.

Is that his plan? To turn my husband against me? Is Nick hoping to break Dave and me apart? It's possible, but if that's what he wanted, he'd tell Dave about the affair, although I'm sure he knows I'd deny it.

Thinking about this is making me anxious. I need to get out of the house. Get outside. Go on a walk to relieve the stress I'm feeling.

As I open the door, I'm reminded of the menu that was left there a few weeks ago. Since Nick's moved here, I haven't had any more surprises left at my door or office or dressing room. I haven't had any notes left on my car. It's all stopped, which tells me it had to be Nick who was doing those things. So why is he telling me he didn't?

I make a full loop around the neighborhood, then another, trying to focus on my surroundings and not think about Nick, but he's all I can think about. What if he's not mentally stable? This little game of his is not at all normal. It's creepy, maybe even a little psychotic, which makes me think he could be dangerous.

"Trent, wait!" a woman yells.

I look up and see Trent, Renee's husband, carrying a suitcase out to his car.

Renee runs after him. "Don't leave! This isn't the answer."

I'm almost at the part of the sidewalk that goes in front of their house, so I stop, not wanting to interrupt.

"I can't stay here," Trent says, putting his suitcase in the trunk. "I need some time to think."

"For how long?" Renee asks, looking like she's about to burst into tears.

"I don't know." He walks around to the driver's side and opens the door. "Tell the kids I'll call them before bed." He gets in the car.

"Honey, please," Renee begs. "We can work this out. Please don't go."

He shuts the door, starts up the car, and backs out of the driveway. Renee watches him leave, her body shaking as she breaks down crying.

"Renee!" I run down the sidewalk and up her driveway to where she's standing. I wrap my arms around her. "It's okay."

"No, it's not okay," she sobs. "It's over. He's gone."

"You'll work this out. I'm sure you will."

She yanks away from me. "Iris, he knows. He knows what I did. And he won't forgive me."

"You told him?"

She shakes her head, tears streaming down her face. "Someone started a rumor at my kid's school." She sniffles. "I'm guessing it was one of the other mothers, but I don't know how she found out unless she knows Joel and he told her. But he wouldn't do that. I know he wouldn't." She stares down at the ground like she's trying to figure this out. "Someone must've seen me with him. Someone from school. If it wasn't a parent, maybe it was one of the teachers."

I can't imagine a teacher doing that, or even another parent, unless they really didn't like Renee. But who wouldn't like her? She's very sweet. She's always helping out around the neighborhood and at her kid's school. And I've never once heard her say anything bad about someone.

"So Trent heard the rumor?" I say. "That's how he found out?"

She nods. "We went to a parent event at the school last night and Trent overheard one of the moms talking to another mom, saying I'd cheated on him with a man I met online. Trent was furious they were saying these things and came and found me. He told me we needed to confront those women and put a stop to the rumor." Her tear-filled eyes rise to mine. "I couldn't do it. I couldn't lie and say it wasn't true. I just couldn't." She breaks down crying. "And now he's gone."

The same thing would happen to me if Dave found out what I'd done. He'd leave me. He'd want a divorce. I'm almost certain of it.

I read somewhere that women are far more likely to take back a cheating spouse than men are. It makes me wonder if I'd forgive Dave if I found out he'd been unfaithful. Part of me thinks I would, but I guess it would depend on when it happened and for how long. When I had my affair, I really thought my marriage was over. If Dave knew that, would he forgive me?

"I have to get inside," Renee says. "Check on the kids."

"I'm so sorry this happened," I tell her. "Is there anything I can do? Do you need help with the kids?"

"No, my mom's coming over. She's going to stay with us until Trent decides what he's going to do."

"I'm sure you two can work this out," I say. "Dave and I work with couples like you and Trent all the time and many of them go on to have marriages that are even stronger than before."

She gives me a sad smile. "I know you're trying to make me

feel better, but it's over. Trent and I aren't getting back together. I could tell when he left just now. I could feel it. He's done. He doesn't even want to try to fix things between us." She glances at the house. "Iris, I have to go. The kids will be up from their nap any minute now."

"Yes, go ahead. But please, if there's anything you need, let me know."

"I will." She runs back to the house and goes inside.

Poor Renee. I feel terrible for her, and for Trent. And for their children. They're such a beautiful family. I hate seeing them ripped apart because of a mistake Renee made years ago. A mistake she deeply regrets and would never make again.

My heart aches for her because I know exactly how she's feeling. The guilt. The regret. Wishing you could go back and change the past. Those feelings never go away. I'm sure some people can have an affair and move on, but not me. Every day, I live with the guilt and regret and shame over what I've done.

As I'm crossing the street to my house, I hear Jane's shrill voice. "Iris!"

I look up and see her smiling at me from her porch. "Hi, Jane."

She steps off her porch and hurries across the lawn, her happy expression replaced with a look of concern. "What happened? Why do you look so glum?"

"Renee." I glance back at her house, not sure I should tell Jane this, but she'll find out soon enough. Jane's very nosy. She keeps tabs on everyone in the neighborhood. She'll notice Trent isn't there and go ask Renee what happened. It'd be better if I told Jane so Renee doesn't have to tell the story again.

"What about her?" Jane asks.

"Let's go inside," I say, not wanting the neighbors to hear. But knowing Jane, she'll make sure everyone knows before the week is up.

She follows me to my house and we go inside.

"So? What is it?" Jane asks.

"Trent found out."

Jane gasps. "You mean about..." She leans toward me and whispers, "The affair?"

"Yes. He moved out. Just a few minutes ago. I was on a walk and saw Trent leaving with his suitcase. Renee was out sobbing in the driveway. I tried to comfort her, but she was too upset."

"I should go over there," Jane says. "I'll bring her some blueberry muffins and maybe some—"

"No, she doesn't want visitors. She's very upset. And her mother's coming over. She's going to stay there and help with the kids."

Jane frowns. "What a shame. If only Renee had never gotten involved with that man."

"Why can't people stay out of other people's business?" I go to the couch to sit down. "Everything would've been fine if someone hadn't started that rumor."

"What rumor?" Jane asks, sitting across from me.

"Someone started a rumor at the school where Renee's son goes. Trent heard people talking about it at some school event he was at with Renee."

"And he believed it? I can't imagine Trent going along with a rumor, especially one about his wife."

"He didn't go along with it. He was going to confront the people who were talking about her, but when he told Renee that, she broke down and confessed. Told him it was true."

Jane sighs. "Well, on a positive note, I'm sure she feels better no longer having to carry around that secret. What a burden that must've been for her, having to hide that from her husband all that time. I don't know how she did it."

"I'm sure it was difficult," I say, thinking of my own situation and how difficult it is for me. "But she was determined to keep her family together, and she knew that wouldn't happen if she told Trent the truth."

Jane cocks her head to the side. "I don't understand you, Iris. You stand up on that stage telling couples how trust is the foundation of a good marriage and yet you felt Renee was right to keep this secret from Trent."

"Every situation is different. In Renee's case, she made a mistake that she deeply regrets. She didn't seek this man out with the intent of having an affair. When it happened, she was tired, overwhelmed, emotional. She wasn't thinking straight. I'm not saying that excuses what she did or makes it okay. I'm just saying that in this case, and knowing how Trent would react, not telling her husband was probably the right choice."

"Speaking of husbands," Jane says as we hear the garage door opening. "Sounds like yours just got home."

"Yes, he was out golfing." I almost tell her he went with Nick but then hear Dave calling for me.

"Iris?"

"In the living room," I call back. "Jane is here."

He walks into the room. "Hello, Jane." He smiles at her. "Did you bring us more of those delicious cinnamon rolls?"

"No, but I'd be happy to make you some!" She's beaming, thrilled that he complimented her baking. She gets up. "I should get going so you two can get on with your day."

I walk her to the door. "I'll see you later, Jane."

"Keep me posted if you hear anything." She glances toward Renee's house.

"Yes. I will."

I open the door and am startled when I see someone standing there.

It's Nick. At my house. Again.

# CHAPTER THIRTY-THREE

"Iris." Nick smiles at me. "Perfect timing. I was just about to knock."

"What are you doing here?" I ask.

"We're going to lunch. Didn't your husband tell you?"

"I didn't have a chance to yet," Dave says from behind me.

"I'm Jane," she says to Nick, extending her hand. "I live next door."

Why is she introducing herself to him? She knows who he is, and she knows I want him to go away, not get to know the neighbors.

"Nice to meet you." He shakes her hand. "I'm Nick. I'm friends with Dave." He looks at me. "And Iris."

He is not my friend. He's not anything to me, except a threat to my marriage.

"Nick works for us," I say to Jane, playing along as though she doesn't already know this. "He just started."

"Yes, I know," Jane says. She looks back at Nick. "She's told me all about you."

"Is that so?" Nick says, like my telling Jane about him means something.

"I told her you were helping us with marketing," I say.

"Would you like to join us for lunch?" Nick asks Jane.

"Oh, no thank you," Jane says. "I already ate."

Dave comes up beside me. "Hey, is something going on with Renee? I saw her talking to her mom outside. It looked like she was crying."

"I'll tell you later," I say.

"It's about her affair," Jane whispers to Dave. "Trent found out and left."

"He moved out?" Dave says with concern. "I guess that explains why she was crying."

"We shouldn't talk about this," I say. "It's none of our business."

"Maybe you two could help her out," Nick says. "Give her some of your marriage advice." He looks at me as he says it. "Since you two are experts."

He's mocking me, and mocking what I do. I want to slap him, but I can't. I have to pretend that he's just some random guy, someone I have no history with.

"I'll let you three get to lunch," Jane says, going past Nick.

"Bye, Jane," Dave says, smiling at her.

Nick comes inside and Dave shuts the door.

"I thought you were going straight to lunch after your golf game," I say to Dave.

"That was the plan, but Nick insisted you join us. You haven't eaten, have you?"

"No, but—"

"Great!" Dave gives me a kiss on the cheek. "I'm going to change and then we can leave."

He goes to the bedroom and closes the door.

Nick walks over to the couch and sits down. "I like your house." He looks around. "You did a good job decorating."

I storm over to him. "Go home, Nick," I say, keeping my voice down. "I mean it. Stop whatever you're doing and go home."

"Yeah, that's not happening," he says with a smirk.

"Why?" I lean down to him, my voice now a whisper. "Why are you here? What do you want? Just tell me!"

Nick puts his arms up along the back of the couch. "I played really well today. Had one of my best scores."

He's talking about golf? Is he serious? Why is he acting this way? Why won't he answer my questions?

"What are you thinking for lunch?" he asks. "Dave suggested a few places, but I told him we should let you pick."

"Did you leave that menu here?" I ask, trying once again to get Nick to tell me what's going on.

"What menu?"

I check behind me to make sure Dave isn't there. "The one for that Indian place. The one we—" I stop and check behind me again.

"He's not there," Nick says. "I'd tell you if he was. And no, I didn't leave a menu here. I have no idea what you're talking about."

"You're lying," I say through gritted teeth.

"I'm not." He shrugs. "But hey, believe what you want."

"Hey, Iris," Dave yells. "Where's my—never mind. I found it." I hear the door close.

"How are things going with you two?" Nick asks.

"Wonderful. Couldn't be better."

He laughs a little. "You really believe that?"

"What's that supposed to mean?" I fold my arms over my chest.

He doesn't answer me, his gaze on the blank TV screen.

"Tell me." I stare at him. "You obviously meant something by that or you wouldn't have said it."

"Not everything is as it seems." His gaze moves from the TV to me, and he has a very serious look on his face.

"Meaning what? What are you referring to?"

He looks behind me. "Ready to go?"

I turn and see Dave, changed out of his golf clothes and wearing jeans and a button-up shirt.

"Yeah, let's go," he says. "I'll pull out the car if you two want to go wait in the driveway."

"After you," Nick says to me as Dave goes to get the car.

Nick follows me to the door. Before I leave, I turn to him. "I'm done playing games. I want answers. I need to know—"

"Iris, stop," he says, his eyes locked on mine. "Leave it alone."

"Leave *what* alone?"

He opens the door. "He's got the car there. We need to go."

This is so frustrating! Instead of giving me answers, it's like Nick's talking in code. Is this another part of his game? Make me guess what he means? Make me even more confused?

"What'd you decide?" Dave asks when I get in the car.

"For lunch? How about that new Italian place we went to a few weeks ago? I can't remember the name."

"I know the place you mean." Dave glances at Nick in the back seat. "You good with Italian?"

"Whatever Iris wants is fine with me."

Dave smiles at me, like he thinks Nick letting me pick the lunch place is proof that he's a great guy.

The lunch lasts for over an hour because Dave and Nick won't stop talking. They talk about golf, baseball, football. It's nothing I'm interested in and all things that seem to draw the two of them closer together. At this rate, they'll be best friends by the end of the week and I'll never convince Dave to get rid of Nick.

"Honey, we should get home," I say to Dave, sliding the check his way since it's been sitting there for ten minutes and he still hasn't put his credit card out. "We have an event tonight."

"Yes, I didn't realize it was getting so late." He finally pays the bill and we leave the restaurant.

"I think I'll go tonight," Nick says as we're driving back to the house. "If you can get me a ticket."

"To the event?" Dave asks. "Yeah, of course. We'd love to have you there."

"You know what's strange?" I say to Dave.

"What?" He glances at me as we wait at a stoplight.

"I haven't received any more mysterious flowers or cards in the last couple of weeks."

"That's true. You haven't." He pulls forward as the light turns green

"Why are they mysterious?" Nick asks.

I look back at him. "Whoever gave them to me didn't sign their name."

"That's strange," he says, as though it wasn't him who sent them.

"We're thinking it's some guy who listens to the podcast," Dave says. "Someone who likes Iris a little too much."

"You should be careful," Nick says to me. "Guys like that can be dangerous."

A chill goes through me. Is he talking about himself? Is he saying he's dangerous?

"Thanks for lunch," Nick says when we're back at the house.

"I'm glad you could join us." Dave gets out his phone. "I'm sending you the ticket for tonight. They'll scan it at the door."

Nick checks his phone. "Looks like I got it. I'll see you tonight."

He leaves and Dave picks something up off the floor. It's a key ring with two keys. "Are these Nick's?"

"They're not mine."

"Go see if you can catch Nick before he goes."

Why can't Dave do it? I decide not to argue with him and take the keys outside.

Nick's still in the driveway, getting out of his car.

I hold up the keys. "Are these yours?"

"Yeah," he says, sounding relieved. "I was just about to go back inside to see if they were there. They must've fallen out of my pocket."

I hand him the keys.

"Thanks," he says. Then he leans down to my ear and says, "Be careful."

I rear back. "What did you say?"

He turns and walks back to his car. He gets in, starts the car, and pulls out of the driveway. Before he drives off, he stops and looks at me in a way that makes a shiver go down me.

I glance away and he speeds off.

What just happened? Why did he look at me like that? And why did he tell me to be careful?

# CHAPTER THIRTY-FOUR

"Hi, Mom," I say, answering her call.

"Hi, honey." Her voice booms through the car speaker and I turn it down. "Are you busy?"

"I'm on my way to the studio, but I can talk for a few minutes."

"Is everything okay? You sound stressed."

"Do I?" I say with a laugh so she doesn't worry. "I'm fine. It's just been a busy week."

It's Friday, and I'm going to meet Dave at the studio. We'd normally go together, but Dave decided to go to the gym this morning. I'm sure he was meeting Nick there, but Dave didn't bother to tell me. He knows I don't like Nick so he's been choosing not to tell me when they do stuff together. The only way I know is if I ask, and even then, Dave hesitates before telling me.

"I wish you wouldn't work so much," my mom says. "It's not good for your health. Are you at least taking the weekend off?"

"Most of it. We have an event on Saturday night and another one Sunday, but then that's it for a couple of weeks."

I was shocked when Dave told me we weren't doing any events next weekend. He said it was a scheduling mishap and that it was too late to book the event hall. So now we get the entire weekend off, which hasn't happened for months.

I'd love to get away for a couple of days. I was thinking maybe we could drive up to Wisconsin, see the fall foliage, get a hotel for a night or two. I was going to suggest that to Dave, but I haven't yet because I'm not sure I want to spend that much time with him. He's been really moody this week. One minute he's happy and joking around and the next he's tense and snapping at me. That's how he was early in our marriage, back when we were having problems. Now I'm seeing glimpses of that again and it's concerning me. I'm hoping it's just temporary and he'll soon go back to his usual self.

"If you're free next weekend," my mom says, "maybe I should come for a visit. Do you think Dave would mind?"

"Of course not. We'd love that, but I'm not sure if we'll be here. I was thinking of taking a little weekend trip."

"Oh, yes, you definitely should. You two could use a break. I'll come some other time."

"Mom, I'm not saying you can't come. I need to talk to Dave and figure out our plans." I pull into the parking lot. "I'm at the studio. I'll call you this weekend and let you know what we decide."

"Sounds good, honey. Have a nice day!"

"You too." I end the call and get out of my car. I usually park in the back of the building so I can go in the door that takes me directly into our office versus going in the front entrance and having to go through the lobby. But I had this strange feeling that I shouldn't use the back lot today, like it wasn't safe.

I keep having that feeling, like I'm not safe. I've felt it all week and it's making me act in a way I normally wouldn't. Like yesterday, I searched the parking lot at the grocery store before I got out of my car. And when I left the store, I felt like someone was following me. I decided to take a different route home that was ten miles out of the way. When I got to the house, I realized nobody was following me and I was just being paranoid.

It's Nick's fault I'm feeling this way. I keep hearing his voice in my head, telling me to be careful. He was probably just messing with me, but my mind took it as a threat and I've been on edge ever since. I really want Nick gone. He's ruining my life.

"Dave?" I call out, going down the hallway that leads to our office.

He doesn't answer, and when I reach the office, I find it's empty. I thought Dave would be here by now.

I toss my purse on a chair and flip through the mail that's piled up on the desk. It's a mix of junk mail and letters from fans. None of the letters are addressed only to me, which means none of them are creepy love notes like I was getting before.

"Iris," a voice says, startling me.

Turning around, I see Nick coming into the room and immediately tense up. "Where's Dave?"

"He's on his way."

"How'd you get in here?"

"Dave gave me a key." Nick gives me a slight smile. "What's wrong?"

"Nothing," I say, trying to play it cool. I walk away from him and go behind the desk. "Why are you here?"

"Dave wants me to listen in while you record the podcast."

"Why? You could listen to it when it's done."

"Didn't he tell you?" His slight smile turns into a smirk.

"Tell me what?"

"He's thinking of hiring me as your producer. You really should've hired one a long time ago. You shouldn't be doing the whole thing yourself, especially now that you have the money to pay someone."

I storm over to him. "We are not hiring you as our producer! You're done here, Nick. I'm going to talk to Dave and demand that he let you go."

Nick's eyes lock on mine. "You really don't want to do that."

"I do. I want you gone. And I'm going to make sure it happens."

"You'd be making a huge mistake."

"It's a mistake to get rid of the man who's trying to destroy my marriage?" I huff. "Of course you would think that."

"Your marriage is a joke. He doesn't love you. Why can't you see that?"

His words are almost exactly what was written on that note that was left on my windshield.

"It was you," I say, pointing at him. "You left that note on my car. I knew it was you. You can deny it all you want but—"

"I didn't leave you a note."

"Stop lying! What you said just now... it was the same thing that was in the note."

"It wasn't me. Why the hell would I write you a note?"

"To let me know you were back in town? To scare me? I don't know, Nick. Why don't you tell me?"

He grabs my arm. "If I wanted to scare you, I have other ways. I wouldn't use a piece of paper."

"Let go of me," I say through gritted teeth as I try to pull away from him.

He keeps hold of my arm. "If you try to get rid of me, Iris, you'll be sorry. I can promise you that."

"Is that a threat?"

He leans down to my face. "It's a warning."

"Iris?" Dave calls out.

Nick lets go of my arm and steps out into the hall. "We're down here. I was telling Iris about our idea."

Dave appears and comes into the office, smiling at me. "What do you think? We've been talking about hiring a producer. Nick's willing to try it, so we might as well give him a chance."

"Sure," I say, faking a smile.

Now is not the time to talk to Dave about this. I'll talk to him when we're alone.

"I want to go over the sound equipment with Nick," Dave says to me. "Then after we record, I'll show him how to do some basic editing."

"You can show him some other time," I say. "It doesn't have to be today."

"I'd like him to start learning this stuff so he can take over. It'll free up a lot of my time not having to do all the production work." He smiles. "Time I can spend with you."

I'm not going to win this argument, and I don't want to fight with Dave around Nick. I'll have to talk to Dave later.

He takes off with Nick while I look through today's podcast episode, which is about how to have difficult conversations with your spouse. That's ironic, given that I'm struggling to have a difficult conversation with Dave. I'm not worried about talking to him. I'm worried about how he'll respond. I'm afraid he'll take Nick's side over mine and insist that he keep working for us.

Dave spends nearly an hour showing Nick the equipment, and then we finally record the podcast. It's usually just Dave and I sitting at a table where our microphones are set up, but today Nick is there. I feel him watching me and keep messing up and forgetting what I was going to say.

When we're done, Dave says to Nick, "It usually goes smoother than that."

"Sorry," I say. "I must be tired. I couldn't get the words out."

"Why don't you go home?" Dave says. "Take a nap."

"I don't need one. I think I'll stick around and watch you teach Nick how to do the edits."

Dave laughs. "Are you joking?"

"No. Why?"

"You hate all that technical stuff."

"I decided I'd like to learn."

Nick gets up. "Why don't we do it another time? I have some personal stuff I need to get done."

"Sure," Dave says. "We can do it this weekend."

I look at Dave, annoyed. "Honey, I was hoping we could do something together this weekend."

"I'll call you later," Dave says to Nick. "Let you know what time will work."

"Sounds good." Nick's eyes meet up with mine for a just moment before he leaves. Is that another warning? Telling me not to get him fired?

Maybe I should wait to talk to Dave. I'm worried what Nick's going to do. He hasn't told Dave about our affair, which makes me think he's here for some other reason. Something more ominous.

Would he do something to hurt Dave? Or me?

# CHAPTER THIRTY-FIVE

"We need to talk," I say to Dave, already feeling nervous.

We're at home, sitting on the couch. I was going to do this at the studio, but decided I'd rather do it at our house. I thought I'd feel calmer here, but I don't. Why am I so nervous? Dave's my husband. I love him. I shouldn't be nervous to tell him this.

"Talk about what?" he asks.

"Nick. I don't want him working for us."

Dave sighs in frustration. "Iris, we've been through this. I get that you don't like the guy, but you need to get over it. He's our employee. You don't have to like an employee in order for him to work for us."

"He's more than an employee. You spend all your time with him. More time than you spend with me."

"Is that what this is about? You're jealous I'm spending so much time with Nick?"

"I'm not jealous," I say, annoyed that he'd think that. "I'm angry that you're not considering my opinion on this. We both own the business, which means I get a say in who works for us."

"Then you should've been involved in the hiring process. I gave you plenty of opportunities to help me pick someone to replace Jeremy and you—"

"Yes, I know. I should've been involved. If I had been, I never would've hired Nick."

"But he's already hired, so why are we still talking about this?"

"I want you to let him go. Or I'll do it. It doesn't matter. I just want him gone."

"Because you don't like him?"

"Because I don't—" I stop before I say something about him not being a good fit for us. Dave will argue that he is, and we'll be talking in circles. I need a better reason. "I don't feel safe around him."

"Why?" Dave asks. "Did something happen?"

"Yes." I pause. "He threatened me."

"When? And how did he threaten you?"

"It was this morning. Before you got to the studio. Nick knew I wanted to get rid of him and said if I tried to fire him, I'd be sorry. Or I'd regret it. Something like that. I don't remember his exact words."

"That doesn't sound like Nick. Are you sure you didn't misinterpret what he said?"

"No. Dave, if you saw how he looked at me when he said it, you'd want him gone. You wouldn't trust him. You'd think he's dangerous."

"Dangerous?" Dave laughs. "Honey, I think you're overreacting. Nick is not dangerous."

"How do you know? You just met him."

"Yes, but I've spent a lot of time with him and he hasn't shown any signs of being dangerous."

"I think he's been following me," I blurt out.

"Following you where?"

"The store. The bank. The house. He's been following me all around town."

"Are you sure it's him?"

"I'm not positive, but it looks like his car, so unless someone else with the same car is following me, it has to be Nick."

"I'll talk to him," Dave says.

"No, you can't tell him I said this. Any of it."

"Then how do I justify firing him?"

"You tell him he's not working out, or that we decided we don't need him."

"He'll know both those things are a lie. And really, Iris, I don't see a need to fire him. I think if we all sit down and have a talk about this, we can work it out."

"Dave, you're not listening." I slide closer to him. "I don't want Nick working for us. If you won't fire him, I will."

"You're not firing him. Like you said, this is a decision we both have to make. You can't fire him unless we both agree to it."

I'm furious he's being so stubborn about this. Unable to sit still, I get up and pace the floor.

"Iris, what are you doing?"

"I'm trying to figure out why you're taking Nick's side over mine."

Dave gets up from the couch as I continue to pace. "Honey, I'm not taking his side. This is business. I finally found someone who's smart, experienced, and understands where we want to take the company. Do you know how hard it is to find someone like that? And now you want us to fire him?

"Yes." I stop pacing and turn to Dave. "I want him gone.

How many times do I have to say it before you'll finally listen to me?"

Dave comes over to me. "How about this? We give him one more week, and if you still feel this way, we'll let him go."

"Are you serious, or are you just saying that to end the argument?"

"I'm serious. One more week."

I nod. "Okay. One week."

I'm disappointed Dave wouldn't agree to fire him right away, but a week is better than having to wait months, or longer than that. One more week and Nick will be gone, assuming Dave follows through with our agreement.

"Oh, I talked to my mom," I say. "She'd like to come for a visit. She suggested next weekend. I told her—"

"No," Dave says, interrupting me. "Next weekend isn't good."

"Yes, I told her another time would be better, but I'm curious why you don't want her to visit. Do we have plans?"

He sighs. "It was supposed to be a surprise."

"What's the surprise?"

He smiles. "I'm taking you away for the weekend. To a little cabin in the woods."

"You've already planned this?"

"Yes. We've had so much going on and it's been stressful for both of us. I thought it'd be good to go somewhere quiet where we can relax and be surrounded by nature."

"That sounds wonderful! I was just going to suggest we take a little trip next weekend. You must've read my mind. So where are we going?"

"A few hours north of here. I checked and the leaves should be changing by then. They might even be at peak color while we're there." He puts his arms around me. "We can go on walks. Make a fire." He kisses me. "Snuggle up in bed."

"I can't wait! I wish we were going now."

"A week isn't that long. Before you know it, we'll be there."

He sounds just as excited about this trip as I am. He's not really the outdoorsy type so I'm surprised he suggested this. But I'm really glad he did. We can go there and celebrate Nick being gone.

Just one more week and he'll be out of our lives.

# CHAPTER THIRTY-SIX

ALL WEEK, I've been counting the days until Nick is gone. It's now Thursday, which means only one day remains before we fire him.

I'm hoping that's what will happen. Dave hasn't agreed to it yet, but I've told him I'm still not comfortable around Nick, which means he has to let him go. That was the deal, and I'm confident Dave will follow through.

He's been spending less time with Nick, and yesterday, when we were all at the studio, Dave didn't say much to him. When he did, it was very business like, not the way you'd talk to a friend. It was a big change from how Dave acted around him before. It makes me wonder if something happened or if Dave is just distancing himself from Nick before he fires him.

My phone rings as I'm driving to the grocery store. It's Dave.

"Hey, honey," I answer. "I'm almost at the store. Did you need something?"

"Yes, we're out of eggs. I forgot to add it to the list."

"Okay, anything else?"

He says something about chicken, but I'm not listening, my attention on a car that's two cars behind mine. It's a blue sedan that looks very much like Nick's and is the same car that I swear has followed me before. But a lot of people have that car so it's hard to tell if it's Nick's or if it belongs to someone else.

"Honey, are you still there?" Dave asks.

"Yes, you wanted chicken. I'll make sure to get some." I turn and see the blue sedan turning as well. It could just be that it's going the same direction I am, but I'm keeping my eye on it, just in case.

"Is everything okay?" Dave asks. "You sound off."

"I'm just trying to focus on the road. I'm driving through a construction area."

"I'll let you go. See you at home."

"Yes, bye." I end the call and turn onto a side street that goes through a neighborhood. It's the opposite direction from the store, but I want to see if that car follows me. I'm a block down the street when I notice the blue sedan. It's a few car-lengths behind me, going really slow.

It has to be Nick. I see an outline of the driver, but I'm not close enough to tell if it's him. Why is he doing this? Why won't he leave me alone?

I call him. It rings several times before he picks up.

"Hello, Iris," he says in an eerily calm voice.

"Stop following me!" I yell at him as I look at the car in my rearview mirror. "I know it's you."

"Iris, I—"

"It's been you this whole time, hasn't it? You've been following me all week! I thought I was being paranoid, seeing things that weren't there. But it was you, wasn't it? Just like it was you who sent me those roses and the card and left that menu at my door."

"It wasn't me. I already told you that."

"You're lying," I hiss. "Who else would it be?"

"Iris, we need to talk. Let's go somewhere. Somewhere private, where we can be alone."

"Are you kidding me? You think I'd agree to be alone with you? After everything you've done? The creepy notes? Following me around? Befriending my husband? You're not well, Nick. You need to see someone. A counselor. Or check yourself into a mental health center. Your behavior isn't normal. This obsession you have with me isn't healthy, and to be honest, it's scaring me."

"Iris, I'm—"

"I don't want to hear your excuses. It's over, Nick. You're going to stop this behavior and go back to wherever you were before. Your job with us is ending. It's ending this week, so you might as well leave now. And if you ever come near me again, I'll call the police. I'm serious, Nick. I'll go to the police if you don't stop this."

I end the call and check my rearview mirror. I see the blue sedan pulling over to the side of the road. I was right. It was Nick. He was following me. He's turning around now, going the other direction.

Did I get through to him? Will he do what I asked? Will he go away? Go back to wherever he was living?

I'm so upset by what happened that I drive home and forget to stop at the store. We have almost nothing left in the fridge, but I can't grocery shop right now. I'm too anxious and tense. I feel jittery, like I just drank a pot of coffee even though I haven't had any since this morning.

"Hi, honey," Dave says when I come into the house. "You want me to grab the groceries?"

"I didn't go," I say, tossing my purse on the couch on my way to the kitchen.

Dave follows me in there. "You didn't go to the store?"

"No. I forgot." I open the cupboard and take out Dave's bottle of whiskey along with a glass. I need a drink, and wine isn't strong enough, given my state of mind right now.

"Honey, what's wrong?" Dave asks with concern as I pour the whiskey into the glass. He knows something's up. I rarely drink hard liquor.

"It's Nick," I say, taking a swig of the whiskey.

"What about him?"

"He was following me. I saw his car behind me and wasn't sure it was him but it was." I take another swig of whiskey. "He's been following me for at least a week. Maybe longer." I turn to Dave. "And I think he sent me those roses and left that note on my car. I know you don't believe me, but it was him. I'm telling you, he—"

"I know." Dave grips my shoulders. "Honey, I believe you."

"You do?"

"Yes." He sighs. "I didn't want to believe the things you were saying about him, but I think you were right. I think he's deeply disturbed. He might even be dangerous."

I can't believe Dave is saying this. Every time we discuss Nick, Dave takes his side. But now he's taking mine? What changed?

"Why are you saying this?" I ask. "Did something happen?"

He nods. "I need to show you something."

# CHAPTER THIRTY-SEVEN

DAVE LEADS me to the office and takes something from the desk. It's a stack of photos.

"I found these in Nick's car," Dave says, handing me the photos. "We went to lunch today and Nick stopped to get gas. While he was at the pump, I noticed his glove compartment had something stuck in it so I opened it and that's when I saw the photos."

I'm flipping through them, feeling sick to my stomach. They're all photos of me, taken without me knowing it. There are photos of me leaving the house, walking down the street, getting into my car. There's even one taken here, in the kitchen. Nick must've taken it during one of the times he was over here. I had no idea.

"He doesn't know I have them," Dave says. "But I'm afraid he'll find out."

I look at Dave, panicking. "What are we going to do?"

"I don't know." He rubs his jaw. "I'm thinking we should go to the police, but I don't know if showing them some photos is enough for them to do anything."

"I'll tell them Nick threatened me," I blurt out. "And I'll show them that note he left me and the card."

"We can't prove those were from him."

"But it's possible they were, so we at least need to tell the police about them."

Dave walks away, then turns back. "You really think we should do this? I don't want to ruin Nick's life. I mean, what if he just has a crush on you and—"

"Dave, this is more than a crush." I race over to him. "He was following me!"

Dave nods. "You're right. We need to tell the police. I can't risk anything happening to you."

"Or you. It's possible he'd do something to you to get to me. Like... try to get rid of you."

"I hadn't thought about that, but I suppose it's possible."

"We need to go right now. We need to tell the police what's happening."

Dave agrees, and we head to the police station. The whole way there, Dave keeps telling me everything will be fine. He's trying to calm me down because I'm a nervous wreck. I'm breathing fast, my foot's tapping the floor, and I keep checking behind me, thinking Nick is following us.

"Try to relax," Dave says as he parks in front of the police station. "I know it's hard when you're worried about Nick, but you're safe now." He reaches over and holds my hand. "I'm right here."

His words don't help. I'm still nervous and feeling like I might get sick. This is all my fault. If I'd never gotten involved with Nick, this wouldn't be happening. I'd be safe. Dave would be safe. And we'd be enjoying a nice evening at home instead of at a police station.

"And this man just showed up out of the blue?" the officer asks after we've told him everything that's happened.

I haven't told the officer my history with Nick. I know it's relevant and would explain why Nick is doing this, but I can't do it. I'm not losing Dave over some stupid mistake I made years ago.

"He's been listening to our podcast for years," Dave explains. "I'm thinking that's how he became obsessed with Iris."

"Can you bring the notes in?" the officer asks. "The ones you think he wrote? I'd like to see them."

"I threw them out," I say. "I didn't think I'd need them."

"Well, if you receive more, you should save them and bring them here."

"We will," Dave says, holding my hand. "Officer, if we're done, I'd like to get Iris home. Just being here is upsetting for her, on top of everything else that's happened today."

"I understand." The officer sets down the pen he was using to take notes. "Unfortunately, at this point, there's nothing I can do." He looks at me. "I know what the guy said to you seems like a threat, but it's actually not from a legal standpoint. And since you can't prove it was him in the car you claim has been following you, we can't charge him with anything."

"So we have to wait for him to harm one of us before you do anything?" Dave says in an angry tone. He gets up. "Honey, let's go."

The officer stands up. "Mr. Larson, I'm sorry I can't do more, but I have to follow the law. I can't arrest someone unless they're doing something illegal."

"Thank you for your time," I say to the officer as I follow Dave to the door.

"What a waste," Dave says as we're driving home. "He didn't seem to care about anything we said."

"He cared," I say. "He just couldn't do anything about it."

"Which means Nick can do whatever the hell he wants to us." Dave grips the steering wheel tighter. "How could I be so stupid? I actually thought the guy was a friend. I trusted him, and this whole time, he's been playing me to get to you." He shakes his head. "I'm sorry, honey. I should've listened to you."

My phone rings. I tense up when I see who's calling. "It's him," I tell Dave. "It's Nick."

"Answer it."

"Are you kidding?" I look at Dave like he's crazy. "I'm not answering it."

"Iris, we can't suddenly treat him like he's the enemy. He'll know something's up with us."

"And that's bad? Why? He should know we're on to him."

"We don't want him knowing that. Not yet. We need to collect more evidence against him so we can get the police to arrest him. If Nick knows we're on to him, he might react by coming after us. We need to pretend everything's normal."

"It went to voicemail," I say, noticing my phone stopped ringing.

"I'll call him when we get home."

"And say what?" My phone starts ringing again. "It's Nick. He's calling again."

"Answer it," Dave says. "And try to act normal."

"Hey, Nick," I say, my eyes on Dave.

"Iris, we need to talk. Meet me at—"

"Sorry, Nick, but Dave and I are on our way home from the store and then we have to make dinner."

"Put him on speaker," Dave says.

"Dave wants to talk to you," I say to Nick. "I'm putting you on speaker." I hit the button.

"Hey, Nick," Dave says in a cheerful tone. "How's it going?"

"Good. I was just calling because I need Iris to re-record part of that ad we did the other day. There must've been something wrong with her mic."

That's not why Nick called. He said he wanted to talk to me. Why is he changing his story?

"She'll have to record it next week," Dave says. "Iris isn't feeling well. She's going to rest."

"Can't we do it tomorrow?" Nick asks. "After you record the podcast?"

"We're not recording tomorrow. We're re-running a podcast from last year. I thought I told you that."

"If you did, I don't remember. Why aren't you recording a new one? Are you going somewhere?"

"No," I say, not wanting Nick to know about our trip. "We just need some time off. Dave and I are both exhausted and wanted some time at home to rest."

"We're taking the whole weekend off," Dave says, glancing at me. "I won't be answering calls or doing any work. We're just going to have a quiet weekend at home."

"Yeah, okay," Nick says. "So we'll talk next week?"

"Yes, I'll call you on Monday," Dave says. "Have a nice weekend, Nick."

"You too."

I end the call. "Do you think he bought it?"

"He seemed to."

"I'm glad you didn't tell him about our trip."

"It wouldn't have mattered if I did. He doesn't know where we're going."

"He could follow us."

"I think we'd figure that out before we got there. We'll be on a two-lane road surrounded by trees without many cars around. We'd easily spot Nick behind us before we reached the cabin."

I sigh. "I wish we could leave right now. Get away from here. Away from Nick."

"We'll leave first thing in the morning." He pauses. "Oh, shoot."

"What?"

"I forgot I have a meeting with Heather in the morning. It's at ten, but it shouldn't take long."

"Can you cancel it? I want to leave town as soon as possible."

"I can't cancel. It's a production meeting. The last one before they make the prototype for the game we're creating. If I move the meeting, it changes the whole production schedule."

"Okay, fine, but you promise we'll leave when it's done?"

"Yes, definitely."

"Where's the meeting?"

"At Heather's office. Allen's meeting me there."

"Can you do it at home? I don't want to be alone."

"It's possible I could call in. I'll check with Heather." He reaches over and holds my hand. "It's going to be okay. I won't let Nick get near you. I promise."

"You can't promise me that. You can't be with me every second of the day."

"Maybe not, but I'll do whatever I can to protect you and keep you safe."

I know he'll try, but I don't feel like I'm safe. I feel like Nick is watching me. I feel like he's going to do something to me, or Dave, or both of us. I just don't know what he's planning, or when he's going to do it.

# CHAPTER THIRTY-EIGHT

**Dave**

Everyone says marriage is hard, but it's even harder when you have to compete for your wife's attention. I've been doing that for years, ever since Iris met Nick. Even after she ended their affair, she was always looking for him, her gaze pausing on any man she thought might be him.

I assumed this would eventually stop, but it didn't. We'd go to a movie and she'd check the theater for him. We'd go out to eat and she'd scan the restaurant. We'd stroll through the park, and her attention would go to any man who walked by, thinking it might be him.

After a while, I couldn't take it anymore. I was sick and tired of competing with this man. I'd already won! I won Iris back. So why was I still competing with her ex-lover?

I learned about their affair by accident. I'd never been to that hotel, but Tom, a guy I knew from the gym, invited me to have a drink there after work one night. His cousin was the bartender and Tom said we could drink for free. I wasn't thrilled about going all the way downtown for a few beers, but it was better than sitting at home, doing nothing. Iris and I had stopped going out by then and were basically separated, although not legally.

As soon as I walked into the hotel, I saw Iris with Nick. They were standing in the lobby, near the back. Nick had his arms around Iris' waist. Hers were around his neck. She was smiling at him. And then he kissed her. I couldn't believe what I was seeing. I hid behind a pillar and watched as they kissed, again and again, until they finally went upstairs to a room.

That was the moment when everything changed. The moment I decided to save my marriage.

Earlier that morning, I'd planned to divorce her. I'd already met with a lawyer and was about to start the paperwork. But that night, when I saw my wife with another man? My competitive nature took over. It became a game. Nick was my opponent and Iris was the prize. I refused to let Nick have her. I was determined to win her back.

It wasn't because I loved her. Any love I felt for my wife was gone the moment I saw her with someone else. I was doing this to win. I wanted Iris to choose me over him. And she did. I won, and Nick lost.

It wasn't easy. Pretending I still loved my wife and wanted to be with her took acting skills I didn't know I had. But over time, I got used to it and became the husband Iris always wanted. I listened. I was attentive. I'd talk about my feelings—not my actual feelings but whatever she wanted to hear. I'd make Iris coffee every morning. Surprise her with flowers. Buy her gifts.

After a year of this nonsense, our marriage was stronger than it'd ever been. At least that's what it seemed like to Iris and everyone else. I was still playing the game, but as far as I knew, I'd won. Nick had left town. He was gone. He lost. And I won.

That should've been the end. I should've told Iris I knew about the affair and divorced her. But then we did that podcast. It was my idea. I was doing it for the experience, not because I thought it would go anywhere. I'd heard about people making millions doing a podcast and wanted to try it myself.

Those early podcast episodes I did with Iris were supposed to be practice for when I developed a real podcast, one that was only mine. I included Iris so I could practice having a guest. We didn't know what to talk about so we talked about us. About our marriage. About how we almost got divorced. There was no outline. No script. It was just the two of us talking.

I never in a million years thought anyone would listen to it. The audio quality was terrible back then. It was painful to listen to, but people still did. Lots of people. They were recommending it to their friends. Making posts about it online. My "practice" podcast was turning into a real thing.

Our audience quickly grew and soon we had companies wanting to advertise with us. Within a few months, the podcast became a hit and was making us enough money that we were able to quit our day jobs.

A podcast about marriage was not what I wanted, but it was too late to start something new. And why would I, when I already had something that was working and making a lot of money? Companies were approaching us with opportunities to make even more money, which was great, but it was getting to be more than I could handle. That's when I hired Allen to be our manager. He and I came up with the idea to develop a marriage-saving program to sell online. I did most of the work, with a little help from Iris, and the day it launched, it was an instant success.

I was thrilled we were doing so well, but there was a downside. Having a business based on my marriage meant I was stuck with Iris. I decided I had to accept that and try to feel something for her again, but I couldn't. Because she was always looking for Nick. I don't think she even knew she was doing it. But I did. Whenever we went somewhere, she'd tense up and her eyes would dart around, checking to see if he was anywhere near us.

Her obsession with him was never going to end. Unless I got rid of him. But even if I killed Nick and Iris was no longer searching for him, I'd still be stuck married to a woman who lied to me and betrayed me.

I couldn't do it. I couldn't have her in my life anymore. She had to die.

It's really quite sad. Iris had so much potential. Our fans love her. They relate to her. She has higher ratings than me. But she doesn't seem to care. She has no desire to be in the spotlight. If it were up to her, we'd do the podcast and that's it. I've passed up so many opportunities because of her, some worth millions.

In a perfect world, I'd divorce her and keep the business for myself, but obviously that wouldn't work. We're known as a couple. It's our brand.

But if Iris happened to die, people would be okay with me running the business without her. They might even praise me for it, saying I'm honoring her memory by doing the work she so strongly believed in. I'd be a hero, the widowed spouse continuing his wife's mission of helping people save their marriage. I can already imagine it. I wish I could jump ahead to when it's actually happening. But unfortunately, I'm stuck in the present, having to deal with Iris.

Part of me feels bad for what I'm about to do, but then I remember Iris cheated on me and lied to me, causing any guilt I was feeling to go away. I gave her one last chance to tell me the truth. The yellow roses. The card. The note on her car. The menu. The hotel brochure. They were all from me. All things that would remind her of Nick. I used what I knew about Nick and his affair with Iris to come up with items that Iris would associate with her former lover. I wanted her to be overwhelmed with guilt and shame, to the point that she'd finally admit what she'd done. But instead of being honest, she continued to deceive me, pretending to be the perfect wife when she was anything but.

Even when Nick himself showed up at our office and began working for us, Iris still wouldn't tell me the truth. Because she's a liar! A horrible woman who deserves to die!

It's finally time to make this happen. Tomorrow it'll all be over. I'm giddy with excitement, like a kid on Christmas Eve. Iris will be gone and I can start my life without her. She'll no longer be holding me back. I can do what I want with the business and be more successful than I ever thought possible.

My phone rings. I see who's calling and yell to Iris, "Honey, I need to check something in the car. I'll be in the garage."

"Okay!" she yells from the bedroom where she's packing her suitcase.

I go out to the garage and answer the call. "Hey, I'm leaving soon."

"That's why I'm calling. I'm assuming we can't talk while you're there."

"I'm afraid not, unless I can sneak out when she's asleep. But I really don't want to be outside in the woods at night."

She laughs. "You're such a city boy."

"I am. I'd much rather be at a nice hotel."

"Maybe when you're back, I could arrange for that," she says in a seductive tone. "I know the perfect place."

"You know we can't be seen in public. Why would you even suggest that?"

She sighs. "Because I'm tired of always hiding."

We'll still have to hide, even when this is over. I can't be dating when I'm grieving. I'll need to wait a few months, maybe longer, and by then I'll be done with Heather. I'm already getting tired of her. She's too young and too needy. I've only been seeing her for three months and she's already demanding more from me than I'm willing to give her.

I didn't intend to get involved with her. Unlike my wife, I've always been faithful, until Heather came on to me in her office one day. She was young and beautiful and made it clear she wanted me. I almost turned her down, but then decided I'd been faithful long enough. If Iris could cheat and lie about it, I could as well. And besides, our marriage was as good as over.

"I need to go," I say. "We're leaving soon. I'll call when I'm back in town."

"When will I see you?"

"I don't know. Maybe we can meet at your office next week."

"I'd love that!" she says, sounding far more excited than she should. We're not dating. I'm not her boyfriend. "See you soon!"

I end the call and go back into the house.

Iris appears with her suitcase. "I'm all packed!" She sets the suitcase down and races over to me, giving me a hug. "Thank you for planning this trip for us. I can't wait to get up there and see all the beautiful leaves and get some quality time with my wonderful husband."

"I'm looking forward to it as well." I smile. "I think we'll have a great time."

One of us will.

The other will be dead.

# CHAPTER THIRTY-NINE

**Dave**

"What do you think?" I ask as I drive down the gravel road, tall trees surrounding us on both sides.

The cabin is just up ahead, completely private and secluded. A lover's paradise.

Or a good place to kill someone.

There's nobody around for miles. Even the loudest scream wouldn't be heard. We're deep in the woods where there aren't any trails so this isn't an area hikers would go. You could dig a hole, bury a body, and rest assured that it would never be found.

But I'll make sure they find Iris. I don't want a missing wife. I want a dead wife. It's the ending I need for the story I'll tell when she's gone. The tragic story of the death of my wife.

"It's beautiful out here," Iris says, gazing out the window. "The whole drive has been beautiful." She turns to me as I shut off the car. "Thank you for doing this. I know you'd prefer a nice hotel to a cabin in the woods."

"I wanted to make you happy." I smile, barely able to contain my excitement.

I'm nervous, but in a good way. My heart's racing, adrenaline's coursing through me. It reminds me of the feeling you get at the top of a roller coaster right before it drops. The thrill mixed with a bit of fear, not sure what to expect, but knowing you're going to love it at the end.

"I'm very happy," Iris says, smiling at me. "I feel like I can finally relax. We're all alone. I don't have to worry about Nick." She rubs my arm. "I really needed this, honey. It's perfect."

"Let's go inside and check it out. Maybe I could get a fire started."

"That sounds wonderful."

We get out of the car and walk up to the cabin.

"This cabin is adorable," Iris says. "How'd you find such a perfect place?"

"I did a search online for cozy romantic cabins my wife would like."

She laughs. "And how many came up?"

"Just this one." I unlock the door, then give her a kiss. "I hope it looks as good as it did in the pictures." I open the door and go inside. "It seemed bigger online, but other than that, it looks the same."

"I love it," Iris says, walking around the small living room. It's connected to the kitchen, and in the back is the one and only bedroom. "It's so cozy." She walks over to the fireplace. "Do you know how to build a fire?"

"I've never done it, but I'm sure I can figure it out. I watched some videos online, knowing we were coming here."

"Oh, honey, that's so sweet."

I didn't watch any videos. And I'm not building a fire.

"Come check out the kitchen," I say, standing next to it.

"Let's go see the bedroom first." She heads toward the room she's not supposed to go in.

"Honey, wait!" I step in front of her and smile. "If we go in there, it could be hours before we come out." I put my arm around her and spin her around so her back's to the bedroom.

"What are you doing?" She laughs.

"Redirecting you to the kitchen. We should make dinner. Fuel up for tonight." I kiss her, a prolonged kiss that will likely be our last.

"I didn't realize you were in such a romantic mood."

"I'm always in a romantic mood with you. And there isn't much else to do here. No TV. No internet. No phone service."

"We don't have cell service?" she asks, sounding alarmed.

"This deep in the woods? I doubt it. Why? Do you need to call someone?"

"No, but it's good to have if there's an emergency."

"We'll be fine." I pause, noticing the bedroom door opening. "Or one of us will."

Iris gives me a funny look. "What did you say?"

This is it. It's time. My heart's going so fast I can hardly breathe.

"How was the trip?" Nick says, coming up behind Iris.

She whips around. "Nick!" She turns back to me and slams into my chest. "Go! We have to get—"

"Iris, stop." I grab her and hold her against me. "Quiet down. He's supposed to be here."

"What?" She gazes up at me, terror in her eyes. "What are you talking about? Nick is—"

"Here to do what should've been done a long time ago," I say, holding her tighter as she tenses up. "You see, honey, I know about you and Nick. I've known for a long time. I went to meet my friend Tom for a drink at that hotel you used to go to. But I never made it to the bar. I was too sick after seeing you with Nick."

My fingers dig into her flesh and she winces. "Dave, please. It was a mistake. I made a mistake. I'm sorry I didn't tell you. I—"

"Forget it, Iris," I say. "It's too late."

"Let's hurry this up," Nick says.

"No!" Iris tries to look back at him, but I'm holding her so tightly she can barely turn her neck. "Nick, don't do this. Please! I'm begging you!"

"You lied to me," Nick says. "You told me you were getting divorced. You told me we had a future."

"No," Iris says, her eyes going back to me. "He's lying! I never told him we had a future! And I said I *might* get a divorce. I didn't tell him it was for sure."

"And that made it okay for you to cheat on me?" I hiss.

"No! Of course not! It was wrong. And I'm so sorry. I never should've done it."

Her voice is trembling and her whole body is shaking. I love it. I love seeing her fear, the sheer terror on her face, knowing she's about to finally pay the price for what she's done.

"You don't have to do this," Iris says, pleading with me. "You can't. We're a team. If I die, our business dies too."

"I've found a way to run it without you." I smile. "I'll be the widowed husband who loved his departed wife so much that he chose to continue her mission to help struggling couples. I've got it all planned out. I already have outlines made for future podcast episodes. Ones I'll be doing alone." I lean down to her face. "Without you holding me back, I'll make more money than I ever dreamed of."

"Dave, come on," Nick says. "Enough talking. This should've been done by now."

I glance at him. "You're right. Go ahead. Do it."

"No!" Iris cries as Nick holds up the knife. "Don't do this! I'm begging you!"

She's struggling to get free, her legs thrashing around, her arms pushing against me.

"Hurry up!" I tell Nick. "She's fighting me."

He raises the knife in the air. My eyes dart back to Iris, wanting to see her expression when the knife slices through her.

She gasps, and her eyes get huge. I almost laugh, but then notice the sharp pain in my side. I look down and see blood soaking my shirt.

"What the—"

"Nick!" Iris screams.

I look to my side and see Nick, holding the knife. He shoves Iris back and plunges the knife into my stomach.

"What the hell are you doing?" I yell, stumbling back.

Iris runs off and I hear the door open and slam against the wall.

My vision turns hazy and the room starts to spin. I grip my stomach and feel warm blood coating my hands.

"Iris!" I hear Nick say.

"What's happening?" I mutter, but nobody answers.

I collapse to my knees, black spots forming in my vision. I fall back and my head slams against the floor.

# CHAPTER FORTY

**Iris**

"Go, go, go, go, go!" I say to myself as I run through the woods, trying to get away from the cabin. It's dark, and I have no idea where I'm going, but anywhere is better than that cabin. With Dave. And Nick.

They were going to kill me. Dave, my own husband, wanted me dead. He was working with Nick. This whole time, the two of them were working together. To kill me!

How did I not put it together? Nick showing up? Dave hiring him? The two of them becoming friends almost instantly? None of it made sense. I should've known something was going on with them. It was all right in front of me, and I didn't see it! But why would I ever think my husband and ex-lover were plotting to kill me?

"Iris!" Nick yells.

He's following me. If he catches me, he's going to kill me!

Where do I go? How do I get away?

If I'd had Dave's key, I could've taken the car, but I didn't have time to dig through his pocket to get a key when Nick was standing there with a knife.

The thing I don't understand is why did Nick stab Dave? If they were working together, why would he want Dave dead?

"Iris!" Nick's voice sounds closer now. Is he catching up to me?

I need to go faster, but it's dark out and I have to be careful so I don't trip on something and fall.

"Iris!" Nick yells. "I'm not going to hurt you! Stop running! Tell me where you are!"

*He's not going to hurt me?* Does he really think I'll believe that? He has a knife. If I'd stayed in the cabin, I'd be dead right now.

"Iris!" He sounds like he's right behind me. How is that possible? Am I that slow? Or is Nick just really fast?

I pick up my speed. My foot catches on something and I lunge forward and slam to the ground. I scream out in pain, then immediately regret it.

"Iris!" Nick yells.

My right ankle feels like it's twisted to the side. It's throbbing and shooting pain up my leg. But I can't stop. I have to get up and get moving. I try to stand and feel someone grab me.

"Let me go!" I scream, struggling against Nick. "Please don't do this! I don't want to die!" I kick at him with my good leg, trying to get away.

"Iris, stop! I'm not going to hurt you!" His voice is softer now and his hold on me loosens a little. "I was never going to do it. I was playing along. I was never going to hurt you."

Part of me believes him, because if he was going to kill me he would've done it by now. And his tone. It's calm, gentle, almost caring. It reminds me of how he was when we were together. Back then, I never would've believed he could hurt someone, which is why I was shocked when he came back and was terrorizing me.

"What do you mean you played along?" I ask. "What did you do?"

"About a month ago, Dave found me. He came to my house. Said some relative of his used to live there and that he wanted to look around. I didn't recognize him at first. He had a baseball hat on and he hadn't shaved for a few days. It wasn't until he came inside and I got a better look at him that I realized it was him."

That can't be true. Can it? Is Nick making this up?

"Why was he there?" I ask. "What did he want?"

"To kill me. I was holding a knife, pretending like I was making dinner, but the knife was really to protect myself. By then, I'd figured out his motive. But he caught me off guard. He grabbed the knife from me and held it against my throat."

"But he didn't kill you."

"Because I made a deal with him. I told him I'd kill you if he let me live."

"Why? Why would you do that? Why would you offer to kill me?"

"So he wouldn't do it himself. I knew he was going to. He hated you for having an affair. He hated both of us. He wanted us dead."

"He said that? He told you he wanted to kill me?"

"Not at first. It was after I made the offer. If he didn't want you dead, he would've killed me right then and there. But as soon as I mentioned killing you, he lowered the knife. Asked me to tell him more."

"Then maybe he wasn't going to kill me. You gave him the idea."

"No, he was definitely going to kill you. He just wasn't sure how. He couldn't think of a way to do it without getting caught. He was afraid he'd end up in prison."

"You're lying."

"Iris, you heard him tell me to kill you. How are you not believing this?"

"Because I don't want it to be true," I say, images of Dave and me flashing through my mind. Us holding hands. Him smiling at me. Kissing me. Telling me how much he loves me. How could he do all that while also planning to kill me?

"I was trying to warn you," Nick says. "That's why I was trying to get you alone. So we could talk and I could tell you to be careful around him and to stop trying to get rid of me. I was trying to help you, Iris. That's why I did all that stuff with Dave. I was trying to keep him away from you. He was getting really angry seeing me with you. Even though nothing was going on, just seeing the two of us in the same room together was setting him off. He kept saying how much he hated you and that he wanted you dead. I was worried he was going to hurt you. That's why I was following you. I was trying to keep you safe."

"How long have you been following me?"

"For weeks, before you even knew I was in town. I moved to Chicago a few days after Dave came to my house. He told me to wait, but I couldn't. I was too worried he'd do something to you. I even considered he might hire someone else to do it. So I moved and started following you around."

"Wait, Dave hired you to kill me? He was paying you money?"

"He would've if I'd done it. I told him I wanted a

hundred thousand. He laughed, like that was nothing. I could've asked for more, but I didn't want to risk him turning me down."

"What about the ad manager job? Why did he hire you?"

"To mess with you. He wanted to see the look on your face when you found out he'd hired me. He wanted to see how you'd react to having me around all the time. He was hoping you'd be sick with guilt and not be able to eat or sleep. He thought it'd make you confess to the affair."

"What if I had? Would he have still done this?"

"Yes. In his mind, it was already done. He'd moved on. He was making plans for the business. Plans for when you were gone."

"What about that note I got? And the flowers and menu and—"

"It was him. It was Dave messing with you. He wanted you to think I was back in town, stalking you, wanting you back. He was hoping that stuff would make you confess about the affair, or at the very least have you constantly on edge, worried about what I might do."

"It worked. I've been a mess for weeks."

"I also think he was doing that stuff to set me up."

"What do you mean?"

"Like if I turned on him and tried to make it look like he was the one who killed you instead of me, he'd have evidence to use against me. He'd tell the police I was stalking you and that I was dangerous."

"I think you're right," I say, remembering how eager Dave was to go to the police yesterday. "He had photos. He said he found them in your car."

"Photos? What photos?"

"Photos of me. He wanted it to look like you were stalking me. He told the police you were obsessed with me."

"Iris, I swear to you, I didn't take those photos. And I didn't write you any notes or send you flowers. It was Dave doing that stuff, not me."

I think I believe him. His story is actually making sense. And he isn't hurting me. We're alone in the woods. At night. If he wanted to kill me, now would be the time and place to do it.

"Why didn't you just tell me this when you got to town?" I ask. "Why didn't you tell me what he was planning?"

"It was too risky. I didn't want you slipping up and Dave finding out that you knew what he was up to. If he had any indication you knew, he would've killed you. I was trying to keep you safe until today, the day we agreed to do it." Nick steps back, but keeps hold of my arms. "We need to get out of here. Can you walk? It sounded like you got hurt."

"It's my ankle. I twisted it. I think it might be broken." I try to put some weight on it. "Ow! I don't think I can walk on it."

"Then I guess I'm carrying you. We'll have to go back and see if we can get a phone signal closer to the road."

"Back to the cabin? No. I'm not going back there."

"Iris, he's dead."

"How do you know? Maybe he's—"

"He lost too much blood. There's no way he's still alive. And if we don't go back where we came from, we'll just be wandering around lost all night."

"I can't. I can't go back there. Not if he might still be alive."

"Then what do you want to do? Wait until the sun comes up? By then, your ankle could be—"

"Wait. Do you hear that?"

"Hear what?"

“A truck. Listen.”

There’s the faint sound of a truck in the distance. Like a semi truck with a loud diesel engine.

“I hear it,” Nick says. “I think it’s coming from behind you. And it doesn’t sound that far away.”

“Let’s go!” I take a step and pain shoots up my leg. “Ow!”

Nick scoops me up like I weigh nothing at all and starts walking, heading toward the road.

This whole time, I thought Nick was the man I had to worry about. I worried he’d tell Dave about our affair. I worried he’d try to destroy my business. And my life. I even thought he might be dangerous.

But it was Dave who was dangerous. The man I thought was so caring and loving. The man I thought would never hurt me... wanted to kill me.

# CHAPTER FORTY-ONE

## SIX WEEKS LATER

**Iris**

"It's such a horrific story," Jane says as we sit at the cafe. "When I told Anne, she could hardly believe it."

"I really wish you'd stop telling people," I say, sipping my coffee. "It's been over a month since it happened. Surely, you can think of something else to talk about."

"It's a very intriguing story," she says, taking her lipstick from her purse. "And one that contains a valuable lesson. I'm doing people a favor by telling them what happened to you."

"What lesson? What are you talking about?"

"Being unfaithful. Lying to your spouse." She opens her compact mirror and checks her reflection. "Everyone thinks they can get away with it, but look what can happen? You could get killed."

"What happened to me isn't typical. And Dave obviously had issues I didn't know about."

"What issues do you think he had?" she asks, gazing into the mirror as she applies her lipstick.

"Anger. Jealousy. Violence. Maybe even a dual personality

disorder. I don't know how else to explain how he could pretend to be the perfect husband while also plotting to kill me."

Jane puts the cap back on her lipstick and drops it in her purse. "Betrayal can drive anyone to violence, even people you'd never think would be capable of it." She checks her reflection in the mirror again. "Just think of all those TV shows where they go back and dissect a murder. Nearly all of them involve a betrayal of some kind, usually between a husband and wife."

"Can we change topics? I feel like all I ever talk about is Dave and what happened."

Six weeks have passed since that awful night at the cabin. Nick and I made it to the road, but our phones couldn't get a signal. Luckily, a guy in a pickup saw us and stopped to ask if we needed help. We didn't tell him what actually happened. We just said we got lost in the woods and that I hurt my ankle and Nick cut his hand, which explained why there was blood on it. The man took us to the hospital and that's when we called the police.

When they arrived at the cabin, Dave was dead. I was secretly relieved. That might sound heartless, but the man he'd become was not the man I fell in love with, or maybe that man never existed and Dave was just pretending the whole time. I hope that's not true, but it's possible. Looking back, I don't think I really knew Dave, at least not like I thought I did.

As for Nick, he's a decent man who truly was trying to save my life. I didn't want him going to prison for killing Dave so I told the police that Nick acted out of self-defense. I said Dave was going to kill us both so Nick stabbed him before he could. I spent hours at the police station explaining what happened, including how Dave was trying to set up Nick to be blamed for my murder. Nick was also questioned and they held him there overnight. I was worried they might charge him with murder, but they released him the following day.

The story was in the news for weeks. It even made national headlines. It got to the point I had to keep the TV off so I wouldn't have to look at Dave's face on the screen and hear the newscasters talk about how a well-known marriage coach tried to kill his wife. It was such a big story that I had people from the media waiting outside my door, wanting me to answer questions. I couldn't take it, so I went and stayed with my mom in Indiana. I was there for two weeks, and when I got back, the story was starting to die down. But even now, over a month later, I still have reporters calling me.

"Have you spoken to Renee?" Jane asks, putting her mirror back in her purse.

"No, have you?"

"Yes, just yesterday."

Renee's house went up for sale a few weeks ago. Trent's living there until it sells. He kicked Renee out and she moved into an apartment. She cares for the boys during the day and then Trent picks them up after work and takes them for the night.

"She's not doing well," Jane says. "Trent wants full custody of the children."

"Why? He's never home, and Renee is a wonderful mother."

"Yes, but she's an adulterer. A judge could decide that makes her unfit to care for the boys."

"That's ridiculous. What she did has nothing to do with her being a good mom."

"She was with that man after just having her child." Jane's

brows rise. "You don't think that would look bad to a judge? Instead of bonding with her infant, she was out fornicating with some man she met online." Jane pauses. "Maybe I shouldn't say it, but I kind of hope she does lose custody. It serves her right for being so careless."

I gasp. "Jane, that's a horrible thing to say! Those children are everything to Renee."

"Apparently not, or she would've been home instead of out with that man."

Jane is being very self-righteous today, even more so than usual. She always thinks she's morally superior to everyone else and it really gets on my nerves. She acts as though she's never done anything wrong, which can't possibly be true.

Her phone chimes, alerting her to a text. She smiles as she reads it. "How nice. Tom's getting married."

"Who's Tom?"

"Barb's youngest brother. Barb's one of my closest friends. I grew up with her. I'm sure I've mentioned her to you before."

"Yes, I think you have."

Jane holds out her phone, showing me a photo. "That's Tom. He's been single for years. It's nice he finally found someone."

"He looks really fit. He must work out a lot."

"He does. He goes to that gym where Dave used to go." Jane sets her phone down. "I'll have to call Barb when I get home and find out when the wedding's going to be."

Jane rattles on about wedding cakes and how she's always wanted to make one, but my mind is stuck on what she said about Tom belonging to Dave's gym. Dave said a guy named Tom invited him out for a drink at the hotel I went to with

Nick. That's how Dave found out about the affair. It couldn't be the same Tom, could it?

The waiter stops by. "Can I get you ladies anything else?"

"No, we'll take the check," I tell him.

"Kayla!" Jane calls out as she waves at a young woman a few tables over. She's getting up to leave, putting on her coat.

The woman waves back, then makes her way over to us. "Hi, Jane. I didn't see you here."

"I didn't see you either," she says with a laugh. "And we've been sitting here for an hour." Jane motions to me. "Kayla, this is Iris. She lives next door, although sadly, she's planning to move soon."

It's true. I can't stay in that house any longer. There are too many bad memories. I'm putting it up for sale next week and moving into an apartment until I find another house. It'll be a smaller, less expensive house since I'm not currently working. My marriage-coaching business no longer exists. Allen said I could've kept it going and rebranded it, but I had no desire to. I wanted to be done with it. Fortunately, it made a lot of money so I'll be fine not working until I figure out what to do next.

"Maybe I should buy your house," Kayla says in a kidding tone. "Then Jane and I could be neighbors."

"Wouldn't that be fun?" Jane says to Kayla. "I could babysit Lily. She's so adorable."

"Aww, thank you," Kayla says to her. "She loves you. She's always talking about you."

"How old is she?" I ask Kayla.

"Five. I have a three-year-old as well." She checks her watch. "Speaking of the kids, I need to go pick them up. It was nice meeting you," she says to me.

"You too."

She smiles at Jane. "I'll tell Lily you said hi."

"Please do. See you on Sunday!"

Kayla leaves and Jane says, "Isn't she sweet? And her husband is the nicest man. They're really a lovely couple."

"How do you know her?" I ask.

"She goes to my church. Oh, and Lily goes to school with Renee's son. They're in the same kindergarten class."

The waiter stops by with the check. "No rush, ladies. Whenever you're ready." He walks off.

"He forgot to split it," Jane says, getting her wallet out.

"It's fine. I'll get it."

"Let me. You can get the next one." She takes out some cash.

As she deals with the bill, my mind is racing, trying to figure this out. Jane knows Tom, the man who invited Dave to have a drink with him at the hotel where he found out about my affair. Jane also knows Kayla, who has a child in the same class as Renee's son. Is that just a coincidence, or is Jane somehow involved? Did she tell Tom to invite Dave to the hotel for a drink that night? Did she tell Kayla to start the rumor about Renee?

"You never told anyone about Renee, did you?" I ask.

"Honestly, Iris, why are we still talking about this?" She sets some cash on top of the bill. "Trent knows the truth now. That's all that matters."

"He found out because of a rumor he heard about the affair. A rumor someone at the school started. Who do you think started it?"

She shrugs. "How should I know? I don't know anyone at the school."

"You know Kayla." I look Jane in the eye. "Did you tell her

about Renee's affair? Was Kayla the one who started the rumor?"

Jane laughs. "You have such an active imagination, Iris. Perhaps you should be a writer."

"Did you tell her or not?"

Jane balls up her napkin and sets it on the table, not answering me.

It was her. I'm almost certain of it.

"What about Tom?" I ask. "Do you know if he knew Dave?"

She tilts her head, like she's pretending to ponder the question. "Actually, yes, I believe Tom knew Dave from the gym."

"Did you tell him to invite Dave out for a drink?" I glare at Jane, my anger building. "Knowing Dave would see me there?"

"So how is Nick?" Jane smooths her hair. "Have you spoken to him?"

"No. I told you, I'm done with Nick. We've both moved on."

Nick is back in the small town he was living at when Dave found him. He sold his house and is renting a place until he figures out what he wants to do. He's thinking of moving to Texas and working for his uncle who owns a bar, but he told me that over a month ago. It's possible he changed his mind. I'll never know because we decided to go our separate ways and have no further contact. We want to put this part of our lives behind us and never revisit it again.

"You can't even be friends?" Jane asks. "It seems a bit extreme to never speak to him again."

"Did you do this?" I ask. "Are you the reason Dave found out?"

"Oh, Iris." She smiles a little. "You already know. I don't need to say it."

It was her. She started this whole thing. Dave never would've known about the affair if Jane hadn't told Tom to invite Dave to the hotel that night. She was setting it up, making sure Dave saw me with Nick. I bet Tom wasn't even there. He was just a pawn in Jane's game. Her sick game to destroy my marriage that almost got me killed.

And then she did it again with Renee. She told Kayla what Renee did and had her start a rumor that would eventually make it back to Trent. And now Renee's living on her own and might lose custody of her children.

Jane destroyed my marriage. She destroyed Renee's family.

Why? Why did she do this?

Jane gets up from her chair. "I need to go, but it was lovely seeing you, Iris." Her eyes pause on mine and she smiles. "I'm making a new recipe when I get home. Cranberry apple cinnamon rolls with maple frosting. Dave would've loved them. But since he's no longer here, you should come by and try them." She winks at me, then walks away.

I'm not trying her rolls, or anything else she makes. My friendship with her is over. I never want to see her again.

# CHAPTER FORTY-TWO

**Jane**

I don't understand why Iris is upset with me. She's the villain here. She's the one who betrayed her husband, then lied about it for years. And how could she have sympathy for Renee? The woman should've been home with her child, but instead she was out doing disgusting things with some man she met on her computer.

Iris and Renee should be happy things turned out the way they did. I did them a favor. They no longer have to hide such a deep, shameful secret. And they're both still alive. I suppose Iris could've been killed, but it didn't happen. I must say, I didn't think Dave had it in him to murder his wife. But looking back, I did always feel a similarity between us. I just wasn't sure why.

If I'm being honest, I wish Dave *had* killed Iris. Watching her pretend to be a marriage expert, knowing she'd cheated on Dave, made me sick to my stomach. She was a liar—a total fraud—and making millions! She deserved to die. And yet she didn't. She's still here, acting as though she did nothing wrong.

I feel no remorse for what I did, not even a little. Dave and

Trent deserved to know the truth. Just like I did. But unlike them, I didn't have anyone leading me to the truth. I had to do all the work myself.

I'd only been married a year when I discovered Richard was having an affair. No one had the courtesy to tell me. No one gave me any clues. No one set out breadcrumbs for me to follow, leading me to the truth.

I was on my own. It was up to me to find out what was going on. It took months of hard work before I finally saw them together and had proof of their affair.

Angela was a nurse Richard worked with at the hospital. She knew he was married. I'd met her. I'd talked to her at the hospital Christmas party. But she didn't care that Richard had a wife. She had no respect for the sanctity of marriage and its sacred vows.

So I got rid of her. For good. And to this day, I don't feel an ounce of guilt. Some would say I should've killed my husband, and believe me, I thought about it. But then I decided against it.

Richard was a good catch, a handsome surgeon with high earning potential. If I killed him, I'd have to start the husband search all over again. And what are the odds I'd find another handsome surgeon to marry?

The point I'm making is that Iris and Renee should be grateful they're here. That they're still alive and well and able to go on with their lives. They fared much better than Angela. Even if it was just a fling and she never intended to steal Richard away, she still deserved to die.

And on a positive note, it had a happy ending. Because after Richard figured out what I'd done? He never cheated again.

Printed in Great Britain
by Amazon

57958731R00169